WALK OF
DEATH

A FORENSIC NOVEL

MIKE TABOR

CENTER HILL PUBLISHING COMPANY

ACKNOWLEDGMENTS

WHEN AN AUTHOR/DENTIST is writing his first work of 'faction,' (fiction based on true crime files), there is a steep learning curve. Without the help from several colleagues, friends and family, this project might not have ever gotten off the ground.

My first salute would be TBI special agents Larry B. Davis and Joe Craig. Without their help, this case would still be cold. Nashville's Metropolitan Police Department has been our right hand since we began our problem solving ventures in dental forensics in 1983. Mr. Herschell Watson, former Chief Forensic Investigator and Dr. Harry Mincer, my forensic mentor, were two influencing professionals who helped me launch this career.

I want to say a special thanks to Dr. Murray Marks and Dr. Bill Bass, whose Body Farm in Knoxville has helped put forensic dental identification on the map. I am grateful to have worked with them on numerous cases over the years. They have always provided me with steadfast friendship and professional support in the many lectures we have given jointly. I am honored to have known these two gentlemen.

Without the essential assistance of the entire team at the Medical Examiner's Office, my ID task would be impossible. Dr. Mike Cisneros, Associate Forensic Odontologist has been a friend and colleague for over a decade, and is always dependable, accurate and reliable.

Launching a writing career with a full time dental practice can be a stressful event. Without extra help and support from our dental team, Kelsey, Heather, Edna, Ali, Kristyn and Miranda, this project would have been very difficult.

Thanks go out to my friend of over twenty-five years and literary attorney, Randy Smith, and my writing coach and morale supporter, Martha Bolton. These are two treasured friends and professional colleagues that I will always cherish.

Our friends were indispensable in helping read the manuscript countless times, looking for extra commas or periods. I think we got 'em all! Victor and Tricia Beck, Mark and Terri Gallant, Steve and Amy Dennison, Debbie Greene, Connie King and Dr. Richard Souviron were my key proofreaders. Thanks so much for everything.

My adult children, Missy and Jayson, are two wonderful people who have given us some of the most precious grandchildren on earth. They have truly been the light of my life.

And finally, my wife Karen, who has endured countless hours of solitude with an ever present smile and never ending support. I am so appreciative of her love and encouragement.

To my readers, I hope you'll enjoy the wild ride; perhaps there's more to come!

WALK OF
DEATH

1

A FEW MINUTES after midnight, in the thick muggy heat of a Tennessee July, a pair of headlights swung sharply off State Highway 48 South, and began to inch along a steep gravel road. Its path seemed to climb vertically up Gatlin's Ridge, an isolated area of Dickson County. Finally the car shuddered to a stop, just feet from the lip of a ravine that disappeared into darkness. As headlights cut out, and two men emerged, their movements became quick and furtive.

The shorter man, with a balding head and short, stubby arms that seemed disproportionate to his rotund figure, gently opened the driver's side rear door. Struggling briefly with a large, unwieldy object inside, he hissed an order to his muscular companion. The other man stooped to help his partner, and, a moment later, they had pulled the limp body of a man from inside the car.

Together, they shuffled to the driver's seat, and arguing in clipped whispers, they awkwardly placed a decomposing corpse inside. With a weak flashlight guiding their motions, the shorter man leaned over and strapped a tattered gray seatbelt across its sagging torso. The head drooped forward, a slime of decomposing greenish gray residue dripped from its mouth and nose. A partially severed tongue dangled by a tiny tissue tag, allowing the segment to lay flat against the corpse's chin.

The shorter one slipped a wedding band from his left hand, and a small, silver pinky ring from his right hand, jamming both onto the body's cold mushy fingers. He removed his watch he had always worn on his right wrist, his trademark since he was left handed, and strapped it onto a limp and soggy wrist.

As he positioned the body securely, the taller man grabbed a container of gasoline from the trunk and began soaking it liberally on the dashboard, upholstery, and corpse. Strong fumes of gasoline were still no match for the putrid odor. He emptied what was left into the trunk and shut the empty container inside. Flames would totally engulf containers, seats, everything, leaving no evidence. They had thought of everything. Or so they thought.

The shorter man put the car in neutral and idled its engine. It rattled as if it were firing on only half of its cylinders. He lit a match, tossed it inside onto the carcass's lap. As flames licked up the corpse's shirt, quickly catching its hair on fire and engulfing its head, they ran to the rear of the car.

"One . . . two . . . *three*," the short man sucked in a lungful of air. Both of them threw their shoulders against the rear bumper and shoved with all their might.

At first, there was a sputter and stall, like a gray elephant picking its way in slow motion down a rocky hill. It threatened to stop halfway down, but then, gradually, it gained speed, then more, and more. As wind fanned more flames, the car's interior lit up like a massive fireball igniting midnight darkness. Suddenly the front end hit a ditch, throwing part of its nose downward. The back end sailed, becoming instantly airborne, and then there began a series of end over end flips. Both front doors were ripped off, glass shattered, and flames began to lash out of either side just as the car slammed into a massive oak tree.

Microseconds after impact, just as planned, the entire car exploded into a ball of raging fire, followed by a second massive explosion that sent sparks and flames skyward. Metal shrapnel and shattered glass flew skyward, causing tremors like an earthquake, releasing a shower of leaves and branches.

Both men stood on the ravine's lip, gazing downward, their dark forms surrounded by thick rolls of fog mixed with black, sooty smoke. A full moon cut through the mist to light their faces.

"How 'bout that?" he muttered. "Wonder how that seat belt is working out for him now?" He laughed at his own twisted humor. His friend only blinked at him in wide-eyed disbelief. It was done.

Mission accomplished.

2

OPRYLAND HOTEL was the crown jewel of Nashville. Country music fans from everywhere flocked to this massive structure each year, seeking a quick glimpse of Garth Brooks, Vince Gill or Dolly Parton. Each of them, and a host of other celebrities, called Nashville home. This was truly the Beverly Hills of country music and everyone living in Nashville was proud of that fact.

Brandie thought this hotel was the perfect venue to celebrate an award her husband, Dr. Chris Walsh, was to receive that evening. It was the Tennessee Academy of General Dentistry's annual meeting, a festive gala celebration honoring one of its own. This year, Dr. Chris Walsh, private practicing dentist and Chief Forensic Odontologist for the Office of the State Medical Examiner was the guest of honor. He was receiving the Academy's 1997 Dentist of the Year award. He had told Brandie that receiving such an honor from his peers would be the most meaningful of his accomplishments.

It wasn't often that Dr. and Mrs. Walsh attended black tie affairs. The two usually preferred a more casual evening with their friends. Tonight, however, would be different.

Their stroll took them past quaint little candy and jewelry

shops, and various 'watering holes' offering world famous Tennessee-made Jack Daniel's Whiskey and Goo Goo candy bars, made famous by The Grand Ole Opry.

"This place is enormous! No matter how many times I come here, I always manage to get lost!' Brandie smiled at her husband's colleagues who had joined them in casual conversation as they strolled together toward to the ballroom.

Walsh's mind wandered as his thoughts carried him to his upcoming speech content. His colleagues might be expecting his content to deal with clinical dentistry. Some would be surprised to learn that he would divert slightly and discuss dentistry's role in murders, rape, child abuse with bitemarks, and mass disasters. For some, it would leave them with haunting memories.

3

"CHRIS! BRANDIE! WELCOME! Tonight's your big night. Great to see you. Your seats are up front to the left of the podium. "Dr. George Campbell, the local arrangements chairman, offered the couple a drink and appetizers from one of the passing waiters.

Brandie nursed a glass of red wine, while Dr. Walsh felt obliged to pay local homage to Tennessee's own, Mr. Jack Daniel. Brandie whispered to Chris, "Remember now, don't you run off and leave me."

Dr. Walsh knew that Brandie would be anxious because the spotlight was on the two of them. She had no appetite, and spent most of her time in nervous chatter, while teasing her food around randomly.

"And now, ladies and gentlemen, it is my distinct honor to introduce to you the Tennessee Academy of General Dentistry's 1997 Dentist of the Year, Dr. Chris Walsh."

Chris was not sure he had ever received a standing ovation. He had given scores of speeches in his twenty-five year career, mostly about forensic dental science and the laws of dentistry in Tennessee. As he made his way to the podium, he looked back and smiled at Brandie. He grinned sheepishly, showing unexpected bashfulness.

"Ladies and gentlemen," he began, "thank you so much for that warm reception. I am honored and humbled to receive this award". Chris went on to thank several members of the audience by name, people who had been influential in his career and Brandie. She blushed and rose to her feet, giving a slight wave and broad smile to the crowd. Chris quickly moved on, knowing how Brandie avoided the spotlight.

"As many of you are aware, I, just like you, am a dentist during the day, but I also have an avocation in forensic dentistry. I'd like to take a few moments to tell you how far-reaching the world of dentistry has become in the field of forensic science.

"To be completely accurate, forensic odontology is not really a specialty of dentistry, but a subspecialty of forensic science. The fields of other sciences we work with include forensic anthropology, medicine, question document examiners, toxicologists, crime scene investigators and more. Having served as Chief of Forensic Odontology, forensic sciences term for 'dentistry', for the State Medical Examiner's Office since 1983, several landmark changes have happened in our court systems that honor dentistry's contribution to the field.

"Our first and foremost thanks must go to Mr. Ted Bundy—yes, *that* Ted Bundy, the serial killer. Ted is responsible for putting forensic odontology on the map. You may remember his last victim was a Florida State University coed murdered in her sorority house in Tallahassee in 1977. Ted bit his victim on the left buttock after killing her and, subsequently, he became America's first person to be found guilty and put to death for murder where every bit of evidence was circumstantial except a human bite mark. Thanks to forensic odontology, Ted was electrocuted on January 24, 1989. That day changed forensic dental identification forever.

"At that time only a handful of states had allowed bite mark evidence as reliably admissible material in a court of law. In 1985, the state of Tennessee had its first opportunity to evaluate bite marks as evidence in the State of Tennessee vs. Castleman. I had the privilege of testifying in that landmark trial. Just twelve short years ago, only seventeen states had allowed its admission. We became number eighteen. Now all fifty states allow it as admissible evidence in courts of law.

"Tonight, I am both honored and humbled to receive this award and to realize I have played some role in helping our profession grow beyond the usual parameters and become a significant cog in the wheel of justice. I can't thank you enough. I will cherish this night forever!"

The applause continued for what seemed like five minutes. Finally, when he felt he needed to return to the microphone, he raised his hand and said, "Hey, I hear there's a few of you who might like to listen to a little classic rock and roll! So whatd'ya say we all get started and dance a little to some old favorites and the music of The Rogues, from Oak Ridge, Tennessee?"

Chris and Brandie enjoyed a vivacious party of their dreams. Three hours seemed like thirty minutes. The couple paused to quench their thirst and take a short break. Out of the corner of his eye, Walsh noticed Sheriff Jake Castleman approaching his group. He was one of the many local sheriffs who had a close working relationship with Dr. Walsh and the Medical Examiner's Office.

"Sheriff, what in the world are you doing here?" Chris said. "Guys, I'd like you to meet one of my law enforcement buddies. This is Sheriff Jake Castleman of Dickson County. Can't tell you how many cases we've handled together. Sheriff, I'm so honored you came."

"Doc, I wouldn't have missed this for anything. Beeper just went off, though. Gotta be heading out. Motor vehicle accident over near Dickson. Pretty intense car fire. May be seeing you sooner rather than later.

"Hope not…for everyone's sake." Dr. Walsh responded.

"I'll let you know. And hey, congrats on your award! You deserve it!"

"Thanks, Sheriff. That means a lot coming from you." The small group exchanged pleasantries as they strolled out to the lobby and their cars. With Brandie's arm in his, Walsh felt a vibration on his belt.

"Happens every time," Chris said glancing down at his beeper for a phone number. "It's Vanderbilt Children's Hospital," he said, then turning back to Brandie. "Let me go ahead and return this call while we're waiting for the car."

Walsh turned in his parking ticket to the valet and pulled out his mobile phone, the 'brick' as Brandie called it, and dialed the displayed number.

"Dr. Walsh, I'm sorry to bother you this late, but I'm afraid we have a bad one. Eighteen month old little girl. Blonde hair, blue eyes. Brought in nonresponsive.

"Mom's boyfriend was babysitting. Says the child fell off the commode and hit her head on the bath tub. Doctors think otherwise. She has a subdural hematoma and a fractured skull. Flat EEG. On life support now. Has a very deep circular wound on her upper thigh. Looks like a human bite mark to me; skin is broken and it is bleeding. Old cigarette burns on the child's stomach; they've scabbed and scarred. ID is here already getting scaled photos. They're also going to try some alternative light source photos, possibly U.V. These wounds are pretty intense. I think they're just keeping her on life support to line up organ donation protocol. Detective Sharp of Youth Guidance has held her boyfriend for questioning. We could use your help right away."

After assuring her he'd be there as soon as possible, Dr. Walsh hung up the phone. The anxious look of despair brought curiosity to Brandie. "What is it?" she asked.

Walsh looked down at the pavement. "You don't even want to know."

4

WHEN SHERIFF Jake Castleman walked out of Opryland Hotel, he and his wife, Alice, were met with a hot, humid night, mixed with a dense fog that cast ominous shadows. "I don't see how anybody is ever able to find their own vehicle here!" he said. Alice started to agree, but then she saw his patrol car in the next row over.

"There it is!" she said.

"How do you do that?" the sheriff asked, impressed. "I was looking right over there and didn't see it."

"Maybe I should be the Sheriff?"

"Well, all I know is I'd sure be lost without you, babe," he said. With those comforting words, he cranked the engine of his squad car and dialed in county wide dispatch. Within seconds he could be brought up to date with the details of the incident.

Dispatch described the incident as an extensive explosion with a car going off the edge of Gatlin's Ridge. There were apparently no eye witnesses, but several locals had called in reporting an explosion and a localized fire from the bottom of a deep ravine.

The drive back to Dickson, which normally would take an hour, was nearly doubled with fog limiting their visibility. Realizing the case might take longer than expected, Sheriff Jake dropped Alice off at their modest farm house on the northern outskirts of Dickson.

"Be home soon, sugar," he said, "I'll call you if it turns out to be an all-nighter. I'm beat, so I'll try to wrap this up as soon as I can."

Once the sheriff had driven to the top of the ridge and peered down into the ravine with a spotlight, he discovered a far more disturbing scene than what he'd imagined. Active flames were still burning, although most of its residue had already been consumed by the fire. Sheriff Castleman drove his squad car a little closer to a white, rusty Chevy station wagon. Three men were standing beside its edge, murmuring in hushed tones. After radioing headquarters, the sheriff approached them.

The Sheriff was disappointed to learn that none of them had actually witnessed the incident; two lived within a mile of the wreck and had been awakened by the explosion. They had arrived on foot, and the third, the driver of the Chevy, had arrived shortly afterward. One of the men, a plaid shirt thrown hastily over his willowy shoulders, was convinced he'd heard some brush rustling alongside the road, but when he'd walked through with his flashlight, he'd found nothing.

"Probably just some wildlife scared by the fire," one of the men said.

"I'm not so sure," the man in plaid answered, shaking his head. "There's something weird about this. Just can't put my finger on it."

No one at the scene noticed the two sets of eerie eyes peering through the woods like four small polished stones. They were taking in every exciting moment of this tragedy.

5

There was little the small town's volunteer fire department could do to save the wreckage; instead, they worked to contain the fire and keep it from spreading to the surrounding foliage. After two hours of dousing, the sheriff called Anytime Wrecker Company. Ray Daltry, one of Dickson County's favorites, was there within twenty minutes.

When he saw the magnitude of the job, Ray shook his head. "I might need another wrecker," he said. "I'll give it a try, but this is awful steep."

Ray had been ready for retirement well before his bank account was. He had wanted to retire several years ago, but the failure of his son, Bryan, to take over the family business had caused Ray to stay with it a few years longer than he had originally planned. Ray was a burly man; quite muscular from decades of hard work, but chronic back pain from heavy lifting and pulling had taken an orthopedic toll on his frame. He had pulled cars from ditches, lakes, ravines, and every conceivable landscape known to man. He was known as a genuine citizen; a Good Samaritan with a bit of an attitude. Though he was quick to complain, he would never leave a man's vehicle in a ditch, even if he didn't have money to pay.

With a series of chains attached to his truck, Ray hoisted himself down the ravine with the skill and precision of an Alpine mountain climber. He carried a two-inch-thick cable connected to a massive hook in his free hand. When he reached the wet and smoldering car, he yelled up his evaluation of the crash.

"Looks like there's just one person in the car. Burned completely up. Can't tell from here if it's male or female."

Ray carefully attached the massive hook to the car's frame and began his ascent back up the steep ravine. The incline was massive, a treacherous climb most would fear to undertake. As soon as he reached the top, he stooped to catch his breath.

"That's over a hundred foot drop! Hell, I'm too old for this," he gasped. "That's what I keep telling my wife."

"You'll never retire," said one of the other men.

"Shoot, if that son of mine would get with the program, I'd sure as heck slow down a little."

After Ray caught his breath, he pushed and pulled three separate levers, and within minutes, the black steel frame housing the charred human remains was once again on top. The sheriff bent down slightly to have a look inside. The local bystander in the plaid shirt insisted on having a look over Castleman's shoulder as well. He groaned with horror. "I ain't never seen anything like that in my life!"

The burnt corpse was leaning on its side; its right shoulder lying on the incinerated passenger seat. The extremities were completely blackened, with all digits missing. The arms, wrists, and legs were drawn up in a "pugilistic" position, a term used in forensic science to describe the drawing up of the arms and legs toward the body's torso, as the water and lactic acid leave muscle tissue. A major portion of the dashboard had collapsed from heat so that its burned remains lay half on the floorboard and half on the head of the corpse.

The right side of the skull and cranial vault had been exposed to the fire's hottest part leaving the upper and lower jaws in an ashen state. The heat had also caused several small holes in the skull, with other portions of boney material flaking away like fine ashes in a fireplace.

The car frame contained no remnants of any clothing or other personal items. The seat springs were blackened with soot, and protruded randomly around the burned body. Even though the license plate had burnt completely off, the VIN number on the front dash, stamped into a much more resilient metal, was still visible.

Ray read out the long sequence of letters and numbers as the sheriff took them down. He immediately radioed the information to the Tennessee Department of Safety. Within five minutes, they had the information they were looking for. The owner of the '92 Honda was Clint Alton Logan of Smithville, Tennessee.

The two counties were about one hundred miles apart, DeKalb being located southeast of Nashville. He knew Sheriff Billy Roswell well, and they would coordinate the investigation and identification in the case on a local level.

Ray shook his head in disbelief. "I just hope and pray the driver was knocked out before that car caught fire. No death is pretty, but this one even gives me the creeps."

6

SHERIFF BILLY ROSWELL of DeKalb County stepped onto the small, concrete porch of a clapboard house in Smithville. A gentle breeze from the southwest provided temporary relief from the unusually high humidity, which had left his uniform top clinging to his skin. He removed his hat and stood for a moment, staring down at a beetle making its way along the edge of a brown woven welcome mat. Before he could let himself get too lost in thought, he lifted his head and pressed the doorbell. These were the moments the Sheriff most dreaded; it was never easy to notify a family of a fatality.

"Just a minute, please," a woman called from inside. He heard footsteps, some shuffling, and a few seconds later, a pretty young woman appeared. Her dyed blonde hair was gathered into a light blue scrunchie on the top of her head. Already, he regretted what he had to tell her.

"Ma'am, are you Amy Logan?" he asked. She didn't answer, so he continued. "My name is Sheriff Roswell. May I come in?"

"Sure thing, Sheriff," she said. The young woman seemed out of breath and in a hurry, as if she might be late for work. She glanced at her wristwatch. "Please come in." She stepped aside and motioned for him to follow her. "Is there something wrong, Sheriff?"

The Sheriff paused and looked up at the ceiling. He stuttered as he struggled to find the right words. "Do you and your husband still own a gray 1992 Honda?" The two stood awkwardly just inside the doorway, and the sheriff nervously ran his fingers along the brim of his hat as he waited for her answer.

"Uh, yes, sir, we do. What is it? Is something wrong?" A concerned look spread across her brow. The sheriff didn't answer right away. It was always difficult for Sheriff Roswell to make direct eye contact when delivering bad news.

"Do you have any reason to believe that anyone other than your husband would be driving your gray 1992 Honda?"

"No, sir, that's the car he drives all the time. He's been gone for a couple of weeks with a buddy of his, but is actually supposed to be home sometime today. Is there a problem?"

"Ma'am, maybe we should sit down."

The sheriff motioned toward the sofa, and the two of them sat down.

"Ma'am, I'm sorry to tell you that your husband, Clint Logan, has apparently been killed in an automobile accident about a hundred miles from here in Dickson County."

A shocked look of horror washed across Amy's face. The sheriff paused for her response; she said nothing.

"Here's what we do know for sure right now. One body burned in a 1992 Honda Civic registered to Clint Alton Logan. We'll need some medical and dental records to positively confirm his identity. We've just received this information a couple hours ago from the Dickson County Sheriff's Department.

"I know this is a terrible burden for you, but I wanted to come and tell you personally. We are working directly with Sheriff

Castleman and his team over in Dickson County." The sheriff's eyes locked on the blue plaid pillow lying on the sofa beside Amy. He couldn't bear to see her facial expression.

For an instant, the young woman's face seemed frozen. Then, she crumpled. "Oh no, Sheriff, please tell me it isn't true! It just can't be true! How can this be? He was almost home from his trip!" She buried her head in the palms of her hands, and wept like a child.

The Sheriff sat very still. He knew from experience that he should wait and allow family members to process the news and then speak later. After what seemed like an eternity, she finally looked up. Her eyes were filled with tears, mascara streaming down her face in helpless desperation.

"Clint had his problems, and we did argue a lot. But I loved him, you know? So what now? What do I do? Where do I go from here?"

Although he'd been on the force for decades, Sheriff Roswell found his voice catching in his throat. His heart went out to this woman, so young and now so terribly bereaved. He carefully explained to her that he would need her to obtain her husband's dental records. Clint's identity couldn't be one hundred percent confirmed without them.

"Dental records? Oh, no... It must be really bad." She'd seen cases like this on television but never dreamed it would happen to her. "Was there a fire?"

"Yes ma'am, I'm afraid there was. A pretty bad one."

Again, she covered her face and sobbed openly. Roswell, overcome by her grief, gently placed his arm around her shaking body in a futile attempt to comfort her. "What about J.D.?" Amy asked. "Maybe he's the one who died. He was supposed to be with Clint. Are you *sure* it's my husband?"

"Don't know anything about anyone named J.D. yet. We're

just in early stages of investigation. It was a pretty intense fire. There is only one body in the car. Dental records will confirm all that."

"Our family dentist is Dr. Bowkamp."

"As far as we can tell, he lost control and went over the embankment at the top of Gatlin's Ridge in Dickson County. That's why we'll need to get some more details of your husband's trip, where he was headed, the route he was taking, things like that, as soon as you've had a chance to recover from the shock of all this."

"Sir, do you mind if I try to call my work and tell them that I won't be in today? I don't know if I can do this or not." Never before had Amy faced such a daunting task. She wondered where she would get strength to get through it all. The Sheriff looked down at his own hands. They trembled with fear and sorrow.

7

Amy stepped into the kitchen to get the cordless phone. She came back in the living room, opposite from Roswell. "Excuse me, officer while I…"

"Ma'am, I'm sorry to interrupt, but I'll be happy to make that call for you, if you need me to."

"No, sir. Thanks, but I have to do this myself. Just please give me a minute. Just stay right here with me." She clutched a wad of wet tissue in her fist.

Amy looked down as Sheriff Roswell was reaching for his handkerchief. Tears were freely flowing down his face. "I'm sorry, Ms. Logan. I'm so overcome by all this that I just don't quite know how to handle it. I know I'm not doing you much good, and that's what my job is supposed to be."

"Oh, Sheriff! You are so sweet!" Amy attempted to wipe another mascara run from her tear-drenched face. The Sheriff had a daughter, Nancy, who was about Amy's age, and the event transferred as a personal loss for him as well. He cleared his voice, stammered a little, and then said, "Let's you and I take a little drive over to Dr. Bowkamp's office. "This way, we'll be able to know for certain. Who knows, he could have loaned the car to a friend." Roswell knew deep down inside that the chances of that happening were slim.

When they arrived at Dr. Bowkamp's office, Amy explained the accident to the receptionist. Fortunately, no patients had arrived yet. One by one, each staff expressed their condolences. Although they hadn't known Clint well, two of the assistants began to cry at the sight of Amy's drawn, lost expression. The office administrator, Helen, escorted Amy and Roswell into an adjoining conference room. Within a few minutes, the staff had prepared a manila envelope containing dental X-rays and clinical notes.

Helen handed the packet to the grieving Amy. "Sweetheart, we are so very sorry for your loss. We usually take photos of all of our patients. Here is a recent picture we took of him during his checkup month before last." She handed the 4x6 color face shot of Clint smiling with a wide grin.

"Oh, thank you so much, Helen. I'll cherish this forever." Amy sobbed.

Roswell drove Amy home, and as he pulled the squad car up the driveway, he apologized again for her loss and assured her that they would be back in touch within a couple of days. At that time, they would let her know results of the comparison. "I don't think the records comparison should take too long. Dr. Chris Walsh usually completes these within twenty-four hours." Amy thanked him for his sincere concern and care.

"Can I call some of your family for you?" Sheriff Roswell asked. "You need to have family close by during times like this."

Amy smiled wearily and nodded to him. "Thank you, sir, but I think I can manage. You've already done way too much."

Amy slowly closed the door of the squad car and made her way up the short sidewalk. Her shoulders were bent, and loose strands of her hair fell across her face. The sheriff watched until she was inside and closed the door. He turned the ignition, passed a trembling hand across his eyes, and pulled away from the curb.

It never gets any easier, he thought to himself.

8

CODY BRITTON's fingers brushed the steel strings of his acoustic guitar, gently drawing a final chord of his last set into the thin, stale air. The notes faded quickly, drowned out by the dry laughter of three not-so-dry drunks sitting in the corner. They were the last patrons left in the place, but they apparently hadn't realized he had stopped singing. It didn't matter, anyway; they were too wasted to even put their hands together in polite applause.

"That might be the last chord I'll ever play in New Mexico," Cody thought. He shook his head and felt himself smiling ruefully. It seemed like an awfully anticlimactic way to close out his last gig.

He absent-mindedly retuned each of the six guitar strings, his ear precisely trained on every note as his mind raced ahead to where exactly his life might turn. He was more than ready to leave New Mexico—there was no question about that.

No one had ever really appreciated Cody's style of music at The Blueroom. He loved the people in Albuquerque; they were really his kind of people, but they had no true appreciation of his craft. The bar where he played had been an Albuquerque mainstay for fifty years, owned currently by a fellow named Roddy.

29

His patrons were the bluest of blue-collar workers, who cared more about cashing their checks on Friday and getting liquored up than savoring the type of country music that Cody had spent years mastering.

Albuquerque was a flat, dusty, cowboy town, one that lacked glitz and glamour that Cody yearned for in his dreams. It was home, and always would be. But Cody was ready to move on, ready to spread his wings and head to Music City.

His tip jar that night was almost empty, but what he made last weekend from moonlighting for the Cutting Horse Show would get him all the way to Nashville if he economized. This, along with his paycheck from his part-time job at the Albuquerque feed store, meant he had enough for a deposit on that studio apartment behind Music Row in Music City, USA. He'd seen it advertised in a Nashville magazine and hoped it was still available. Barely getting by in Music City sounded like heaven compared to plodding through this local smoky bar for the rest of his life.

Cody planned to survive on his savings for a few weeks until he found a job even if it was in some music executive's mailroom. Garth Brooks started out that way, selling cowboy boots at Boot Country in Goodlettsville, Tennessee for years before his time finally came. Faith Hill had found her way to Nashville all the way from Star, Mississippi, and she'd worked for Reba McIntyre's fan club until her big break came. If it could happen to them, it could happen to Cody. He knew it just as sure as he knew his name.

He'd read about the Rainbow Guitar Bar not far from Music Row where he could sing his songs for record company royalty on "Writer's Night." It would certainly be a far cry from singing here at the Blueroom Cafe, where the beer was cheap and the women were stale. Besides, Cody had heard that Roddy was planning to call it quits after twenty-five years in business. He was getting too old to be bartender, bouncer, and bookkeeper, and wanted to move to Oregon to be closer to his kids. If Roddy could make a big change at his age, Cody could certainly make an effort to get out of his rut.

While he was apprehensive about the hard work, rejection, and uncertainty of a career in the music business, having regrets about not even trying was far scarier. Music had been on his mind since he was eight years old—ever since his mother, Cayla, first entered him in a talent show sponsored by the Lion's Club in Pocatello, Idaho. It was the first thing he'd ever won. He'd gotten a blue ribbon for *"Home on the Range,"* which Cody played on his first store-bought ukulele. Cayla had taught him to play the ukulele when he was just five years old, and she had always been his biggest fan. She was a remarkably brave woman with great strength and a thirst for adventure. Nothing fazed her. Maybe that's where Cody got his courage to try new things.

The closest Cayla ever got to a professional music career was playing the mandolin and singing on Cal Gregory's Country Countdown, a local version of the Grand Ole Opry to country music fans in the Pocatello area. But her plans took a backseat to real life when she married the love of her life, Don Britton, a salt-of-the-earth, hard-working, good man.

When Don was killed suddenly in a car accident in the spring of 1977, Cody was just ten years old. A drunk driver crossed the centerline as Don was coming home from working the graveyard shift at a tire plant outside of Pocatello. Cayla was left alone with only a minimum wage job in a fabric store and a young mouth to feed. But she was determined. She took in sewing and alterations for extra money. Cody's clothes were perfectly clean and pressed, and there was always good food to eat. Every Sunday, Cody sang in the church choir, and Cayla bragged on her son's voice to everyone she met.

In the summer of 1979, Cayla moved with Cody to Albuquerque, New Mexico for a higher paying job. She thought that being able to better support her son might help her with the deep-seated grief she couldn't seem to shake since she lost Don.

But in March of 1987, exactly ten years since Don's life had tragically ended, Cayla was diagnosed with stage-four breast cancer. The disease was devastating, swift, and fatal. She passed away in four short months. It rocked the very foundation upon which Cody, who was only twenty at the time, had been raised.

If Cayla Britton had been alive now, she would have urged him to go after his dreams while he had the chance. This was the time to put his plans in motion and become another singer seeking fame and fortune in Tennessee. He had as good a shot as anyone. Maybe even a better shot. He just had to get there.

9

CODY HAD READ all about the American South in magazines—lush green hills, sprawling lakes, and rushing rivers everywhere. But he'd never actually been east of the Mississippi River. He read in *Country Weekly* magazine that some of the country stars had mansions on Old Hickory Lake and in the Great Smoky Mountains. He couldn't wait to have a look for himself.

Going from a one bedroom efficiency to a mansion on a hill meant he'd have to live frugally. He might have to sing for his supper on the streets, sweep out bars and maybe even wait tables in cafes in order to make a name for himself. But he didn't doubt that his talent would be noticed sooner or later. He wouldn't fall through the cracks. He was just too determined and stubborn for that to happen.

He was still struggling with one detail, however. The name "Cody" wasn't a sexy, commercial name for the music business. He couldn't picture it on an album cover. It just wasn't memorable enough. Using the first syllable of his last name, he thought "Britt" would work, but he hadn't settled on a new last name yet. He thought the name "Britt Britton" sounded like a television anchorman. Maybe he could be a one-name act like Cher or

Elvis. So far, there wasn't anyone in country music known only by his first name. Not unless you counted Hank or Waylon.

Cody shook that question from his mind. There would be plenty of time to worry about marketing himself once he arrived in Nashville—he could mull over it as he emptied the trash at the RCA building. Why, that's how Kris Kristofferson got started, or so Cody had heard.

Just as Cody was starting to draw himself back into the reality of the Blueroom Cafe, a piercing, nasal voice cut across the dingy barroom.

"You think yer gonna hit the charts with that last one, huh, Cody?" It was Rafe, the owner of the local pawnshop and a regular barfly at Blueroom.

"We'll see." Cody really didn't want to continue the conversation with this bunch.

Cody scoffed to himself as he returned to delicately tuning the strings of his guitar. He couldn't leave these bums behind fast enough. But then, suddenly, his memory caught up with him, slamming into place like a dull wrecking ball hitting his chest.

There *was* one person who Cody truly would miss. Christine Browning, the resident bartender at the Blueroom. He had to admit that their friendship had developed into much more; he was in love with Christine. That bleach-blonde, blue-eyed cowgirl had a smile that would catch anyone's eye. Her petite, five-foot-four frame and well-proportioned figure were more than enough to make most of her customers drool with desire. Her classic attire for work at the Blueroom was a pair of cutoff blue-jean shorts coupled with a Blueroom Cafe t-shirt, carefully knotted up in the back to show her biscuit brown tummy, flat as a washboard. Tiny brown toes, usually painted with bright orange or blue toenail polish, decked out her characteristic black flip-flops.

Cody often found it next to impossible to keep his eyes and mind on his guitar when Christine was working. That was what scared him. He was so intent on his music career that he practically saw any distraction, even one involving testosterone, as a violation of his long-term plans.

He had told Christine countless times that she didn't deserve to spend the rest of her life pouring beer into frosty mugs and sweeping up spilled popcorn past midnight. And she had reminded him in turn that she would certainly welcome a change of venue; all Cody had to do was extend the invitation. Christine saw nothing at all wrong with raising her future family in Nashville.

Christine had dropped out of high school in the eleventh grade to help her parents with past-due bills. She started as a short-order cook in the kitchen of the Blueroom Cafe, but quickly graduated to full-time bartender by the time she was eighteen. No one, Roddy included, paused to consider the fact that she was underage and serving alcohol in a bar in New Mexico.

Cody knew that their relationship was really something special. They spent countless hours in one-on-one conversation, going as far as to confess to each other what they were looking for in a spouse. Christine hadn't been shy; she made it quite clear that someone just like Cody was just what she was looking for. She'd only had one boyfriend, and that relationship fizzled before it really got started. Every man she had met since then had been measured against the "Cody yardstick."

Christine couldn't take her eyes off Cody from the moment she saw him. He was her lifelong ideal of handsome—tall with dark hair and eyes. She loved to run her fingers across the dark stubble on his face and down his neck, over his smooth olive complexion. She knew it embarrassed him when she was so forward, even when they were alone, talking long past closing time.

It was no secret to the regulars that Christine wanted a "passel of young'uns" who looked just like the talented and sexy crooner of the Blueroom Cafe. One night, she unabashedly told an audience about how she could picture Cody's famous brooding face on a big poster hanging in her bedroom . . . but she admitted she was holding out for the real thing in her bedroom someday soon.

"Sweetie, I want those big brown eyes singing to me all night," she'd whisper lowly to Cody as he finished up his last set.

Without a doubt, she wasn't alone in her feelings. He felt a warm rage inside him when they were alone. It was all he could do to rein himself in, stubbornly reminding himself that Nashville was still just out of his reach, and how he needed to stay focused if he was ever going to get there.

Christine was off tonight, and Jerry was filling in. He knew the goodbyes would be so hard. "Maybe I should just slip away into the darkness," he thought. It wasn't what he really wanted to do, but it was the easy way out.

10

SUDDENLY, Cody jumped up from his stool like he had been shot. He had been sitting on that rickety stage tuning a guitar for God knows how long in a deep trance. He had been plucking and re-plucking notes that couldn't get truer if Chet Atkins were playing them.

"What the—?" Cody actually spoke out loud to what was now a totally empty room. It was like he had been in a trance. How long had he stared at the floor, tuning his guitar? He let out a sigh of relief when he realized that Rafe and his drunken buddies were long gone and no one had witnessed his zoning out.

But just as he did, a recognizable voice came from the back of the dimly lit, smoke infested bar.

"Hey, sweetie! You knocked that last tune outta the park! Too bad there were so few people to hear it. But look what I got." Christine held up a battered but functioning portable cassette recorder that she had slung loosely around her neck. It had been capturing every precious moment that she could now cherish forever of her Cody's music.

Christine ran to Cody through the smoky room, her flip-flops popping like bubble wrap. Her blonde hair, carefully braided in two pigtails, held nearly as much spring and bounce as her plump breasts, freely housed in her snug Blueroom Cafe t-shirt.

"Oh sweetie, it was awesome!"

"Thanks, sweetie." The pair had affectionately begun calling each other "sweetie" about three months earlier, even before they knew how much the pet name really revealed about their true feelings for each other.

As Cody pulled Christine's body tightly against his, his mind was nearly overcome with passionate rage. Oh, how he wanted this woman! But Cody felt sure that it had to be one way or the other. Stay here with Christine and give up his dreams of becoming a country star, or head to Nashville and give up a future with Christine. Never did it enter Cody's mind that he could have the best of both worlds.

"I thought you weren't coming down tonight," Cody breathed into Christine's sweet smelling hair. "Don't get me wrong; I'm tickled you're here."

"Sweetie, do you honestly think I'd stay away from seeing your last show, that is 'til we see you next on the *Grand Ole Opry*? I've even got you on tape now, and I'll wear this little machine out!"

Cody simply couldn't resist the impulse to pull his lips to hers in a passionate embrace.

After what seemed like an eternity, Christine gently drew away. "What's the name of that last song, anyway? I hadn't heard that one before."

"It's a new tune I wrote last night. It's called *I Will Return*."

Christine was still in his arms. Her royal blues eyes gazed intently into his, and she asked, "Is that a promise? *Will* you return?"

Cody responded as if he had rehearsed this for years, just in case the subject ever came up. "Sweetie, I will be back, I promise. To get you."

Christine broke into a broad, coy smile. "Now, what exactly does that mean?"

"Well, sweetie, I will be sending you a plane ticket to Nashville as soon as I can get myself situated with a place to stay and some income. Who knows, you might even like the place."

"Now that it's gotten right down to it, I don't know if I can stand to see you go. What am I gonna do? The Blueroom is closing down, and you're leaving. It just seems like my whole world is going to collapse, all at the same time!"

"Now don't you go thinking like that. You know, my granddaddy told me an old saying a long time ago, and it's really stuck with me. He said, 'If it's meant to be, you can't stop it, and if it's not meant to be, then you can't make it happen.' That's what we really have to believe in."

"Oh, I knew you'd have some deep philosophical way to explain it to me. You are so smart, Cody."

He gave her a funny look. He knew she hardly ever called him Cody.

"Well," she said finally, "I suppose I'll tell you why I showed up here tonight. I want to help you close up, and then I want you to come over to my apartment. I have to give you a proper sendoff. I will not take no for an answer." Her smile radiated from her gorgeous, round face. "Please don't turn me down."

Cody gazed into her eyes, thought a minute, and said, "Sweetie, that's something that I've wanted for a long, long time. But I was afraid it would just make it harder on both of us when it got time for me to leave. I tell you what, how 'bout you go on back and get some sleep? I'll pick you up tomorrow around noon. We'll fix a picnic and spend the whole day together. How does that sound?"

"So you're not coming over?"

"I want more for us than that."

"You mean…?"

"I said I'd be sending for you, didn't I?"

"That sounds like a proposal to me."

"A promise of one, anyway. But let me get settled first. I want to do it up right."

Christine reached up again and planted the longest and wettest kiss on Cody's lips that he could remember. Cody knew Christine would be a part of his future. One day soon she would carry his name everywhere she went. She would be counting the days.

11

It was half past two in the morning by the time Cody finished breaking down all his gear. It felt really weird, taking down the speakers, amps, and mikes that had been such a bedrock of his musical career for the last few years. If he never smelled cigarette smoke again, it would be too soon.

Thoughts of Christine and some last-minute regrets were streaming like a movie in his head as he walked down the street to his room, two flights above the Town and Country Restaurant. That was another smell he wouldn't miss, old cooking grease clinging to his clothes. Everything at the Town and Country was fried, even the coffee. But it had been a good breakfast place for him in the wee hours after work.

He climbed the rickety stairs above the restaurant, ready for one last lonely Saturday night in his grimy little room he called home for three years. Struggling out of his cowboy boots, smoke-logged jeans, and black t-shirt, Cody stepped in the shower and let hot water run over his face. He was tossing around the idea of shaving his signature two-day-old beard, but decided against it. If he was going to be a scruffy hitchhiker next week, he might as well look the part.

Stepping out of the shower, Cody felt as though he had washed off a year's worth of going nowhere. He plopped down on his rickety twin bed. Next to his guitar was his legal pad of half-written songs, which was stacked atop a three-ring binder full of music he had written since he was fifteen. Somewhere in this binder was a hit that would go platinum. These prized possessions, his only worldly goods, could be slung over his shoulder in one guitar case and a backpack. He would travel light to reach the top. As soon as he got his paycheck from the feed store at the end of the coming week, he'd be ready to start thumbing his way east.

This felt right. All of it…except leaving Christine.

He turned out the light and, as he had done since he was a little boy, said a prayer that morphed into more of a conversation. He talked to God about the years so far and how he might not have been the best example to others but how he intended to make up for it with his music. He ended his prayer by giving thanks for a place to sleep, food to eat, and enough resources to share with friends he might meet along the way. He prayed for guidance and the wisdom to begin this new chapter in his life.

With that, Cody set the alarm for 11:00 a.m. and drifted off to the best sleep he had enjoyed in years.

12

CLINT LOGAN ROLLED OVER and hit the snooze button again, groggily noticing that his wife Amy was already in the shower, having sprung out of bed at the first alarm. Her secretarial job at the bottling plant meant they could at least eat and make the house payment until he could replace the job he had lost two months ago. And that wasn't the first time. Amy was growing tired of supporting Clint.

This was the time of day when it all started replaying in his head, when he first opened his eyes in the morning and realized that he wouldn't have a paycheck coming in today, or any day in the foreseeable future. No more happy hour drinks with his buddies. No more tickets to the ballgame. That was the worst part of being out of work. Having to ask Amy's permission to spend money really stung Clint's pride, especially since Amy had gotten so smug about being the only breadwinner.

Amy was trying to decide what to wear to work. She was obviously annoyed that her husband was still in bed. She noticed him restlessly tossing in bed, trying to decide whether or not he should get up.

"When are you going to apply for that unemployment?" Amy asked—the same refrain she'd been singing every morning for three weeks, and he was getting tired of hearing it. "Jeanine said her husband got good money from that until her sister got him that job at the printing shop."

Clint wasn't listening to a word Amy said. His eyes were fixed on her shapely figure, which cast an even more tantalizing shadow on the door of the bedroom closet. She was wearing a yellow and blue striped bra and bikini panties, highlighting her buxom breasts. She was standing with one hand on her right hip; her left leg was bent up at an angle, with her left foot resting against her right knee. She stared at her wardrobe indecisively, index finger pointing against her cheek.

"What a little sexpot this morning! Any chance you could call in and be a little late? Might be a chance to catch up on some sugar."

Amy looked stunned. "Clint, are you serious! You're gonna make me lose my job! One of us has to bring in a paycheck! Get off your ass and get a job like the rest of us do around here. It might just be a good idea for you to take a swing at pulling your weight around this place."

Clint mumbled something to himself. Then, louder, he shot back at Amy, "I'll take that as a qualified, 'Thanks, but no thanks.'"

She didn't see him give her the finger. She was fumbling with her watch and big, hoop earrings. "There's a pot pie in the freezer, and it'll take an hour to cook, so follow directions on the package and put it in the oven around four thirty so we can eat when I get home."

"I'm callin' Jimmy Dale when I get up, and we might go somewhere."

"Suit yourself. But I swear, Clint, if you're there laying up drunk on the couch when I get home, I'm leavin'!" Amy warned, taking one last look in the full-length mirror on the door. She liked her outfit, not her husband.

When Clint first had met Amy, she was just a skinny little bleached blonde working behind the counter at a pawn shop on Second Avenue. She was impressed with his Harley-Davidson Clint had parked out in front when he came in to hock a pistol his grandfather had given him.

They cruised down Broadway together in lunch-hour traffic and sped west on River Road, stopping for a beer at a little joint on the water and watching the sunset. She was unlike any girl he had ever met—a free spirit with an idea that money—somehow—would always land in her sexy little lap.

13

THE NEXT MORNING couldn't arrive soon enough for Christine. She hadn't given a second thought to what she would include in the picnic basket. That was low on her priority list. She had a sneaking suspicion that this would be a day for her and Cody's memory book.

Just the right amount of blush, just a touch of eyeliner. She didn't need much—she already had way too much natural beauty; her cute little pigtails from the night before now replaced with long flowing curls that framed her beautiful face. Cody had told her once that she was pretty enough to be a cover girl. She smiled to herself at that wonderful memory. She wiggled her hips slightly from side to side, allowing the white cotton sundress with spaghetti straps and pink lace to slither down her little waist. She would be embarrassed if Cody knew she had been primping for nearly two hours.

The knock at her front door reminded Christine that the most wonderful day of her life was about to begin. She skipped across the living room rug as if she were gliding on air, her bare feet seemingly floating across the room. With one smooth swoop and a broad smile, she opened the door to the most handsome man she had ever seen.

Cody wore a pair of freshly washed black jeans that strategically accented all the manly shapes that Christine so wanted to touch and feel. His black roper style boots were polished perfectly. He wore his freshly ironed white linen shirt like he was ready to model in New York City.

"Oh my gosh, sweetie! I think I'm in love!" Christine giggled like a teenager who just got her first kiss.

"Hey, sweetie! Wow! It's gonna be hard to pay attention to the picnic basket with somebody pretty as you sitting right next to me." His equally broad smile glowed with mutual excitement. He stretched both arms out to give her a big hug, but soon found his lips pressed against hers in a wet kiss that they both wished would never end. With eager anticipation, she pulled him from the front porch, their lips still locked tightly.

Christine had never felt a burning desire like this. Her hands groped every inch of his muscular shoulders, sliding down to embrace his lower back and then his butt. Cody needed little encouragement to reciprocate.

"Whoa now, sweetie!" Cody laughed as he half-heartedly tried to break himself free from Christine's grip. "We better finish this later. I need to help you make some sandwiches."

It was obvious that Christine was a woman on a mission. Cody was not going to escape without what they both so desperately wanted.

"You know, I can eat sandwiches tomorrow, and the next day and the next. I don't know when I'll see you again."

With that, her tight little hip nudged her front door closed, and, without losing that ironclad lip-lock, she blindly reached behind him to lock it in one smooth motion. Finally, she came up for air, grabbing Cody's hand. With a wink and a smile, she said, "Follow me. End of story."

Cody gave no resistance. He was at her mercy. All their inhibitions were suddenly gone. Christine's heart was pounding with desire. They found their way quickly into her bedroom, modest but spotless. Still tightly clutching Cody's hand, she sat down on the side of her bed and pulled him down beside her. Placing both her hands around the back of his neck, she resumed the passionate kisses that had already sent him into orbit.

Cody's hands no longer felt awkward. He gently caressed every square inch of her back, sides, and then, slowly, her breasts. Christine's breath quickened; Cody's muscular chest expanded and contracted with increasing velocity. She groaned lovingly with each passing moment. Her hands slowly and methodically slid under Cody's shirt. His rocky abs seemed to vibrate with desire. It was as if every button in both of their bodies had been switched to the 'on' position. Cody managed to free one hand and reach for his shirt, beginning to unbutton it.

Christine smiled at his efforts and gazed into his midnight brown eyes. "No. Let me do that." With that, she replaced his hand with hers and slowly, one button at a time, she began the amorous task of slipping each pearly gem out of its individual buttonhole. She giggled with delight. His breathing was becoming a slow gallop.

Cody began to groan with desire. He reached up to slide off her cotton spaghetti straps of the sundress. "Is it my turn now?"

Christine giggled again, saying nothing but placing her right index finger on his lips. She shook her finger from side to side as if to say, "Nah nah nah. Not yet! I'll let you know when it's time. It won't be long."

When the last button surrendered, Cody's shirt hit the floor. Christine's pink polished fingernails glistened like diamonds in the sunlight through her bedroom window. She ran her hands down his two-day-old beard, massaging his neck and scalp as she moved to his shoulders, back, and finally his abs again.

Next came Cody's belt—a rich, black, handsome piece of cowhide that shone like a new penny. Christine's inhibitions were completely gone by now; she was operating on pure animal instinct. She groped blindly for his buckle, and in one swift motion, it was free.

Christine paused briefly, looked up to meet Cody's eyes, and smiled. He started to say something, but she smiled again, looked back to her treasure, and pushed him back flat on her bed. Her lips and tongue gleefully explored the playground of Cody's well-developed stomach and chest. As her mouth found new and exciting areas to explore, her left hand managed to find the top of his jeans button.

"Okay, sweetie. It's your turn now."

Like a polished actor right on cue, Cody rolled Christine over on her back, and gently felt the soft, delicate skin on her face as he continued to shower her with never-ending kisses. Slowly, his hands migrated toward her breasts and the front button of her sundress. As his wrist gently rubbed across them, she groaned loudly. She grabbed Cody's hand and gave him full and complete direction to all the places she insisted he visit. She was in outer space.

A wave of sensation, somewhat primitive and unfamiliar to either of them, began to build as their urgency reached its peak. They became animals, gripping and gnawing at each other with muscular jerks and lunges. Within moments they were both naked. Two sets of hands sped up their exploring as the writhing and moaning continued to mount. Cody rolled over on top of Christine. He was puffing like he was about to finish a marathon.

"Sweetie, please! Please!"

White lights, bells, whistles, sirens. Christine felt it all. She could finally express the love she had for this man. As he arched his back and groaned loudly, she fell into a mixture of laughing and crying inexplicably. She just didn't want it to end. As the tears rolled down her cheeks, she shook with uncontrollable emotion.

They both lay still and motionless, staring at the ceiling. Sweat was pouring from all the pores of their bodies. Christine's hair was plastered to her forehead and cheeks as if she had been roping cattle all day. Her face shone with a contentment that she had never experienced before in her lifetime. Cody shook his head from side to side and gasped, "Whew! That was off the charts!"

Christine laughed out loud, tears still rolling down her cheeks. Her makeup was already long gone, but Cody would never have noticed. Her natural beauty radiated through.

"What's wrong, sweetie? Are you okay? Why are you crying?"

"Nothing. It's a girl thing. All I know now is that I died today; my life is complete."

"Sounds like a good name for a song. I may have to work on that one. That was absolutely wonderful! I've been waiting a long time for that."

"Me too."

Just as she'd expected, the day did become the most memorable of Christine's life. She and Cody shared their treasures with each other another three or four times that afternoon, each one carefully documented in Christine's diary. Later, she would be able to cherish each precious moment. The two of them laid in Christine's bed, reliving all the memories that they had made, all the way back to the first time that they locked eyes. The first time they met each other. The first time that they called each other "sweetie." Of course, Christine claimed to have been carrying Cody's torch way before Cody had a clue. Cody completely denied that, just claiming to be the one who was better able to hide his emotions.

Christine didn't know what she was going to do when the Blueroom Cafe closed up and Cody left town. They talked about that for a long time. Christine had promised herself that she wouldn't be too persistent about her desire to come to Nashville, but she was certain of one thing. If Cody hadn't been so wrapped up in his first love, singing country music and making it big in Nashville, she would already be on her way to raising his children. That was what she wanted more than anything else in the world. But she was smart enough to realize that for her dream to have any chance of coming to fruition, she would have to be patient and work herself into his country music plans.

"Can I ask you something?" she whispered. "Since you're leaving in just five days? Can we spend as much time together as possible? Who knows when I'll get to see you again."

"The devil himself couldn't keep me from seeing you again. I'll be back."

"I love you more than anything in this world," Christine confessed.

"Sweetie, I love you more."

14

MRS. SCOTT WAS clearing the breakfast dishes when her phone rang. She didn't care for Clint and never tried to hide that fact from anyone. She blamed Clint for whatever trouble her son, J.D. and Clint had experienced together. And she never had figured out what that nice girl Amy saw in him.

"Jimmy Dale, honey, Clint has to talk to you," Mrs. Scott called, bristling as she tossed the cordless handset onto her son's bed. Jimmy Dale propped the phone between his pillow and head, too lazy to hold the receiver in his hand.

"Jimmy Dale! 'Sup? Pick up a six-pack and some chips and get over here. I've got an idea you're gonna like, man." Clint barked out his marching orders to Jimmy Dale as he always did and didn't wait for a reply before hanging up.

Less than thirty minutes later, as if summoned by a king, Jimmy Dale burst through the door with chips and suds. He was singing some country song he'd heard on his truck radio. He tossed the cold six-pack to Clint and lay down on Logan's king-size bed, burying his face in Amy's pillow.

"Man, this better be good. I ain't used to gettin' out this early," Jimmy Dale grumbled, his voice muffled by the goose down.

Clint popped his first beer of the day, sat down with his back propped up against the headboard, and hatched his plan.

"I've got it all figured out, J.D. This time next week, we'll be sittin' pretty at a casino in Vegas, my man. Go home and get your stuff packed. You said you were due vacation from the market. We both need to get outta town for a couple of weeks. Make some easy money. Clean some cobwebs out of our minds. We're gonna drive straight through, and we're leavin' after lunch."

Clint tossed his beer can aside and disappeared down the hall. When he returned, he was carrying a giant duffel bag, which he over-filled with wadded jeans, wrinkled t-shirts, and dirty socks.

Jimmy Dale rolled over to watch his friend running around, opening drawers, and slamming closet doors as though he had been told to evacuate.

"What the hell are we gonna do in Vegas?" Jimmy Dale's eyes were still closed when he asked, as if he were trying to get back to sleep.

"We're gonna make us some money. Big money. Enough money for you to quit your job at the market. See? Right here… Look… On television right now." Clint said, as he pointed to his TV set and slipped into a t-shirt, mussing the few wisps of hair he had left on top of his balding head. "It's that Sharon Stone movie. It's so cool! We can get in on these poker games and blackjack, and we can win… We can win, buddy! There's so much money out there, man, and there's stacks of it with our names all over them. Women, too, my man."

"I don't know how to play poker." J.D. wasn't that enthusiastic.

"Don't, worry. I'll teach you."

Clint could get into an almost manic state that drove Jimmy Dale crazy sometimes. He was in that mode now, talking fast and swooping around like a bird—packing, throwing clothing, and dumping the contents of his dresser drawers on the floor. He left his bedroom and returned again, waving a small jewelry box above his head.

"Here it is. This is our seed money," Clint said, balancing the box with his fingers as if he were showing off Egyptian antiquities at Sotheby's.

Sliding the box top open, Clint revealed a large stack of cash—money that Amy had been squirreling away. She kept her secret box on top of the dresser in their spare bedroom.

"Holy smoke! These are all mostly Bens under this one-dollar bill!" Clint was moving his lips silently, counting the bills, his eyes getting bigger and bigger. He counted quickly.

"Twenty-five hundred dollars! She's been adding to it since I last counted it. Little sneak's been holdin' out on me! We can make a lot of money with this. Man, we're there!"

Jimmy Dale was sitting up in bed by now, sipping a beer and watching Clint's head spin like a top. "Don't you think she might miss the money if you take it?"

"Oh, come on, J.D.! We need a little extra cushion for our bankroll. We'll triple this in no time, and I'll put it back when we get back. She'll never miss it!"

"I dunno about that. That's your call."

"Well, get up and get goin'!" Clint ordered. "Be back over here by three o'clock—packed and ready to help me drive straight through. And don't you even think about coming over here without some money. I ain't financin' this whole trip."

Just as planned, Jimmy Dale's dad dropped him off in front of Clint's house with his bag and an envelope stuffed with $1,500. It was all his mother had; she wanted her little Jimmy Dale to have a good time on his vacation. He lied when he told her he was going with Clint and Amy to Panama City Beach. He also lied and assured her that he had cleared it with work. She never would have given him money to gamble away in Vegas. She'd worked too hard and saved too long.

Actually, J.D. was surprised that his mom would let him go anywhere with Clint, even with Amy supposedly chaperoning. According to her, he wouldn't have gotten in trouble with all that "dope" in the first place if it hadn't been for Clint.

Clint was already waiting impatiently in their driveway, sitting behind the wheel of his Honda Civic and smoking his first from a new carton of cigarettes. Jimmy Dale climbed in, rolled down his window to avoid the smoke, and closed his eyes as Clint left Smithville's city limits and headed toward I-40 West.

Jimmy Dale had a lot on his mind. His boss didn't buy his story that he had a "family emergency". He couldn't tell him about going to Vegas; that would get back to his mom. He'd make it up to his boss when they got back in town. Right now, he was just trying to catch forty winks and avoid driving as long as he could.

The sunset shone like an artist's brush as the "Welcome to Memphis" sign passed in their rear view mirror. Clint was getting chatty about his anticipated fortune he was going to win at the blackjack tables, a fortune he had already spent in his mind.

"Just think," Clint said, poking Jimmy Dale in the ribs to wake him, "when we come back through Elvis Country, we might be riding in a chauffeured limo! It happens every day, you know . . . to someone. It might as well be us!"

Clint was getting sleepy, but they had more miles to put under their belts for the first night. He tried to stay awake by explaining to Jimmy Dale about a new book that he had read on a guaranteed way to win at blackjack tables in Vegas. It had to do with card counting, an illegal system requiring a great deal of memorization and usually only mastered by a genius.

By keeping a mental record of cards that have been played, the player supposedly has a little edge—he can calculate when there is more or less likelihood of certain cards surfacing. By the time Clint got through with the basic overview, J.D. was snoring.

15

As quietly as he could, Dr. Chris Walsh turned the handle and inched open his back door. He couldn't make out any shapes or objects in the shadowed hallway; lights were off and it had been dark for several hours. For a moment, he paused and listened.

The house was quiet.

Walsh let out a sigh, closed the door gently behind him, and moved slowly down their hall. He felt strangely aware of his own breath, wondering for an odd moment whether it sounded as loud on the outside of his body as it did inside. Just then, his briefcase struck the wall beside him with a dull thud.

Dr. Walsh muttered. He'd gotten so focused on trying to breathe quietly that he'd drifted in darkness and walked right into the wall. The dull thud caused a few expletives, but triggered a sudden stir of Mollie and Millie, the couples' two canine children. Both dogs began howling as ferociously as they could, making every effort to protect their domain.

He set his briefcase down and passed his hand over the wall, feeling for any light switch.

With a loud click, the room flooded with light.

"Hey there!"

Walsh jumped.

Across the room, his wife Brandie was standing in a robe in the doorway between the kitchen and living room. She had just pulled the cord of a standing lamp next to the door, and her fingers still hovered on its gold fringe dangling back and forth.

"Brandie!" Dr. Walsh exclaimed. "Holy smoke!! You scared the crap out of me!"

Brandie smiled. "Did you really think you could sneak up on me, honey? Not with these two bloodhounds here to protect me."

Millie and Mollie were never more than six feet away from their mom. Millie, a West Highland Terrier, welcomed Chris with her lovable bark. Her sister, Mollie, nicknamed "clueless", a nine pound Bichon, was a little priss with a tail as fluffy as a French plume. She whined for Brandie's attention whenever she hugged her husband. It was clear Mollie thought that she was better than anyone else in the neighborhood.

"I wasn't trying to sneak up on you!" Walsh said, putting on his best imitation of an offended kid. "I was trying not to wake you."

Brandie laughed. "Oh, come on, it's hardly ten o'clock. Besides, you told me you'd be getting in late. I waited up for you." She tossed her head and disappeared into the kitchen. "You hungry?" Walsh heard her call over her shoulder. "Did you get anything to eat?"

Dr. Walsh didn't answer right away. "I might take something little, thanks".

The couple had their daily rituals and routines. He usually made his medical examiner's stops shortly after seeing his regular dental patients around five. That might put him home anywhere from six to eight in the evening, depending on his forensic case load.

It was a second marriage for both of them; their kids were grown; they had no children between them, but they both treasured his/hers. They also enjoyed being empty nesters. Chris' son was a junior in college in Birmingham, Alabama. His daughter had just graduated from University of Alabama and had recently begun working on her MBA degree while employed by Southtrust bank in Birmingham.

Brandie had one daughter, who had recently married a physician, working on his pediatric residency. They lived in Memphis. Brandie and Chris both were looking forward to having grandchildren someday.

As Brandie stood at their refrigerator, pulling out a Tupperware container, Walsh smiled to himself. Absent-mindedly, he started getting out a plate and silverware. Suddenly Brandie stopped; the refrigerator door was still half open. She stood staring at the Tupperware, her nose wrinkled in disgust. Her nose was so sensitive, Chris claimed she could work backup to the bloodhound units.

"I just fixed this chicken last night," she said. "How could it go bad already?" Then… "Do you…do you *smell* that?"

Dr. Walsh paused, pointing his nose into the air, twitching it from side to side. "I don't smell anything," he said. He crossed the kitchen and stretched out a hand to take the container of chicken from Brandie. He knew where this conversation was going, but waited patiently for it to unfold.

As he came toward her, Brandie recoiled, her face frozen between disgust and amusement. "Christopher!" she almost shouted. "It's you!"

Dr. Walsh felt all the blood rush into his face at once. The morgue. He'd spent three hours at the State Medical Examiner's Office, working on a decomposition case. "What do you mean, me?" He knew exactly what she was talking about, but played ignorant. Both thrived on teasing each other.

"Ugh!" Brandie tossed the Tupperware on the counter and started waving her arms in front of her face. She was half-laughing, half-grimacing. She started shooing him out of their kitchen.

"I'm so sorry—I didn't even think about—" Dr. Walsh stammered as he backed away.

"Shush! Garage! Now! Remember, that was our agreement? Millie, go on girl, go out and keep your daddy company while he undergoes decontamination!" Millie barked, following him through their living room, out toward the garage.

"But—where am I supposed to… What do you want me to…?"

Now she was laughing through her barked orders, one hand covering her mouth to shield her from the stench. She was in good spirits, but he knew she was serious. Once she realized the odor's source, she wanted no part of it!

The door swung shut, and Dr. Walsh found himself once again standing in darkness, with trusty Millie right by his side. Mollie had stayed behind to protect her mom. "The snowballs," as Chris often collectively called them, were truly as special as anyone's children. He always teased Brandie about her care for her the "children," and often commented that their dogs live better than most kids in North America. Chris chuckled at the number of times he'd complained that Millie and Mollie eat dinner before he did and they even got their food microwaved. Brandie's characteristic response was always the same, "What's your point?"

He fumbled along the wall until he found a light switch, flipped it, and blinked a few times as his eyes adjusted. Walsh chuckled to himself. He had such a good time teasing with Brandie. They both loved making each other laugh.

He'd been a forensic specialist for more than two decades— so long that he forgot how strange it must seem to others that he spent his nights in a forensic morgue. No company. Just unidentified human bodies. Mostly charred from a fire, decomposed or completely skeletonized. None were pretty and most smelled worse. When Nashville law enforcement discovered an unidentified victim, Walsh was often their first phone call.

That particular night, he'd been working on a drowning case. The victim hadn't been recovered until at least ten days after death. If there was one thing Dr. Walsh had learned from years of this work, it was that death and decomposition reduces everyone to the same state. We all look, feel and smell the same, and it wasn't very pretty. He had promised Brandie he would wear scrubs while in his morgue so any lingering odors wouldn't pollute their house. Tonight, he had forgotten. It was no wonder Brandie's sensitive nose had picked up on his evening activities.

Walsh chuckled to himself. "I can't smell a thing! You must be making this up!" In fact, it had been their chief topic of conversation on their first date. As they'd strolled along the beautiful streets of the Music City after a dinner, Brandie had smiled devilishly and reminded Christopher, "In my next life, I want to be a detective." Three dates later, she'd convinced him to bring along some of his files from closed cases. Those stories always fascinated her.

Dr. Walsh pulled on his robe ventured back in. "Is the coast clear now?"

"Straight to the shower!" she shouted as soon as she heard the door open.

Walsh laughed and started down the hall, but just then, he heard a muffled beeping behind him. Picking up his briefcase, which he had left in their entranceway, he recognized it was his mobile phone was ringing.

Walsh fished the brick out, knowing that a call this late would probably be another one from the Medical Examiner's Office. He was right.

"Hey Doc, it's Jerry from the M.E. office. Sara asked me to give you a call. I know you just left here and it's late, but we've just gotten a call from countywide. There's been a trailer fire off Dickerson Road. Pretty much leveled. Supposed to be a young mom with three small kids. Burned to the ground. Thought you needed a heads up."

16

NIGHTFALL BROUGHT them close to Little Rock, Arkansas. By
then, Jimmy Dale had finished his catnap, and Clint was about
to doze off behind the wheel. He had been relying on a whole
thermos full of coffee to keep his eyelids open, and now, he badly
needed to give back some of that coffee. They wheeled their
Honda into the next Stuckey's truck stop.

"You want me to drive a while?" Jimmy Dale said, chomping
on a newly purchased pecan roll and figuring he should at least
offer to relieve Clint.

After their Honda was filled and bladders were emptied, J.D.
started his shift. Clint fell asleep before they passed the next mile
marker. J.D. hadn't been driving long before he started getting
sleepy again. He turned on the radio to find some country tunes,
his favorite kind of music. The sudden blare of the music woke
Clint from a deep sleep. He jumped like he was shot.

"Numb nuts, what in the hell are you doing?" Clint shouted.

"Look, man. I almost ran off the road a couple times back
there. I'm not used to driving this long."

Clint looked at his watch. "Long, hell! You've only been

driving two hours. I've been driving all afternoon! How 'bout helping me out just a little."

"I'm sorry, man. Maybe I shouldn't have come. I didn't get much sleep last night, and I'm kinda nervous about all of this anyway. You think I'll get fired from the market for lying? I really don't understand gambling enough to be good at it."

Clint thought to himself for a minute. Maybe he was being a little hard on his buddy. This trip was going to be a marathon, not a sprint. They had to believe in each other and cover each other's backs. It dawned on Clint that he was going to have to manage most of this trip, but he knew he could still handle it. It wasn't exactly how he had it drawn up in his mind, but it would still work.

"I tell you what, J.D. How about I stay awake, and we talk to keep each other alert? We gotta save our meth; you know we didn't get away with very much, and I don't know how hard it's gonna be to run up on some out west."

"Oh, gosh, I forgot to tell you," J.D. exclaimed. "I was able to get two ounces from Wayne Bob this morning. His cousin finally came up with that contact who is helping them out."

Clint perked up instantly. "Awesome, man! Good job! That's gonna sweeten the whole trip! Tell you what. Let's celebrate. What's the hurry, anyway? I'm gonna find us a Holiday Inn or something, and we're gonna kick back! J.D., you are da man!"

Jimmy Dale wasn't sleepy any more. Knowing that he had a really good inventory of crank changed Clint's entire attitude of the trip.

The next bottle-green I-40 road sign told the boys they were on the outskirts of North Little Rock, Arkansas. Time to sit back, kick back, and enjoy. For the next forty-eight hours, life for Clint and Jimmy Dale went on pause. Vegas could wait.

17

"CLINT? YOU OKAY?"

The Oprah Winfrey Show was being broadcasted, but was muted. The red light on their telephone blinked steadily. Jimmy Dale looked at his watch; it read three-thirty. The light through their blinds told him it was afternoon, but he had no idea what day it was.

Jimmy Dale didn't know where he was. A "Do Not Disturb" sign was still up, and the chain was still fastened. They hadn't left the room; they just crashed and burned right there on the spot.

"Hey, Clint. Wake up. You okay? Where are we?"

"You know what time it is? I mean, you know what day it is?"

"No. But who cares? Aren't we somewhere near Little Rock, Arkansas?"

"Oh, yeah. Now, I remember. J.D. fumbled for the remote control and turned it up. *Headline News* was showing clips of Americans celebrating with Fourth of July festivities.

Jimmy Dale thought a shower might help him clear some cobwebs. Hot, steamy mist soon filled their bathroom. It *did* feel good to him. He felt like he was starting to get his thoughts back. Back where he could worry some more about his job status back in Smithville.

After Clint's shower, he felt more like himself with renewed enthusiasm for their trip ahead.

"Boy, J.D. That is some mighty good stuff. Wonder where Wayne Bob came up with that?"

"I dunno, but I'm so hungry, I could gnaw my arm off."

Jimmy Dale couldn't remember when a Waffle House breakfast had tasted so good. He also couldn't remember if he had ever tried to read their menu when he was sober. He couldn't get the "scattered, smothered, and covered" hash browns down the hatch quickly enough.

J.D. continued to marvel at the Southwest's vast flatlands. He reminded Clint that he had never before even crossed the Mississippi River. An occasional cactus or tumbleweed was a chilling reminder to him of his childhood days watching cowboys and Injuns battle it out in this kind of territory on TV.

Their route of travel took them due west through Oklahoma City, and then on to Amarillo. The guys were excited to cross the half-way point to Vegas. Unfortunately, it was also the city in which their chariot's air conditioner blew. By then, the daytime temperatures were hovering around ninety, with nighttime lows only reaching the high seventies.

The boys stopped by a Honda dealer in Amarillo; upon learning that cold air would cost six hundred dollars, Clint quickly decided that it was not in their budget. But it did seem like a good place to have a nice dinner before converting over to a nighttime driving schedule.

Sunrise greeted the duo as they wheeled into Albuquerque. Even with the meth, they decided it was time to get one more days' worth of sleep in a real bed before making the final nonstop to Vegas.

The Honda was beginning to show signs of its age, and to

make matters worse, the boys weren't exactly good stewards of their chariot. Crumpled up cigarette packs, Mountain Dew cans, and potato chip wrappers were strewn across the backseat and floorboard.

"I'm gonna shut one eye for just a bit. Wake me up if you get the least bit sleepy," Clint said.

"Okay, but I've got to have my country music."

Clint replied, "Okay, but I'm leaving my window up so don't blast me out. He would go along with anything now. As each mile got closer, he could visualize his soon to be found fame and fortune. Little did they know what type of fame and fortune lay around the corner.

18

CLINT AND JIMMY DALE must have looked like some version of the Beverly Hillbillies, both hanging their heads out of their windows, jaws drooping with wonder as their minds processed everything. J.D. was most impressed with an advertised ninety-nine-cent breakfast. Clint was excited to find out that they could see Willie Nelson perform at Caesar's Palace.

Circus Circus Hotel and Casino had a billboard advertising rooms for nineteen dollars. Clint won out, and the boys decided on the world-famous Circus Circus Hotel and Casino. Since neither had a credit card, the hotel required a $500 cash deposit to cover their tab. Room 7426. "Can you believe it J.D.? We're here! Let's just take our time, slow and easy, and we'll be in the money before you know it."

"I'm going to get me one of those ninety-nine-cent breakfasts. I don't care what time it is. I might even eat two."

The boys turned heads wherever they walked. J.D. thought it was because they looked so cool. Clint knew that was the case. Other gamblers may have had a different opinion. "Check this action out, J.D." All they could see was what seemed like miles of casino tables and rows of machines with lights and bells. Jimmy

Dale was intent on absorbing all the sights and sounds, but a flashing light from above caught his eye and turned his attention to directly overhead. They were the center ring performers for the "Greatest Show on Earth," happening right above all the casino action. J.D. only had eyes for the circus show. He wandered around in a daze like a nine-year-old seeing a trapeze bar for the very first time.

"Whaddaya think, so far?" Clint asked.

"I don't know what to say. Never seen anything like this in my life. It don't even seem real. Don't think I've ever been to a circus before, have you, Clint?"

Clint ignored Jimmy Dale.

They strolled to the entryway, and a massive, dark gray electronic door slid open. Their next stop would be The Bellagio.

"Twenty-five dollars on hard eight is a bet!" the stickman shouted as Clint made his first bet. Jimmy Dale was salivating as a gorgeous blonde cupped two shiny red dice, rubbed them on both breasts. She then kissed them, giggled to her mate and let the 'bones' fly.

"Eight, eight. Winner eight. Eight is a winner!" The stickman verified each payout. The crowded table shouted with approval. Clint's loud voice, recognizable by everyone, led their cheers.

He had just made a 'proposition bet' and had turned $25 into $200. The stickman quickly slid the green chip back to Clint along with two brand new shiny black ones. "This is like stealing! I knew it would be like this!"

Jimmy Dale didn't hear a word. He was still watching the blonde angel of darkness, who was being comforted by a short, fat, Middle Eastern man with a beard.

Two hours into their casino action, it was clear to Clint that having Jimmy Dale with him in a casino was like trying to gamble with a four-year-old. All J.D. could do was gawk. At lights. At women. At money. He would occasionally look up, making certain each trapeze artist was still performing. A quick count revealed that they had won $575 already. All he could do was give a quick acknowledgment to Clint's results at the table, and then go back into his own world.

The boys walked out of The Bellagio and continued their stroll. Clint was eager to go get a steak, even though J.D. was still full from his three ninety-nine-cent breakfasts. But Clint wanted to celebrate. "I've never felt this good in my life. Just made $575 having fun in just two hours." He never felt as good as he felt right then. If he managed his money right, he could make this last forever.

He stopped at a payphone and called Amy. He knew she wasn't going to be happy with him. By now, she had definitely discovered that he had "borrowed" from her mad money box and left it bare.

"Tell you what I'm gonna do, baby. I'm gonna wire you back $300 as soon as I find a Western Union office. I've already hit 'em up for $575. Give me just a day or two, and I'll have it all right back in your little box."

"Whatever." Amy showed little emotion. She didn't like the idea of being married to a thief.

Clint couldn't understand why that still didn't make everything okay with Amy. "Must be a woman thing," he commented to J.D. as he got off the phone.

J.D. wanted to side with Amy but knew that would not set well with Clint.

The boys stopped in at Caesar's Palace. They both had heard of that casino. Clint changed a $100 bill for four green, $25 chips. He walked up to a roulette wheel, calmly placed a $25 chip on the black square and watched its wheel roll. The ball stopped promptly on black seven. Before J.D. had even finished his new round of gawking, Clint had watched the wheel stop on four consecutive black numbers. "That's another $675 in a little over two hours. Hell, this is like stealin'! That's $975 for the day. I'm ready to drink some whiskey! Then I'll make another fortune." What they didn't realize was that the fortune they were about to discover would rock their world forever.

19

THURSDAY WAS THE best day yet. Clint wound up at a blackjack table that gave him a run of three blackjacks in a row, along with winning hands in eight out of nine that he played. Clint had pocketed $2,780.

Deciding to keep his word to Amy, he found a Western Union office where he wired all of her stolen money. Paid in full. Now, she should be thrilled, Clint thought. He never did fully understand why that didn't make things okay between them.

Friday was not a good day. Lady Luck had turned her back, and it was not fun. Clint won every $10 bet and lost every $50 bet. Back and forth, all day and half the night. After tallying the latest damage, Clint discovered that he had lost $600 for the day. He then realized the one thing that gamblers invariably fail to understand until it happens to them: losing $600 is a lot more painful than winning $600 is pleasurable.

Clint's anger was barely controllable. Once they were back in their room, Clint threw things around in anger, looking for an argument to pick with anyone. He couldn't find it, but he did run across a wad of meth in his shaving kit.

"Hmm! Haven't had any of this in a few days," Clint figured. "Right now I'll just shove a little of this back." With that, he created a couple of lines, rolled up a $100 bill, and snorted deeply the entire first line. He paused, looked up to the ceiling to keep his nose from dripping. It was already running like a faucet.

"J.D., you want a hit?"

"No thanks, I'm into this bull riding on TV. Man, I really love this place! I could stay here forever!"

Shrugging, Clint pulled a second line into the bill without waiting for the first one to take effect. He was angry, and this would take care of it all.

It was now 1:00 a.m. J.D. was snoring, and Clint was wired and mad. He had paid Amy back, but it left him out of cash. He dug into J.D.'s stash. He put three $100 bills in J.D.'s envelope and stuffed the rest down his pockets. He wouldn't spend that $300, and their room was covered by the deposit. He headed downstairs to prove his point. These Vegas jerks weren't going to take his money without a fight. Especially now, when he had crystal meth on his side.

The meth caused a euphoria that completely wiped out his inhibitions—plus his ability to rationalize the mechanics of gambling. Within a matter of an hour of angry "double up and catch up," Clint was totally busted. He had nothing. That pushed him over the edge. A fellow gambler started laughing with his buddy about something totally unrelated, and Clint accused him of laughing at his casino losses. An ugly confrontation ensued; bouncers had to escort Clint to his room.

This, of course, woke J.D. up, who just wanted to know, "What the hell is going on?"

"Come on, J.D. Get your stuff packed. We're outta here. Screw this place!"

"Where we going?"

"Home. As soon I get a couple hours sleep, we're outta here!"

Now J.D. was really confused.

Clint knew he was wired. J.D. was half-asleep. For hours, he laid in his bed and stared into darkness. He tried not to think about how much pleasure he had experienced when he was several thousand dollars ahead of the game. Finally, he fell asleep.

The following morning had both guys rising in a better frame of mind. Even though they were broke, they had had fun and learned some life lessons.

"There ain't no free lunch," was J.D.'s only way to explain Clint's bad turn of luck. He was proud of his slogan and acted like he made it up for its first-ever debut. That made Clint laugh, in spite of his bad mood.

While waiting for J.D. to shower, Clint channel surfed. His eye caught on a commercial with Ed McMahon pitching a low-cost life insurance program. It reminded Clint of the policy Amy bought on him several years before when a new insurance benefit package was offered to all employees at the bottling plant.

Since casino table games didn't seem to be his pot of gold, Clint's attention suddenly started circling around the life insurance policy. He wondered how he might devise a plan to cash in on his policy for $250,000. That would be pretty sweet, Clint thought. He was tired of working for a living. He was ready to make money by *thinking* —all he had to do was disappear, have Amy cash in the policy, move somewhere else, and they could live happily ever after.

Faking his own death; it was perfect. And he could talk Jimmy Dale into helping. But first, he'd have to think through the logistics.

J.D. was certainly not ready to leave Vegas, but it was time to head back home. They climbed in the trusty "ol' Hoopty" after polishing off the last of their ninety-nine-cent breakfasts.

With the lights of Vegas receding behind them, Clint carefully tried to explain the concept of faking his own death to Jimmy Dale. Basically, right before they got home, they would search for a homeless guy or hitchhiker. All they had to do was knock him off, then place his body in Clint's Honda, crash it, and make it look like it was Clint who was killed. The life insurance company would cut Amy a check for $250,000. Seemed pretty simple.

J.D. and Clint would split the money, and Clint and Amy would move somewhere else where people didn't know them. And everybody would live happily ever.

Throughout the journey home they would keep an eye out for their prey. Someone who was about the same age and size as Clint would be ideal. Clint was sure Amy would go along with the scam. The money would get her to do anything. But what if he was wrong?

20

THE SIGN ABOVE the chain link fence read, "University of Tennessee Forensic Science Research Facility." Dr. Stanley Gowen carefully searched a large key ring that would open the massive padlock. Dr. Walsh and his dental hygienist, Lana, waited nearby.

During their three-hour drive to Knoxville from Nashville, Dr. Walsh had told Lana what to expect from "The Body Farm," and warned her it was indeed everything the name implied. It was the official University of Tennessee anthropological lab, established to study "Time Since Death," using actual cadavers placed in outdoor circumstances replicating crime scenes. By recording insect activity and photographing bodies as they decayed, the Body Farm's research would help crime scene investigators determine how long an actual body had been lying in a particular location.

The Body Farm was located behind The University of Tennessee Medical Center maintenance building along the banks of the Tennessee River. Only a couple miles away, inside UT's Neyland stadium, were administrative offices, classrooms, and a bone bank storage facility.

"Glad you guys could make it today," Dr. Gowen said as he popped the lock on the gate. "Thought I'd give you a little tour of our research facility. Sorry it's so cold now, but at least it won't smell so bad."

Dr. Gowen hesitated a moment before entering. "Now guys, please remember one thing before we continue. We like to remind all our guests here at the Body Farm that we treat each of these bodies with the utmost respect and dignity. When they were alive, each person made a conscious decision to donate their body to science and help us learn valuable information to assist investigators in solving crimes. For that generous gift, we are eternally grateful. Were it not for these individuals, we would have nothing to study. It's okay to laugh and joke around a little; this kind of work requires a little dark humor or you'll go stark raving mad, but we must never lose the real sense of respect and appreciation for what these people here have given us."

Both Walsh and Lana looked at each other but said nothing. They were impressed with Dr. Gowen's reverent treatment of human life, even after death. Lana was already getting goose bumps as Gowen's words echoed through her mind.

Dr. Gowen ushered Dr. Walsh and Lana through the gate, beginning his guided tour of one of the most unusual sights in scientific research.

"On these three acres lie approximately one hundred bodies in various stages of decomposition," Dr. Gowen said. "About twenty-five of them are buried for future archeological study. As you wander from station to station, you can see each experiment being conducted by graduate students and scientists. Within their bodies lie millions of bits of information that can provide valuable clues to puzzles."

Dr. Gowen led them through the stations, narrating as they

toured. "Our main emphasis here is to conduct human body decomposition experiments. We try to document measurably visible changes in each human body as it decomposes under a variety of circumstances, both environmentally and elementally.

Lana nodded her head. It was creepy but she loved it.

Dr. Gowen pointed to the first body, which was partially covered in brush and leaves. "When a body is found in the woods or a field, one of the first bits of information the cops want to know is how long the body has been there. Many times, that will help direct them in one path or another in the investigative process. If, for example, it is determined that a body has been there two months, and a person of interest has been in Europe for three months, then that would be valuable information in determining 'who dunnit.'"

"This is fascinating!" Lana exclaimed.

Dr. Gowen seemed to feed off her interest, and the fact that he was among colleagues energized his explanations. "It is," he agreed. "It's certainly exciting when a forensic scientist can finally put the last piece of a puzzle in place for police—especially in a cold case.

"We document weather conditions, temperature, wind velocity, humidity, cloud cover, and all that. We combine this information with photographs we have taken every twenty-four to forty-eight hours for an entire year. During this time, we have an opportunity to measure all types and sizes of insects that eat and decompose human tissue," Dr. Gowen explained.

He motioned toward another corpse, like a game show host showing off fabulous prizes. "Each body has a *residence*, as we call it here, of about a year. It takes that long to study each body from start to finish. Bodies that are placed out in the summer decompose fast in summer months, begin to slow down in fall, almost halt in winter, and then begin to re-decompose again in spring."

They continued their stroll through each workstation, which were in some cases so bizarre that they looked almost unreal. "Each experiment is conducted under a slightly different set of circumstances. Take this one for example." Dr. Gowen stopped before a body wrapped in a shower curtain. "This research is being done to compare the relative rate of decomposition of a body wrapped tightly in plastic compared with one not wrapped at all."

At the next station, two bodies lay side by side. These bodies were "fresh," having been placed in this scenario only a few days before. One was a young white female with a gray sweatshirt and black sweatpants. She had a heavily soiled tennis shoe on her left foot and her right foot was bare. A tiny red rose with black thorns intertwining its stem had been tattooed on the inside ankle of her right leg. Her fingernails were nicely painted, and her hair appeared to have been professionally colored. The right side of her head had an irregular gash extending from just above her right ear across her forehead to the lateral edge of the left eyebrow. Portions of her skull were sunken in a jagged shape. Brain matter and viscera exuding out onto the ground. Dr. Walsh's eyes fixed on this wound, stories of how her life must have ended immediately racing through his mind.

"What happened to her?" Lana just had to know.

"Car wreck with open head trauma. This type of case is quite valuable, as it more closely simulates what cops find in the woods when someone has been bludgeoned to death. The maggots actually get a head start here. Their meal is already sitting out there ready for them."

Lana rolled her eyes in grotesque disbelief.

"Now, here right next to her," Dr. Gowen continued, "is her laboratory partner. A twenty-five-year-old man placed here three days ago. He's wearing street clothes and is wrapped loosely in a plastic shower curtain. You'll notice that the terrain is slightly sloped, like on a small hillside. Its foliage canopy will let little direct sunlight hit these bodies, even in winter when leaves are down."

Their attention fell to the adjacent corpse, which didn't look like a body at all.

The tour continued through the wooded property, which was mostly flat land. Various native hardwood trees, white oak, maple and hickory proliferated well in east Tennessee, providing a moderate cover of foliage. All of this was meticulously planned as critical components of each research project.

The terrain changed slightly, becoming more rocky and damp as their path proceeded toward the southwest corner. In front of them was an old, rusted-out, 1989 Chevy. Its original color was impossible to determine. Its right front fender was missing. All glass was blown out. The trunk was open. Lana peered inside.

Greenish yellow colored flesh splotched with burgundy patches greeted her; a human arm and leg protruded from its partially closed trunk.

Lana's curiosity was irresistible. "May I?" She lifted the trunk lid to have a better view of the body. It was a male of undeterminable age, wearing no clothing. His skin had turned a gray/bluish splotch, since it had not been exposed to direct ambient air. "Oooh!" Lana had just gotten her first real scent of that characteristic odor of decomposing death. She felt nauseated.

"This shows relative deterioration of human skin when it is

covered versus uncovered. By the way, check out the backseat!" Dr. Gowen gestured.

Lana stuck her head through the back window to have a closer look. There lay a mostly decomposed mound of gooey flesh and soft tissue, comingled with an orange and white "Go Vols" t-shirt that had once had long sleeves in better days.

"You can see that insect activity from last summer and fall has contributed to advanced deterioration of clothing this body wore. This one has been here for about five months," Dr. Gowen explained.

"Are any of these bodies embalmed?" Lana asked.

"No. We can't get good data from embalmed specimen, since those found at a crime scene are not embalmed. Good question, though." Gowen smiled at both and checked to see if Lana had recovered. "You okay? We can stop any time."

"No, I'm fine, thanks. Let's keep going." She wasn't very convincing.

An old bathtub had been placed at the next station. It was half filled with brown, murky water and sticks, leaves and other debris.

A body was leaning over the bathtub, face down in the water, partially held underwater by a piece of firewood. Its arms were in the water and legs were on the ground in a semi- kneeled position. "This compares the influence water has on the relative decomposition rate of submerged skin versus dry skin from the waist down."

Gowen reached in his laboratory jacket pocket and produced a metal examining probe. He used it as a pointer and demonstrator to show the soft and mushy texture of decomposing skin. "Notice how you can see skin slippage starting to occur now." He placed his probe in the bathtub and touched the back of the cadaver.

"The probe pushes right on through the skin, like it's a soggy bar of soap left in a hot shower. That is called 'saponification.' The skin almost turns to fat or grease. It's one of the biochemical stages in decomposition."

Dr. Gowen straightened up, paused, and asked, "Do you have any questions?" Neither said a word.

21

CLINT AND JIMMY DALE stopped for coffee and fuel a few hours outside of Albuquerque and then got back on I-40 East. Jimmy Dale was at the wheel. Clint made a pillow out of his sleeping bag in the backseat and was just dozing off when J.D. startled him with a loud yelp.

"Clint, hot damn!" he whooped. "We've got yer ride to Music City!"

Clint jolted up and peered out the back window as Jimmy Dale slowed down to get a better look. A man was hitchhiking eastbound on the I-40 shoulder, his guitar case serving as a road sign showing his destination. The word "Nashville" shone in reflective tape down the side.

"There he is! J.D. I think we have our winner." Jimmy Dale pulled over on the shoulder and stopped about a quarter mile ahead of the hitchhiker.

Clint got out of the backseat to make way for the new passenger. "Hey man, we're going your way!" he yelled, waving his arms.

The man jogged up to the Honda, his clothes drenched with sweat. Relief washed over his features, and then a big smile. His sandy brown locks of hair were unkempt from the wind on the interstate. He was dressed in a red plaid shirt with faded blue jeans and brown roper boots. His possessions were limited to a guitar case and a khaki colored duffle bag. He wore a red bandana tied around his neck. A wheat colored woven cowboy hat provided poor relief from the scorching sun.

Clint held out his hand. "Hey, I'm Clint! Come on, we'll set you down right square in the middle of Nashville, buddy. That's exactly where we're headed. Maybe you can help us drive."

"Hey man, thanks!" The young man clasped Clint's hand in his. "In Nashville I'm planning to go by Britt, but for now, everybody calls me Cody."

"Nice to meet you, Britt—or Cody. Climb on in. I'll put your bag in the trunk. With this heat, you'd better hang on to your guitar."

Cody nodded. "I really appreciate it, guys."

Clint tossed his bag in the trunk while J.D. was offering their new friend a cool drink of bottled water from their cooler.

"You guys came along just in time. This heat is unbearable!" Cody downed the entire bottle's content in one quick gulp. He used an already soaked bandana to wipe his face. "Can't tell you how much I appreciate this."

"Sorry about the A/C," Clint said. "It died on the drive out. When we get up to seventy, the breeze is pretty good and it's not so bad. Wind makes it noisy, though."

"Listen, guys, I'm just thankful you stopped to help."

"No problem. We're looking for somebody like you, to keep us company," Jimmy Dale said. "You play that guitar?"

"I try. I'm a singer and songwriter. Gonna give it a shot in Music City." Cody grinned. "I can't sing in beer joints forever. I gotta make some money while I'm still young enough to take the rejection."

"Well, sit back and take a load off," Clint said. "We'll stop for a little grub in a couple hours. Gotta have gas by then, anyway. He cranked up a country radio station, and Cody leaned back in his seat. The wind from the open back window blew over his face, drying his sweat-soaked hair.

He couldn't believe his luck in finding a ride that would take him all the way to Nashville. Maybe God was looking out for him after all.

22

I**T WAS COOL AND DARK** when Jimmy Dale pulled into a parking space at a truck stop just west of the New Mexico-Texas border. Cody was dozing in the backseat but woke up as soon as the car stopped. The weary travelers climbed out and stretched their legs.

With his mind still on the task at hand, Clint found a comfortable booth in the back. The friendly waitress kept hot biscuits coming and coffee flowing as the three laughed and stuffed their faces. They talked about politics, economy, and women. Cody shared his stories about singing in a beer dive in Albuquerque.

Cody also shared with his new friends about Christine and how hard it was to leave her. "I was real close to bailing at the last minute. I got awful close to that li'l gal, and wouldn't you know it—didn't realize it until right before leaving. I reckon I'll send her a plane ticket to Nashville as soon as I get my feet planted. She's the closest thing I've got to a home."

Meanwhile, Clint and Jimmy Dale told their stories about their trip to Las Vegas, and how they went from rags to riches and back to rags. Afterwards, Cody grabbed the check before their waitress could even lay it on the table. Treating these nice guys to supper was the least he could do.

It was Clint's turn to drive again, but Jimmy Dale was buzzed from three cups of coffee while at the truck stop, and there was no way he would be able to sleep now. From the passenger seat he craned his head around to look at Cody.

"Hey man, sing me that song you were telling us about at supper. The one you wrote."

"*I Will Return*? That one?" Cody asked.

"The one that's gonna be your first hit," Jimmy Dale said, nodding.

"A live concert would be just the thing to keep me awake, buddy!" Clint said, smiling at Cody, then shooting Jimmy Dale a strange look.

Cody pulled his guitar case from the floorboard and maneuvered the instrument into position in the cramped backseat. He retuned each string and began picking the opening notes with the skill of a classically trained guitarist. The boys rolled up their windows; it was now cooling off and they could hear better with the wind noise quieted. His crystal clear voice filled the car, and from the first note it was obvious to Clint and J.D. that this wasn't just another Music City drifter, but a seasoned professional who had simply postponed his pursuit of stardom until his time was right.

When Cody hit his last note, J.D. was beside himself. "Oh, man. You wrote that? That's gonna be a hit, man. I know my country music and that's gonna be played on every radio station in the US, and I heard it first! Man, let me be your manager, you're gonna be rich!" Jimmy Dale was positively gushing.

Clint cut his eyes at J.D., and Cody noticed a cold stare in the rearview mirror.

"Didn't you think it was good?" Jimmy Dale shot back at Clint.

"Oh . . . uh . . . absolutely, Cody, that's a hit for sure. I . . .

just don't think Jimmy Dale realizes what it would take to be a successful manager," Clint said, clenching his teeth in frustration.

"Well, I listen to country music all day long," Jimmy Dale said, speaking with authority now. "We have it over the sound system in the store, and I keep up with who's who in this business. I'm tellin' you, you got what it takes. And I know it when I hear it! We could make some real money together."

"Thanks, J.D. You'll get all-access passes to my gigs, I promise," Cody grinned and assured Jimmy Dale—stopping short of promising him a managerial spot in his music career. He slipped his guitar back into its case and propped it up beside him, then put his head back and closed his eyes.

"You know, guys, I really believe things happen for a reason. You guys just happened to come along at the right minute and saved me from a long day of misery on I-40. I hadn't been out there but a little over an hour; don't know how long I would have lasted in that oven, if ya'll hadn't saved me. Somehow, I feel like I've known you both forever. You know since we all live in the area, or at least I will soon, there's no reason we can't continue this friendship once we get to Nashville!"

Both Jimmy Dale and Clint nodded. There might be one reason.

23

THE SUN WAS HEATING UP, and Clint woke his sleeping passengers for a quick breakfast stop. As they climbed out of their chariot, Cody offered to fill up, saying it was only right that he should pitch in.

"Thanks, man. I'm gonna bust if I wait another minute," Jimmy Dale said, as he patted Cody on the back and hurried inside.

Jimmy Dale was already at the urinal when Clint came in and checked under stalls for feet. He didn't want anyone to hear what he had to say.

"Okay, we need to make some decisions here. When do you think is the right time to do this?" Clint asked.

"Doin' what?" J.D. stared ahead as if he had no idea what Clint was talking about.

"You ain't still gonna go through with this now, are you? I mean I'm really startin' to like this guy!"

"Look, J.D. How short is your memory? We didn't pick up this guy to find a new fishing buddy. We got a plan to carry out, and it's time to get our plans going."

"Well, I can't kill him. He's a good guy. A good singer, too, and

I've always wanted to know somebody famous. Shoot, I could manage this guy and make us all rich."

"You know how long that takes?"

"You know how long twenty-five to life is?"

Jimmy Dale was backing out. Clint had to think fast.

"Look, Jimmy Dale, we're in too deep at this point," Clint said, his voice raspy. "If you back out now, you can kiss your cut of the deal goodbye. I'll have the cash. He'll be dead, so you ain't managing nobody and you ain't gonna get squat either, 'cause if I get caught, I'll just say that you were in on this from the start."

"You'd lie? Throw your own buddy under the bus?"

"If I'm willin' to kill, I'm willin' to lie!"

Clint stared at Jimmy Dale in the dirty mirror that hung over the sagging sink. Jimmy Dale felt betrayed but didn't know what to do. "He'll forget you faster than you can say your freakin' name; the minute he hits Division Street."

"You can say whatever you want to say, Clint. You're just jealous 'cause I thought of managing him first. Screw you, man! I'm tired, and you're crazy! I ain't killin' him! He's a good songwriter. Don't that mean nothin' to you?" Jimmy Dale threw his paper towel on the floor and stormed out to meet Cody.

When Clint returned, J.D. and Cody were in a conversation over who had sold more records, Conway Twitty or George Strait. He had no interest in joining their conversation. Clint pushed the eggs around on his plate, hoping their topic would soon shift. He was worried over J.D.'s apparent reluctance to cooperate. His thoughts were focused on the details of implementing his plan. J.D. kept asking for more song titles, and Cody was writing a postcard back home.

After several minutes of awkward silence, Cody broke the ice. "Guys, I got to hit the john before we head out. I'll be right back."

Clint squirmed awkwardly in his seat. He knew he had to address this issue with J.D. sooner rather than later. "Look, J.D., unless we totally throw this plan out, we have our guy right here. It's time to start our plan. Now, it comes down to this. Do you or don't you want to split half of $250,000?"

J.D. stared at his half empty breakfast plate. He paused and stared out the window, avoiding any eye contact with Clint.

"Well, what's your answer? Are you in or out?"

"I guess I will, but I don't really want to." J.D.'s face shone already of shame for what they were about to do. "How 'bout you doin' it instead of me? You're the one that don't have any hesitation about it all. I mean, what if you kill him and don't never get any of that life insurance money? Have you ever thought about that?"

"Look, I need you to whack him while I'm driving, since it's my car. I'm just more familiar with drivin' it. We have to be rolling while our whackjob happens to make sure there are no witnesses." Clint knew that logic was weak, but felt he could sell J.D. on the idea. "As far as not ever gettin' the money, I know for a fact that Amy has a $250,000 life insurance policy on my sweet ass. I've seen our policy and even know right where it is at home. Pay premiums on it every month with payroll deduction."

J.D. continued to stare aimlessly at their table countertop. "I can drive your car pretty good. You whack him."

Clint slumped in his seat. He was losing patience with J.D. and he was trying hard not to show it. J.D. was trying every way possible to get out of it. "Well, we could ask him if he wants in on the deal with us and we'll hunt for somebody else."

Clint shook his head in disgust. "Are you serious? Tell the guy we were gonna knock him off, but changed our minds and decided to look for someone else, but now we want to see if he wants to chop the deal three ways instead of two because he writes good songs? Come on, J.D.!" Clint was desperate now and he knew it. It was time to pull out all stops.

"Man, I really need you to help me with this plan. I've spent a lot of time figurin' this out. Will you please help me do this?" Clint was totally against this plea tactic, but he was having to play his ace card now or else the game would be over. His face and tone of voice now resembled persuasion. Clint leaned in toward J.D. and refused to lose direct eye contact as he made his final plea. A thick bead of sweat appeared above his upper lip. His mouth was dry, his hands were shaking.

J.D. slowly looked up from his plate until he gradually made eye contact with Clint. He managed a weak smile. He struggled to say the words he didn't want to say, but Clint so desperately wanted to hear. "Ok, Clint, I guess you're right." Clint grinned joyfully as he slapped him on the shoulder just as Cody sat down. He wiped the perspiration from his upper lip.

"You guys 'bout ready to roll?"

Clint jumped up cheerfully from their booth, "Yeah, guess we better. I got this check fellas."

With that, the threesome loaded up in the "Hoopty" and headed down I-40. Clint was driving and suggested Cody ride up front to keep him awake. They still had a couple more days to cross Texas, so there would be more time to finely tune J.D.'s method of murder. Clint finally had it the way he wanted it. Or so he thought.

24

THE HOURS CREPT BY at a snail's pace. The inside of the car felt like an oven and smelled like a locker room. The wind noise competed with conversation. J.D. fidgeted in the backseat, picking at a loose string on the seat's upholstery.

Jimmy Dale's mind raced with anxiety, his palms sweating. He could feel his heart pounding in his chest. He focused on the back of Cody's neck and tried to forget all the good times they had had in the last two days. But a promise to Clint could not be broken.

Gazing at the floorboard, J.D. spotted one end of a bungee cord sticking out from under the driver's seat. He reached down, picked it up, and began a careful examination. It was about eighteen inches long with a black shiny hook on each end. The polyester woven fabric was a deep green with a black line through its center. He hooked each thumb with either end of the cord and stretched it as far as his arms could extend.

J.D.'s mind was racing now. Could he do it? Should he do it? Was this the weapon? When was the right time? Can I do it without him knowin' I'm doin' it? Clint hadn't given him any of those details. His poor brain couldn't fully process all his emotions. He relaxed the tension, and the cord became one fifth its size. He nervously wound the cord around his wrist, then each finger, then every other finger. Then he began to tie it in knots, shaking violently through all these motions. His breathing was erratic and quick. He nervously rocked back and forth in his seat, as if he were in a rocking chair on his mother's porch. He continued a paranoid glance over each shoulder, as if to confirm that no one was behind him to observe this evil deed.

Clint was carefully observing the back seat performance in his rear view mirror. Clint glanced to his right to confirm that Cody was still asleep.

Clint cleared his throat, hoping to catch Jimmy Dale's attention, and yet not wake up Cody. Finally J.D. looked up and into the rear view mirror. There he saw Clint shaking his head back and forth and giving him the familiar 'kill' signal with an index finger sawing across his throat. Jimmy Dale nodded into the mirror; he got the message. The time was now. Or was that what that signal meant? J.D. wasn't sure, but knew he couldn't ask Clint.

His hands trembled with fear. His breathing had turned to panting. He could hear the air go in and out of his lungs as he stared at the back of Cody's neck. He could feel every pounding of his heartbeat, the gurgling and gushing of his own blood through his veins.

He looked down at the cord and grasped it in the middle. He slowly tightened his grip on each end of the cord. Now he was squeezing. He looked down at his shaking hands; his knuckles were white from the intense pressure.

Clint was trying his best to keep one eye on the road, and the other eye's time split between Cody and Jimmy Dale. The longer Cody slept, the better, from Clint's point of view. He really wanted to settle J.D. down but didn't want to risk waking up Cody. He had given up on eye contact in the rear view mirror. Twice he turned his head halfway around, stared dagger-like glares into Jimmy's eyes as he quickly looked away.

J.D. thought the message was now. Or was it?

J.D.'s thoughts were racing now. Maybe Clint was right. Maybe Cody was a loser. Maybe Cody *would* consider taking him along as manager, but only until he made it. Then he'd drop him. Maybe Cody thought J.D. was just a big, dumb joke, like Clint had said. J.D. was so confused, and so nervous.

Like a bolt of lightning from a darkened sky, J.D.'s sudden impulse resembled an epileptic seizure. In one swift move, Jimmy Dale grabbed the cord by both ends, brought it over Cody's head and neck, and pulled with all his might.

Clint turned and watched in shock and disapproval, trying to keep control of the car's direction. *He hadn't given the signal! What was this loose cannon doing now?!*

"What the hell are you doing?" Clint nearly ran off the interstate, he was so shocked at the action. He looked off his right shoulder and saw a face of panic and desperation. Like an angry tiger, he quickly tied the loose ends around the back of his headrest.

Before he knew what had happened, Cody's lifeline airway was cut off. He coughed and struggled violently, shoving his feet onto the dashboard and kicking at the windshield. He grabbed the cord with both hands as he fought, trying to stretch it far enough to catch his breath. It didn't budge. The seatbelt and shoulder harness restricted his efforts to fight back.

Cody's mind was racing. What was going on? Why was this happening to him? He had thought these guys were his friends. Was this really happening or a dream?

He knew he had to survive. He *would* survive. As he struggled to breathe, he reached for Clint and the steering wheel, but Jimmy Dale grabbed his arm and twisted it over the back of the seat. Cody's mouth opened in a soundless scream as his forearm popped like a dry branch.

Clint struggled to keep their car on the road as Cody clawed at the steering wheel with his other arm. It almost sent them out of control and careening off a guardrail.

Cody was still kicking at the windshield, but losing strength as his life slowly left his body. He felt his body turning cold. All he could see was Christine's face. The sound of his own blood howled in his ears. Cody turned his face upward and his eyes darted wildly back and forth.

His mind formed silent, desperate prayers in what would be his last few seconds on earth. Everything turned into a bright, white tunnel. Cody felt his body lifting, floating as if it were weightless. He saw Christine suspended before him; then, only light.

Cody was gone.

25

"**W**HAT THE HELL HAVE YOU DONE?" Clint glanced into the rearview mirror at Jimmy Dale's frozen face. He swung the car sharply onto a deserted exit ramp.

"I didn't mean for you to do this *now*, numb nuts!" Clint screamed as he got out of the car to confront J.D.

"You said you wanted him dead, so that's what you got. Now you don't want him dead. Make up your mind!" Jimmy Dale yelled at the top of his lungs as he got out and slammed the door with his foot. He'd had just about all he could take of Clint Logan. His eyes darted back and forth in raged fury, as he glared at Clint with a maniacal rage. He started toward Clint with both fists cocked and loaded for combat. "You bastard! I can kill two as easy as one!"

When he saw Jimmy Dale's gigantic frame looming over him, Clint took a step back. He'd temporarily forgotten that his sidekick, while not the sharpest knife in the drawer, could still take him down in seconds.

"Jimmy Dale, we are a thousand miles from Nashville! No air and a piece of junk car. This place is gonna smell to high heaven before too long!"

"Well, that's your problem now, isn't it? Look, you roped me into this thing and we both know it. I've tried to help you with your stupid damn game, and now I can't even kill a man good enough to please you! I'm a good mind to just whip your ass right now. I'm sick of you trying to use me like some kind of monkey."

Clint knew he had better change the climate, and quickly. "C'mon, J.D. I'm sorry, buddy. I'm stressed just like you are. But we got to stick together. Let's just settle down, take a deep breath, and things will work out. We've got to figure out our next step."

Cody's body was sitting upright, his head and neck tied tightly to the headrest. His cowboy hat had somehow ended up in the back seat floorboard during the scuffle. His face had turned blue and his eyes were open and bulging. The whites of his eyes were a deep red. His mouth hung open, a whitish-red froth rolling out on his chin. He had bitten his tongue nearly off, and the inside of his mouth and back of his throat were full of thick, dark blood. Clint opened the door and winced at the sight as he forced himself to move in closer. He was going to puke. He grabbed his pocketknife to cut the bungee cord loose from the seat. Cody fell toward the door and nearly onto the pavement. Clint hurled a sizeable volume of vomit over the front fender.

J.D. stood motionless, as if in a trance. Clint wiped the vomit residue from his mouth with his shirt tail. "Shit! This is disgusting!"

"Can you help me with this?!" Clint hissed. "We can't make a mess. Blood is dang near impossible to clean up. It'll smell forever! Worse than puke!" He motioned for J.D. to put Cody in the backseat. "Check his pockets and take his shirt off. We'll put one of mine on him. Cover him up with that sleeping bag, and if any cops stop us, we'll tell them he's asleep."

"They won't see he's blue?"

"They're not gonna get close enough to see him. Now, come on!" The two boys used some spare rags to wipe up Cody's blood, which had spread over most of the front seat. Jimmy Dale was moving in slow motion, still trying to process recent events.

Ready or not, his buddy Jimmy Dale had carried out his wishes. Now it was up to Clint to follow through with his plan. They were a long way from Nashville, even further from where Clint had planned to stage the accident in Dickson County.

Clint grabbed the guitar and Cody's duffel bag, checking for anything that might identify its owner. When he was satisfied nothing could be traced, he took the belongings into the woods and dumped them unceremoniously. "I smell sumpen' already, and he ain't even been dead five minutes. I think he messed in his pants." J.D. raised the shirt he had just put on Cody and examined his jeans. A dark wet stain shown around the zipper. "What I smell ain't pissin' in your pants. How we gonna get rid of that smell?"

Clint ignored him. They would worry about that later.

J.D. softly talked to Cody's body, as if the murder had never occurred. "It weren't nothin' personal, buddy. You were just in the wrong place at the wrong time. Sorry it had to end this way. I kept your songbook, though. Got it right here. Maybe I'll try and get some of your songs sold."

Clint interrupted J.D. "Man, you're losing it! The dude is dead. What in the hell are you doing talking to a dead man? And you can't keep that songbook, or go pitching any of his tunes. Are you crazy??? It's gotta have his name in it somewhere."

"I am too keeping the damn songbook! If his name is in there, I'll rip it out. I'm keeping his songs, Clint. I ain't never killed a man before. Especially one that I really liked."

No one witnessed two men moving a body from the front

seat to the back. No one witnessed a guitar or a backpack full of clothing being dropped off in the woods. It certainly seemed like they had just gotten away with murder. At least for now.

For the next few hours, there appeared to be no witnesses to anything. There was no one nosy enough to peer into the backseat, no one to wonder why someone would be sleeping wrapped in a goose down sleeping bag when it was one hundred degrees outside.

Clint felt pretty good about their whole situation. J.D. could not have felt worse.

26

THE NEXT TWENTY-FOUR HOURS seemed like a month to both men. Tension filled their car. Clint worried about J.D.'s lack of commitment to their scheme of madness. The conversations were shallow, with J.D. giving one word answers to Clint's attempt to reestablish their relationship. Nothing seemed to be successful.

Suddenly, up ahead, blue lights flashed and sirens screamed. Clint's plan had hit another roadblock. Literally. Both lanes of I-40 East were shut down; and curious gawkers brought all westbound lanes to a stop. Cars were at a total standstill and drivers were standing outside their vehicles, talking on mobile phones and visiting with each other.

"You've got to be kiddin' me!" Clint gritted his teeth and beat the steering wheel with each word as he neared. The radio DJ reported a local temperature of 101 degrees; with the humidity it felt hotter than that. As they came to a stop, their interior felt immediately like a sauna; they would only be able to stand a few minutes of conditions like this.

"What do we do now?" J.D. had no good ideas.

"Let's just roll up the windows; we can't let this smell out, in case somebody walks by." They threw their cooler, maps, and bags of trash on top of Cody's body, and got out to walk around like everyone else. They figured the activity might draw attention away from their car and its contents.

Several of the truck drivers shut their rigs down, kicked their shoes off, and fired up their portable televisions. Some just stood outside their rigs, talking with fellow truckers and smoking cigarettes on the shoulder of the interstate.

Clint felt a need to remind J.D. of their story. "Look, here is our line. We are just on the way back from Vegas. Our car has no A/C, and it is packed with clothes and junk from our trip. We lost all our money in Vegas, so we can't get our A/C fixed. We're just anxious to get home. Got it? And let's just hope that no one asks us why we're keeping all the windows rolled up if we ain't got A/C. But we just can't afford to leave them down. Not this close to people."

J.D. glared back at him with a scowl. "You think I'm crazy or sumpin'? Just because I just killed a man don't mean I'm crazy!"

J.D. started walking west down I-40, while Clint walked ahead to survey their situation. They agreed to meet back in fifteen minutes.

About a quarter mile down the road, J.D. met a pair of Texas Rangers chatting in the median, their blue lights flashing. He panicked. The paranoia that frequently accompanies meth users had begun to kick in. What would he say to the troopers if they questioned him? His first reaction was to run, but he knew that might draw unnecessary attention. No one runs anywhere in a traffic jam. And certainly not in this kind of heat.

The rangers finished their discussion, and each headed to opposite sides of the interstate. It seemed to J.D. that one of the rangers was walking directly toward him. J.D. began to wonder if he smelled like death, too. Surely he reeked of it— the stench must have soaked into his hair and clothes. Just breathing made him nauseous. Better not to get too close to anyone, he thought.

J.D. spotted a rig driver with the cab door open, sitting on his cab step smoking a cigarette. He walked close enough to get out of the ranger's way, but not so close that the guy could get a whiff of him.

"Hey, pahd'na. How's it goin'?"

"Better if this mess would clear up. Right now, I wish we were gettin' paid by the hour instead of the mile."

"So where you from, buddy?'

"Wichita. How 'bout you?"

"Nashville. By the way, any word about what's holding us up?"

"Nah. But here comes the law. We can ask him what's going on." The man nodded to the ranger who was walking toward him. J.D. froze. Then, he waved a "see you later" and kept walking.

His basic instinct of fight or flight had gotten the best of him and before he knew it, he was three rigs back and in a dead sprint. He stopped to catch his breath, and then turned around to see what was happening.

It suddenly dawned on Jimmy Dale that he had just pulled the bonehead move of his life. He cussed at himself instinctively as he walked back toward the rig where the ranger was engrossed in conversation with the truck driver. He had to wander back up to the two and act like nothing had happened, like he was just out for a morning jog down I-40.

When J.D. returned to the rig, the ranger had engaged the driver in friendly conversation. Jimmy Dale's huffing and puffing did seem a bit out of character for a group of people who were bored stiff waiting for time to pass in the heat.

"A tractor-trailer rig jackknifed 'bout two miles ahead," the ranger said by way of explanation. "Be cleared in about thirty minutes. Everything okay, sir?"

"Uh, sure."

"You're sweating and out of breath. And, well, we don't need no heat strokes out here."

"I'm fine, really. I was just running to get the kinks out of my legs. Been cooped up in a hot car for hours and the engine keeps overheating."

"Overheating, huh?"

"Yeah, but…"

"I bet it's your thermostat. Didja check it?"

"Yeah, yeah. Don't think that's…."

"Where's your vehicle, sir? Nothing's gonna be moving here for a while. I'd be happy to give you a hand."

J.D. flinched. "I think we'll be ok."

"Look, we all three might as well go check it out for you. It may be something we can fix," the truck driver said.

No matter how much Jimmy Dale tried to object, the ranger and the truck driver seemed insistent on helping. As the three men walked back against the grain of the stalled traffic, J.D. felt the sweat dripping down his neck. All he could think about was what he would say if the interfering helpers noticed the rank odor.

The three men got back to their 'Hoopty' at the same time as Clint. When Clint saw a uniformed officer standing by the door of their car, he froze.

"Is there a problem, officer?" he asked, discreetly narrowing his eyes toward J.D. "J.D., did you ask the officer for some help?"

"No, no," the officer answered. "Your friend here was just telling us about your engine overheating. Just thought we'd take a look. May just be a stuck thermostat."

J.D. said nothing, but silently held his breath. Could this be the beginning of the end? Would this blow their cover?

"Do you have to pop a lever from inside to open your hood on this model?" the ranger asked. He felt under the hood for the lever and waited for an answer.

Quickly, Clint took control of the conversation. "Yes, sir, it sure does. Let me give you a hand with that."

He circled the group and made his way to the driver's door. He held his breath, hoping no one would notice he had locked his car and all the windows were rolled up in the blistering heat. There was no wind, and he felt sure that someone would notice the odor as soon as he opened the door. His hands shook as he struggled to get his key into the lock.

Finally, the lock popped; Clint jumped into the driver's seat, slamming the door shut behind him. All his attempts to seem casual and appreciative were failing miserably. The putrid and toxic odor was overwhelming as Clint fumbled on the underside of the steering wheel. He first released the emergency brake, then the door to the gas tank. Finally, his trembling hands found the right lever, and he gave it a desperate tug. *Thump.* The hood of 'Hoopty' popped up.

"That's it! You got it!"

The ranger waved and nodded as Clint leapt out of the car and slammed the door shut behind him, before any more death scent could exit the vehicle. His lungs breathed a sigh of relief; they also welcomed the fresh air.

The officer slowly raised the hood of 'Hoopty.' Its hinges squeeked like an old wrought iron gate that badly needed oiling.

He and the truck driver leaned over the engine to observe the radiator hose that housed the thermostat. After a few short moments of silence that seemed like eternity, the ranger announced, "Looks okay to me. But you better have a garage check it as soon as traffic opens up. Don't see how you guys could go another mile in this heat with no air."

"A garage. Yes, sir. We'll do that. Thanks so much for your help." Clint didn't know if they were out of the woods or not.

"I don't know what it might be, guys. Wish I could help you more. Gotta go check my radio and see what the traffic status is now." He turned around to walk back, but then paused at the driver's door. "Say, you fellas smell that? Like something's dead."

The ranger slowly walked around the car, sniffing, to see if he could locate any reason for the smell. Clint and J.D. were too paralyzed to move.

"You hit a deer?"

"No, officer," Clint quickly answered.

"No road kill in the ditch or on your bumper or anything like that," the ranger said. "Damn, that is really rank!" The officer looked with curiosity at all four windows rolled up. He said nothing, but he looked at both boys. When he got no response, the ranger shielded his eyes to avoid the glare and peered more closely inside the vehicle.

"What's in the car, boys?"

Clint responded before J.D. had a chance. "Sir, we've been on a bender from Tennessee to Vegas and now back again. We've practically been living in the car for two weeks and it's like a train wreck in there. Come to think of it, that could be part of our problem. We're not the best housekeepers when it comes to keeping our 'Hoopty' clean. Probably just some old food."

The ranger looked directly into Clint's eyes, and Clint gave a polite nod of appreciation. His breath had already caught in his lungs and his nerves were frayed. Then the ranger's eyes roved over J.D.'s face. Jimmy Dale moved his head downward, staring at the pavement, his jaw clenched.

"Well guys," the ranger said slowly. "Be careful, you hear? Have a nice day." He shook his head, mumbled something under his breath, and walked away.

J.D. and Clint both felt like a decade had just been shaved off their lives.

27

As THE BOYS CROSSED into Arkansas, the smell continued to mount, and so did the tension. Clint and Jimmy Dale didn't talk much. There wasn't much to say. Every few minutes, Jimmy Dale would glance back over his shoulder, as if to confirm Cody's continued presence.

"Stop craning your neck to look back there, man. You'll call attention to the cargo!" Clint warned. "He's there. Can't you smell him? That's what death smells like. Wait til this time tomorrow. You'll see what I mean. It'll get worse before it gets better. And stop fidgeting, you're makin' me nervous!"

"Stop telling me what to do! I'll look wherever the hell I want to!" Clint could tell he had a different Jimmy Dale on his hands than before Cody's death.

"We're screwed, man. We shouldn't oughta have done this," Jimmy Dale whined. "He was a nice guy . . . He didn't deserve none of this!"

"I didn't deserve to lose all our money in Vegas either."

"Well, yeah, you kinda did. You were betting with it. This guy didn't do nothin' but take a ride with us. And this whole thing is really creepin' me out—that song he sang about comin' back after dyin'. You think he could really do that?"

Jimmy Dale stopped talking and looked back once again at the blanket-wrapped body. "You don't believe in that stuff, do ya, Clint? I mean . . . that spirits come back?"

"Stop it, J.D.! Don't start in with that crap! I don't wanna hear it! That dude ain't comin' back, I don't care what his song says!"

It was obvious J.D. heard nothing. His mind was concentrating on the soul of Cody. Whether out of mere curiosity, guilt or a subconscious hint of morbidity, he couldn't help but turn back the blanket to catch another quick glimpse of Cody's face. It would be the fifth time he checked it in the last three hours.

As he peeled back the corner of the blanket, J.D. was forced to hold his nose with his other hand. Cody's face was now barely recognizable compared with two short days ago. The whites of his eyes were now a brownish red, bulging to nearly complete protrusion from each eye socket. J.D. had already tried to close his eyelids, but that was impossible. Even the slightest pressure on his eyelid caused the eyeball to protrude even farther. The tanned stubble of his three day old beard had transformed into a swollen mass of multicolored slime, with colors of grayish green splotches surrounded by yellow and brown pigmentation The tongue was nearly bitten off, except for a small piece of soft tissue that allowed the swollen severed segment to dangle down upon his chin.

Cody's neck was swollen and distended with bright burgundy and green irregular blotches. There was a dark brown line around the throat area where the bungee cord had done its deadly work.

Three large flies had found their way into the car and competed with J.D.'s attention to the decomposing body. J.D. tried to swat them away. They flew away, circled the head and then relit on Cody's face. As J.D. swatted again, one of the flies crawled up inside the nose, crawling through a greenish brown exudate that drooled out of both nostrils.

"Buddy, I am so sorry for what I done. I wish I could make it up to you. Don't know what I was thinkin'." J.D. hung his head in shame as he carefully placed the blanket back over his face.

Clint shook his head in disbelief but said nothing; he was now dealing with an emotional cripple that had to be handled with quiet caution and concern.

At the next fuel stop, Clint rolled up the windows as he filled the tank, so the smell would not permeate the service station. Still hundreds of miles left to go in the unrelenting heat, the stench was getting worse with each passing minute. Clint returned to the car with an aerosol can of bathroom air freshener. He hated the way those things smelled, but the odor of death was worse. He had no choice but to unload half a can in hopes of masking a portion of the odor.

Clint drove his car exactly within the speed limit and obeyed every traffic law so as not to attract any unwanted attention. There was no more J.D. driving the 'Hoopty'. Clint could not predict J.D.'s behavior from one minute to the next.

The wind whipping through the open windows helped tone down the reek of death. As long as the car was moving and the air was circulating, Clint figured they had to deal with this until they got back to Tennessee. They had no choice.

Jimmy Dale turned his face toward the swift breeze the open window provided. He insisted on hiding his emotion from Clint and let the breeze dry his welled-up tears. He didn't know where all the sadness he was feeling was coming from. But there was a feeling in his gut that he couldn't explain. All the while, the haunting music of Cody's last song wouldn't stop playing in his head: "*I will return.*" What did Clint know about these things anyway? he thought to himself. Maybe corpses really do return.

28

THE GREEN INTERSTATE SIGNS told the boys they were only an hour from Memphis. Finally, it seemed that they might have a chance of returning to middle Tennessee safely. Clint shook his head in disgust as he remembered his comments to J.D. just a couple weeks ago about how they were likely to be chauffeured back to Tennessee in a limo. "This sure isn't how I had this drawn up in my mind when we came through here the other day. Instead of a limo, we've got a broken down piece of shit for a car with no air, hauling around a maggot infested corpse trying to find a good place to blow it up and make it look like me."

J.D. offered no insight to their predicament.

"I guess the thing to do is to get as close to Nashville as we can before we blow this thing up. That way, we can hook a ride back to Smithville and wait to see how long it takes to get our cash.

"There's a place near Dickson where my cousin and I used to sled in the winter. He claimed it was the highest place in Dickson County. Place called Gatlin's Ridge. It's out in the middle of nowhere near highway 48 just north of town. It's about two hours from Memphis. We'll camp out tonight after we blow it up and get an early start tomorrow morning. That should put us back in

Smithville sometime tomorrow afternoon or night. Then, we'll just have to wait and see how the chips fall from there.

"I'll have to lay low 'til the cops confirm that it was me in the wreck, and then I guess we'll have a funeral or something. Amy will help us with the details. You wave cash in front of her little face, and she's likely to do anything." Clint failed to realize that his intense planning of this scheme had not proceeded past this point, and he really was lost as to how to implement the scheme from here.

J.D. looked apathetic and somewhat lethargic. He was emotionally spent. "Do you think we ought to call her to let her know about the plan?"

"No. Just in case she's pissed. It's always better to ask for forgiveness than for permission."

J.D. looked puzzled but hesitated to give his opinion. Finally, he said, "I think you're making a mistake by not talkin' to her about this. I mean, we can't make this happen without her help. Don't you think she needs a little heads up?"

Clint wanted to put off facing Amy as long as possible.

29

On the surface, so far, it had been the perfect crime. There had been no other eyes to see them shove the old Honda down Gatlin's Ridge. Not at midnight in the middle of nowhere in Dickson County, Tennessee. There were no witnesses. Only Clint, Jimmy Dale, and Cody.

And now Cody was ashes.

Curiosity was something Clint could never control very well. He insisted they hang around and watch the drama unfold, as locals would be sure to show up any moment. He motioned for J.D. to follow him to the top of the ridge on the other side of the road. It would prove to be a perfect vantage point for them to watch the discovery unfold.

Clint winced in pain, his bad knee threatening to give way at any moment. His chain-smoking habit was also taking its toll as he and Jimmy Dale dashed along their escape route. His lungs were on fire, and his body begged for more oxygen as the two ran as fast as their pitifully out-of-shape bodies could take them.

In the faint glow of their cheap flashlights they could barely see the hill across the road. The full moon showed a thick growth of honeysuckle, poison ivy, and saw briars, which made it almost impossible to walk upright. They had to crawl on their hands and knees up most of the steep embankment to reach the top of the hill.

Their clothes were soaking wet; they were exhausted and bleeding from saw briars and thorns. The black smoke from the fire was mixed with thick mountaintop fog.

As they hovered, looking down at the fire, Clint's mind wandered to the one part of the plan he had considered in great detail on the trip home—the funeral of the late Clint Logan who died in a tragic car crash in Dickson County. He was certain that he would be laid to rest after one of the most elaborate and heartbreaking funerals anyone in his hometown had ever attended. He would be a legend.

He also imagined how many chiggers he would be scratching tomorrow morning. Perhaps it was punishment for the dastardly crime he and J.D. had committed. He couldn't help laughing to himself. A few chigger bites and a little poison ivy for $250,000? He could live with that.

Suddenly, the boys heard voices. Clint motioned for J.D. to be still. With the painstaking effort of a paratrooper, Clint pulled himself up over the crest of the ridge, entirely hidden by the brush. He had to check out the crime scene. The full moon that had been their ally earlier, now threatened to give away their hiding place.

Clint could just make out the silhouette of two adults standing by the ravine. He couldn't clearly hear their conversation, as their backs were turned away. The smoke and fire still billowed from the hollow below.

J.D. moved slightly to find a more comfortable position. "Shhh!" Clint whispered, as if scolding a four-year-old for talking too loudly.

"Sorry! My butt's falling asleep."

"You think you're miserable? How do you think Cody feels right about now? Careening the car down a ravine like that." Clint laughed at his own sick humor. J.D. didn't think it was funny at all.

"Ya know Clint, that's purty bad to say stuff like that. Don't you have no respect for the dead?"

"Oh hell, J.D. You know I'm just kiddin'. Give me a friggin' break!"

"Just quit making jokes about the guy. You're gonna piss him off and he really will come back!"

"Whatever."

The gentle purr of a car's engine arose in the distance. Clint perched carefully, hoping to once again catch a glimpse of their crime scene. The car turned out to be a white Chevy station wagon. As it arrived near the accident scene, Clint crouched down a little lower.

The headlights of the car lit the side of the briar thicket, and the boys remained motionless.

The Chevy moved toward two silhouettes that were now lit up like actors on a stage. As far as Clint could tell, both of them were men and had arrived apparently on foot as no other cars were in the area. They greeted the driver of the Chevy as he got out of his vehicle, leaving the motor running and his headlights on to help illuminate the area. Because of the steepness of the ravine, most of the headlight beams failed to shine down to the bottom of the still-burning inferno.

Now, Clint could hear bits of the conversation quite clearly:

"I'm afraid it's gonna catch the rest of the brush around it on fire."

"How long you been here?"

"Any idea what happened?"

"Going too fast to make the turn, I reckon."

J.D. signaled to Clint as if he had something important to say.

Clint ignored him. J.D. signaled again. Clint waved him off again. Then came a loud and distinct sneeze. It scared Clint so much he actually jumped. J.D. had tried to keep it in, but all his futile restraint made it come out even louder.

"What in the hell . . . ??? Nevermind!" Clint shook his head.

"I couldn't help it!" J.D. whispered, again way too loudly.

Clint motioned downward with his hand, reminding Jimmy Dale once again that they weren't alone and to keep it quiet. But it was too late.

One of the three men had obviously heard the noise and looked up like a startled deer.

"Did you hear that?"

The tallest man turned on a flashlight and walked toward the noise he had heard. J.D. grabbed the back of Clint's right arm. He was shaking so intensely the leaves were rattling underneath his arms. Clint gave him the 'sealed lips' sign; J.D. nodded his head in acknowledgement. Clint's mind was racing with fear, frustration, and regret. He would give anything to undo his last few days. The sweat on his brow dripped into his eyes causing a ferocious burning sensation with blurred vision. He futilely attempted to wipe his eyes with his mud-stained hands. It only made things worse. Every move by either boy seemed to cause amplified noises that were sure to give away their presence.

J.D. was in even worse shape. His breathing was rapid and irregular. He had long since gnawed all ten fingernails down into his cuticles, causing dried blood to cake around his nail bed. His entire body shook with terror; his eyes trained back and forth from silhouettes of Clint, looking for new directions, to the new position of the trackers.

"Guys, either of you have a gun?" one man asked, now close enough for Clint and J.D. to overhear every word. "I'm purty sure there's somebody hid out over there," he said, pointing to where Clint and J.D. were hiding.

The man turned around and walked the twenty paces back down the embankment.

Clint reached his hand around to place it on top of J.D.'s. They were frozen. It was too late to run; the noise would be a sure giveaway. It appeared that their capture was eminent.

"Here's a .38 if you need it." He reached into his glove compartment and brought out the handgun. "You're welcome to use it. Just be careful over there. Might just be a coyote or sumpin'? Or…?"

"Whatever it is, I'm fixin' to find out."

Clint heard it all. He knew they were as good as dead now.

30

THE TALL STRANGER retraced his original steps, this time armed with a revolver. His flashlight beam seemed even brighter as it danced around bushes and trees. "Wish I had my bloodhound with me right now."

Clint and J.D. couldn't breathe. Their lungs were screaming for air, but any noise at this point would give away their hiding place.

The man took a couple more steps up the hillside, stopped for a moment, and turned around. The full moon lit him up just enough. He wore a black and red checked flannel shirt with a khaki colored hunting cap. His shirt tail was out, partially hiding his protruding belly. He shouted over his shoulder. "Maybe I'm losing it. Are you sure neither of you heard anything? It came from right over in this area. I swear there's somebody over here. And I swear I smell gas. Coyotes don't carry gas with 'em."

He took a couple more steps toward J.D. The man's left foot couldn't have been more than ten feet from Clint's right hand. Both boys shut their eyes in fear. They couldn't bear to look at the beam of light dancing erratically as they combed the landscape.

J.D. had to breathe. Gently, he released air out of his lungs and, without a sound, took in another breath. He opened his eyes just as the man nearly stepped on his outstretched leg. How the flashlight had failed to shine directly on J.D. and Clint baffled even them. It seemed that at any second, he would step on their back.

Suddenly, just as he was inches away, J.D. felt another sneeze coming on. Whatever brush they were in was wreaking havoc on his allergies. He squeezed Clint's arm, trying to give him some kind of sign of looming danger. Momentarily, another sneeze would blast out of J.D. and their hideout would be discovered.

They were doomed.

But just when J.D. thought he couldn't hold it in a second longer, another set of car lights arrived. Blue lights were flashing. Headlights showed *THP* on the side. The Tennessee Highway Patrol had arrived.

The tall man turned around quickly, muttered something under his breath, and ambled back. On his way down he stepped on a dead branch that popped loudly. He gasped and nearly lost his balance, producing a string of choice profanities that made his friends chuckle. In that same instant, J.D. let out his muffled sneeze.

"Careful there, Adam," his buddy laughed, "you ain't twenty-one anymore!"

The patrolman got out of his squad car and joined the three men below. Their attention turned to black smoke as it continued to rise. Flames seemed to have diminished; the boys could no longer see any light.

The scratching blare of THP's radio became a welcome distraction. Slowly, Clint sat up, holding J.D. down. If he could move without making too much noise, then he could get J.D. up, and they might be able to slide their way down.

After coming within an eyelash of having their cover exposed, they needed little encouragement to lie motionless. They had already regretted their curiosity in hanging around to watch this melodramatic conclusion.

It wasn't until they made it to the bottom of the ridge that the boys finally felt some sense of relief. Looking up, they could see a faint blue glow as emergency lights reflected off the scattered cloud cover.

After they had regained their composure and caught their breath, Clint motioned for J.D. to follow him. Clint whispered, "I think Highway 48 loops back around down here. We'll get our bearings from there."

Clint knew that with any more encounters like that, their destiny would be sealed. Sealed in prison.

31

CLINT AND J.D. REACHED Highway 48, but their bearings weren't there to meet them. Nothing looked familiar, especially in darkness.

"Well, where do we go from here?" J.D. asked.

"I don't know!" Clint snapped. "Guess we'll just flag down that sheriff when he drives by and ask him for a lift." Clint's sarcasm showed his patience was wearing thin. It was irritating J.D.

"Ya know, Clint. I'm gettin' damn tired of hearing you tell me what I shoulda done!"

"Just shut up and let me think!"

The sooner he could get home and get away from Clint, the better J.D. would feel. He finally recognized that their friendship was changing. J.D. spotted a small rock overhang down near Obed Creek that ran parallel to Highway 48, about thirty feet below.

"How 'bout over there," J.D. said, pointing to an overhang. "We could hide out there 'til morning…and 'til we come up with a plan."

Clint and J.D. were physically and emotionally spent, so the patchy moss on the rock floor seemed as inviting as a memory foam mattress. Within minutes, they were both sound asleep.

A loud muffler on a vehicle several feet above them startled Clint just as sunrise appeared. At first he was disoriented in the unfamiliar surroundings of their bedroom. But the all-too-real memories of last evening's activities quickly reminded him. He looked over at J.D., who was still peacefully snoring away. Clint grumbled to himself out of both jealousy and disbelief.

"How does he do it?" he said aloud. J.D. raised an eyebrow, and then opened one eye.

J.D. yawned with his whole body like a Siamese cat. "Ok. What's the plan? I'm starving!

"The best way for us to get back to Smithville is to hitchhike," Clint said. "We'll hitch a ride down 48 over to 40. From there, we can get a lift home."

The only thing Clint had was a small knapsack with two extra tee shirts and one pair of jeans. J.D.'s backpack carried the flashlights, two tee shirts and Cody's songbook. Assessing their condition, they decided to change into their fresh clothes; they thought they might get a ride sooner if they looked more presentable.

After thirty minutes of walking south on 48, a late model Dodge Ram truck approached. J.D. quickly painted a smile on his face and stuck his thumb out. The truck driver drove past them slowly, no doubt sizing them up. But then, he slowed and came to a stop about a hundred feet past the boys. He stuck his head out and yelled.

"Morning, guys! Out awful early, ain't ya? Where ya headed?"

"Nothing like morning air in your lungs. We're actually heading over to Smithville, but any distance in that direction would sure be appreciated."

"Smithville, huh?"

"Yeah, I know it's off the road a bit. But we thought we'd try to git down to 70, or if there's a truck stop at 48 and I-40, could you get us that far?"

The man appeared to be a local, perhaps in construction, judging from contents. The truck's entire front seat was covered with mounds of papers and fast food wrappers.

"No room up front, but if you boys don't mind riding back there, I can run you down as far as Dickson."

"Great, thanks! We're much obliged!" Clint said.

Both boys hopped in, and found a spot to sit among empty concrete bags, cement mixers and trowels. Clint grinned to J.D..

"How 'bout this for good luck?'

"Just hope he's not some psycho killer." J.D. remarked. "Can't be too careful these days. I mean look what happened to Cody when he started hitchhiking."

Clint glared at J.D. but said nothing.

The wind chill factor wasn't suited for their clothes, but the price was right. Somehow they managed to nod off. Their nap was interrupted by a blast from a Tennessee Highway Patrol car.

"What now?" Clint gasped, his heartbeat pounding.

"So much for luck," J. D. said. "He's pulling us over. What are we gonna do now? This just ain't worth it, Clint! My heart can't take this anymore. Let's just..."

"Calm down, man! We got no choice. All you gotta do is stay put."

The amplified sound of a megaphone resonated, "Please remain in your vehicle. I'll need to see your driver's license and registration papers."

Clint gasped.

32

THE OFFICER EXITED his vehicle, placed his flat broad-billed hat confidently in place, and approached the truck. He apparently had not noticed Clint and J.D., because he did a double take when he turned and saw them. He nodded and continued talking to the driver. The truck's engine was still idling so they couldn't hear.

"What should we say if he asks us anything?"

"*You* say nothing. You let me talk. And I'm not saying a word unless he asks me a direct question. We'll just have to wing it. What other choice we got?"

The officer gathered paperwork and took it back to his vehicle without acknowledging the boys. After reading information off to someone on his police radio, he then put the paperwork down and began writing. After what seemed like thirty minutes to Clint and J.D., the officer returned, stopping briefly to quiz Clint and J.D.

"Gentlemen, this driver here a friend of yours?"

"No, sir," Clint hurried his words, "We're just hitching a ride with him. Why? He done something wrong?"

"Where ya headed?"

"Cookeville, Tennessee, sir."

"What's your names?"

Clint hadn't intended for their conversation to go on this long. He ran some names through his mind. "Name's Clay Salinger, sir, and this here's my buddy J.D. Sullivan."

"Just getting back from Las Vegas, officer," J.D. quickly offered. "Had some car trouble over in Arkansas and no money. Been hitching rides ever since. Just trying to get home, sir."

"Can I see your license?"

"Well, that's just it officer," Clint said. "Neither one of us has a driver's license."

"You got an I.D.?"

"We've got a license, sir. Just not on us."

"That's right, sir."

"How'd you get from Vegas to Arkansas without a license?"

"We, uh…"

"I'm gonna need to take a look at your I.D., fellas."

As Clint and J.D. exchanged nervous glances, the officer got a call on his radio. He listened, looked at his wrist watch, then walked up to the driver and held a brief, muffled conversation. All the boys could hear was, "Alright, be careful now, Freddie." He returned his paperwork and headed back to his squad car. Without stopping, he muttered, "Your lucky day, gentlemen."

The truck resumed its heading south on state highway 48. The road sign ahead told Clint they were only fifteen miles north of Dickson. Clint's hands were shaking like jellyfish. J.D. was speechless, a rare situation for him.

In less than thirty minutes they had made it to the junction of I-40 and 48. The driver pulled into a truck stop.

"Boys, this is about as far as I can take you. Got a little lucky back there. Thought Smokey was gonna nick me for speeding, but he seemed more interested in knowing about you two than anything else. Anyway, good luck to you guys. Hope you make it home ok."

Clint thanked him. He and J.D. climbed out of Freddie's truck and out of another cobweb of deceit. At least for now.

Their finances were in shambles. Collectively, they had about $33, just enough by Clint's assessment to eat breakfast and find a ride east toward Cookeville. J.D. didn't eat much, forgetting that an hour ago he could have gnawed his own arm off from hunger.

"I just wanna get back home and start this whole week all over," Clint said.

"How you gonna start anything over when everybody in town's gonna know you're dead before you even git back. Shoot, there's probably been family and friends coming and going all day."

"That'd sure be something to see," Clint said, romanticizing the moment. "Gets me a little choked up, you know." He smiled as if visualizing his imagination. J.D. couldn't follow his fascination.

"When you gonna tell Amy 'bout all this mess? She's not gonna be happy, ya know."

"Well, that's another thing I'll have to worry about later. Gotta do it in person. Hope she'll understand. Bet she will when she sees her cash prize she's gonna get for her trouble. It'll take them a week or longer to run numbers. By then, we'll be tucked away back at the house. So you really think a lot of people will come to express their condolences?"

"Get us a ride, Clint," J.D. said, shaking his head.

Within twenty minutes, Clint had befriended a truck driver hauling for Big Ten Express, and he convinced him to take along two stranded travelers. The driver had a load going back to Cookeville, which was just about twenty miles north of Smithville. The boys were elated, as they figured they could hike from Cookeville. Pitch black darkness inside their new temporary ride would be perfect for getting in another nap.

J.D. propped himself up in between sacks of soybeans and cornmeal, and managed to get to sleep within minutes. Clint, on the other hand, was mentally wrestling with his alternatives from Cookeville to Smithville, and exactly how he was going to sell Amy on his master scheme. Since he hadn't spoken to her in over a week, he knew she was still seething over his theft of her personal cash stash even though he had paid her back in full. He hoped he would find her in better spirits.

Slowly the eighteen-wheeler rolled into a rest area about two miles from Highway 111 South, just east of Cookeville. The sounds of latches clacking and chains loosening thundered in their ears, as the trailer's back door opened. Bright sunshine rushed in, temporarily blinding them.

"Guys, this is as fer as I can git ya. You know how to get to Old Kentucky Road? That's your best bet."

"Oh yeah. We're from around here. Listen, man, thanks so much. If I had any money I'd sure give it to you."

"No problem, guys. Always glad to help a man in need. Been in your fix myself a time or two."

As the rig rolled out, the boys waved in appreciation.

If that driver only knew…

33

OLD KENTUCKY ROAD was home to these boys. Hitching a ride should be easy. Either could hike home blindfolded with no trouble. Unfortunately it was about eighteen miles and they were both spent. They managed to thumb a ride over to Old Kentucky and 70.

Clint and J.D. knew it was about eight to ten miles to Clint and Amy's house, but they were running on adrenaline. Chances would be high that they would be recognized by a friend or neighbor so there was no more hitchhiking. The last few miles would give them some time to process this whole mystery saga; make sure they hadn't left any gaping holes.

"We did a good job of blowing that Honda up. Bet they couldn't tell that body from a dinosaur egg," Clint said, almost proudly. "Soon as they sign off on that death certificate, the $250,000 will be in the mail. But now, listen here…" Clint said. "Since Amy bought the life insurance policy through her group plan at work, I figure it's only fair to split the money three ways."

"Cut her in on the deal? But won't that give you two-thirds? You being married and all?"

"So you gonna cheat Amy out of any money? Being a widow don't mean nothin' to you?"

"Well, no, I didn't say that. Just don't think...*a full third*? You really think it's worth a third?" He didn't pursue the subject any more, but didn't feel good about it either.

"She has gotta help us a lot for this to work."

J.D. agreed, but still had reservations. "It just seems like what I done should be worth at least half."

They continued walking in silence toward Logan's house. But so much had changed in such a short amount of time. Clint began to contemplate.

"Maybe Amy and I will just move out of town and start all over," Clint said. "I'll change my last name, maybe get one of those FBI-like makeovers. I could afford it. A new face, everything. Life'll be perfect again."

"When was it ever perfect, Clint? You and Amy fought constantly."

"Yeah, but who fights when you're rolling in dough?"

"Well, are you sure that's even what Amy wants? I mean ya hadn't even asked her about any of this yet?"

"She'll be ok with it." Clint kicked a rock extra hard and sent it spinning completely across the highway. "She better be ok with it."

The last few miles of their trek took them by a local convenience store. "Hey, you think we ought to duck in here at Highway 70 market and call her? I mean just to make sure everything's ok at the house and all that."

"Naw, no need in it. The main thing to remember is that you and I had an argument in Dallas, you left on a bus, and hadn't heard from me since. Otherwise, everybody's gonna ask how come you didn't get killed in the car wreck too. You follow?"

This time J.D. kicked a rock as hard as he could. He said nothing. Clint spoke up again.

"Say, man, I know sometimes I kinda talked down to you during this whole thing, like you were a dumbass or something. Well, I just wanna say, I mean, we practically grew up together. And sure, we did some stuff we hadn't planned on, at least not like we planned it. But let's not let any of that get between our friendship. Right, bro?"

J.D. walked along, with both hands in his pockets, looking down in front of him. "Why you sayin' all this stuff now?"

"Well, for no particular reason other than…."

"Well, then, we ain't got nothin' to talk about then, do we?" J.D.'s pace didn't change; his voice didn't change. Neither did his gaze. He kicked a wrinkled Miller Lite can and it bent in two pieces, wrapping around his right foot. The apology dangled, leaving Clint confused and concerned. His relationship with J.D. had been strained ever since they left Vegas.

J.D. said almost nothing during the last mile. One-word answers to direct questions from Clint was all he'd offer. His withdrawal continued to concern Clint. How he was going to hold J.D.'s interest and loyalty?

34

Dusk was fast approaching when they made the last turn onto Possum Holler Road. Both guys stopped in their tracks and starred at each other in horror when they saw Clint's house. There were at least half a dozen cars parked in his driveway and along both sides of the road.

"Sunuvabitch!! I can't believe it!"

"Hey, that's my mom and dad's car over there. We're screwed!"

"Now hang on, J.D. Just cool it a minute! Let's think this out. We hadn't planned on this happenin'." Clint was having to think fast, and he wasn't ready for that. He took a deep breath, keeping a firm grip on J.D.'s arm while closing both eyes and tilting his face toward the sky. "Ok, look. We gotta hide out here for now, just to make sure that no body is gonna come in behind us." The pair slipped down into a ditch-like thicket that would hide them and yet still be within earshot of the Logan house.

"Guess the State can run those VIN numbers purty fast. I'da thought it would have even melted that VIN; that's what I was bettin' on," J.D. was in panic mode.

"Can you friggin' believe that! Not in a million years did I think they could have finished workin' a blown up car that quick!"

J.D.'s attention refocused on his parents. "My mama and daddy probably think I'm dead too. I hadn't had a chance yet to tell nobody 'bout our fight in Dallas. I hope mama's not cryin'. Gosh, Clint, I gotta let her know quick that I'm ok. I mean I gotta let her know now!"

"J.D.!" Clint said, pulling him back, "You gotta work with me a little on this. We're gonna let your mama know, at least what she needs to know, in just a few minutes. So just hold on. You understand me?"

"Yeah, I understand."

Clint and J.D. waited at least an hour.

Finally, J.D.'s parents were first to leave. Clint watched J.D. as he sat up with excitement. Clint settled him down, although J.D.'s breathing remained rapid and strained.

"Thanks so much for your love and support, Mr. and Mrs. Scott." Amy said. Clint strained to see her face, but could barely make out her silhouette "I hope we hear good news about J.D. soon."

Clint continued to hold J.D. steady by grasping his left forearm tightly. "Ya gotta hang on just a few more minutes."

"Ok, ok. I know."

J.D.'s dad held his wife's hand as she took slow and deliberate steps towards their car. She paused a moment to wipe her nose with a hankie in her other hand. She had a lost and depressed look on her face. Her many wrinkles seemed exaggerated, J.D. thought, but it was hard to see. They slowly got in their car, turned around right in front of the boys, headlights glaring straight into their hunched bodies. Their blue late model Chevy slowly pulled away, until nothing could be seen but dim taillights.

J.D. was like a bulldog on a short leash. He was one grip away from tearing down the road after his parent's car. "Just hold on, man! Gimme another minute, we gotta tell Amy first!"

J.D. was impatient.

It was another fifteen minutes before the last departure. This time Amy turned the porch light on, which prevented Clint from seeing anything but silhouettes and shadows. But he did hear Amy say to the departing couple, "We'll know more details tomorrow and I'll let you know."

A few minutes later, each light in the house, one by one, was extinguished. "Ok, I think we're clear. Let's go up the road a bit and come in through the woods and go in from the back porch. Maybe she left the back door open."

Slowly and deliberately, the boys crossed the street a hundred yards up from Logan's front door. Their modest home was surrounded by woods, with no immediate neighbors. As their path took them a few hundred yards deeper into the woods, they turned left and followed the land Clint knew so well. The full moon shone just enough for them to navigate the adjacent land and up to Clint's back porch. Each step was purposeful and calculated.

Emerging from the woods onto their cleared back yard property, Clint whispered, "If it's locked, let me knock. Gotta try not to scare her." J.D. nodded in agreement. Clint crept slowly up toward two concrete steps that led to the back door. Just as he approached the first step, there was a sudden black blur at his feet. He looked down, but it was too late. A black feral cat chasing a rat suddenly shot between his legs. He lost his balance and fell onto the first step of the back porch. His nose and cheek struck the concrete ledge, blood streaming from his nose and a gash on his left cheek. A chorus of expletives decorated the fall. J.D. was glad it was dark as midnight, so Clint wouldn't notice the laugh J.D. could barely hold back.

Clint wiped his bloody nose and cheek on his shirttail and sleeve. "Shit! This is a great welcome home for Amy! I probably look like a serial killer!" He looked down at his shirt to examine his blood loss. "Have I got most of it off my face?"

"I guess. I really can't tell." J.D was helpless; it was too dark. He gave a gentle tap on the window, stepped back to look at J.D., and took a deep breath. After a few seconds he repeated. Both men's faces were covered with sweat. Clint's facial bleeding had resumed.

After what seemed like forever, a faint voice came from inside. "Just a minute." Amy clicked on the light switch as she approached the back door in her black bathrobe and bare feet. Without another thought, she clicked on their back porch light and unlocked the door. Out of the corner of her eye, she caught a blur of a man coming at her with a bloody tee shirt, wringing with sweat and smelling like a locker room with crimson streams flowing from his nose and a gash on his cheek. She screamed.

"Amy, it's me!"

Amy stood speechless. There, standing before her, was a body or ghost of the man whom she had been mourning all day. Amy screamed again. Her blood curdling cry resonated through the valley with an unfading echo.

35

CLINT WAS NOT EXPECTING such a shocked response from Amy. "Shhhhhhh! Amy, it's me, Clint! Can't you see? I'm ok. It's all a big misunderstanding. We didn't think you would have heard about the wreck this fast." He paused a moment. She was in shock. Her hands rested on one of the chair backs of their kitchen table. Her face was pale, her brow covered with sweat. Her hands shook uncontrollably. She was unsteady on her feet, and began to lose her balance. Her eyes stared blankly into and through the backs of Clint's eyes, as if she was imagining. "And look, you can see J.D. is OK too."

Amy seemed non-responsive. Her eyes rolled back in her head, as if she was having a seizure. She began to hyperventilate. "Holy smoke? Amy, You, ok?" Her knees buckled under her, she slumped to the floor, the left side of her head striking the corner of the kitchen table.

The events happened so quickly that neither J.D. nor Clint could react fast enough. It was as if it was happening in slow motion as they saw her sleek black bathrobe slide slowly to the floor and her lifeless body lay crumbled in the garment.

"Holy shit! Oh my God! She's cut pretty bad! J.D. was down on his knees immediately attending to Amy's injury. Clint was fast forwarding in his mind as to how they would handle the next few hours if Amy was hurt really bad. J.D. gave curt and pointed directions to Clint, a rarity in their relationship. "You got a first aid kit here? If so, go get it quick! She's bleedin' pretty bad!

"Uh, I think we do, but...... I can't remember where she kept it. Let me think...... Oh, yeah, it's downstairs in the laundry room. Over the dryer is a cabinet. I think it's up there."

He stared at his lifeless Amy as she lay sprawled awkwardly on the kitchen floor. Blood that had already pooled by her was the size of a dinner plate. She coughed sporadically; her breathing was irregular and shallow.

"Clint, go get it for us now, please! Hurry up, this is bad!"

Clint rose and made his way downstairs to retrieve the kit. J.D. quickly tore open rolls of gauze, adhesive tape and a brown bottle of antiseptic. "Now get me a bowl of hot water." J.D. noticed his hesitation. "Hurry up, man!"

Clint complied but with no sense of urgency. J.D. blotted Amy's temple and carefully applied the antiseptic. "Amy? Can you hear me? Amy, do you know where you are?" He shook her gently, with a sense of panic in his voice. "Amy, please open your eyes!" He gently slapped both sides of each cheek, and shook her slightly. She was out.

J.D. caught Clint's eye. He resented Clint's apparent apathy toward his wife's accident and injury. "I think she just fainted, but the blow to her head is what's buggin' me. What do you think, Clint, she's your wife."

"How the hell should I know? It's not like we can call 911 or they'll wanna know who we're talkin' to. That would give us both away, we can't have that. J.D., can you tend to her for now 'til I can think about this a while. Buddy, we are stuck in the mud up to our axle!"

"Get me the damn hot water! Now!" J.D. was out of patience.

Over the next hour, J.D. would not leave Amy's side. Direct pressure on the head wound got the blood to finally clot. He had tied a wet gauze and bandage around her head.

After being chastised by J.D., Clint began to make excuses. "I thought about calling 911 from our house phone, report the emergency and we just get outta here. I was planning on staying here at the house with her, but if paramedics come, I can't be here. If you leave her by herself 'til 911 arrives, then you'd have to worry about what story she might tell if/when she wakes up. We haven't even had the chance to coach her on our plan."

J.D. was looking at the scenario from a totally different perspective. "I just wish there was some way to know if there was somethin' else we could be doin' for her. I mean, what if she's got a concussion or a brain tumor, or something' like that. Who can we call? What would we do?"

"J.D. I have no idea! We can't call nobody!! Buddy, this whole damn thing has gone so far off path already, that I wouldn't venture a guess for nothin'. No sense in remindin' me that you said this scheme wouldn't fly in the first place."

"Clint, while you're rattlin' on there, how 'bout getting' me a plastic bag with some ice cubes in 'em. Hurry, please." Within minutes, a cold compress was applied to Amy's head.

Clint and J.D. carried Amy to the sofa in the living room, propping her head up so they could get access to the cut. J.D. sat on a stool by her head as she remained motionless. He removed the gauze from her head wound, and reapplied the medicine. J.D. was starting to get worried. What possible way could they get Amy to medical attention before something life altering might happen? Or even life ending.

36

SHERIFF CASTLEMAN'S next order of business would be to contact Dr. Arthur Templeton, former state medical examiner. Dickson County was one of only a few regions left that still relied on Dr. Templeton for assistance in forensic death investigation. He did seem a little disheveled and disorganized, especially lately, but locals felt sorry for the way he had been treated after serving the state for so many years. The local District Attorney made all those types of decisions.

"Doc, we've got an unusual situation here up on Gatlin's Ridge," Sheriff Castleman began. "A Honda rolled down a ravine, hit a tree, and exploded. The fire pattern is a little odd, so we've got fire arson on it now. One dead, can't tell if it's male or female. Car registered to . . . a Clint Logan of Smithville. Can you meet us sometime today?"

Dr. Templeton arrived at the Dickson County Hospital Morgue, where the incinerated remains were being temporarily held.

Sheriff Castleman pulled up in his patrol car as Dr. Templeton prepared to begin his investigation. "Doc, I've got some dental x-rays from the family yesterday. This thing happened night before last. The sheriff held the small strip of x-rays up to the sunlight for Dr. Templeton to see. They showed several silver fillings and a couple of crowns.

"Should be pretty easy to confirm," Dr. Templeton said, as he took the strip and strained to look at it from different angles. "We'll have a look."

"Want me to call Dr. Walsh? He handles all TBI work and most of the state. I'm sure that's who you still use?"

"Yes, but we won't need to in this case." Dr. Templeton patted the sheriff on the arm. "Looks like this one is pretty cut and dried."

The sheriff wondered how Templeton could know it was "cut and dried" when he hadn't even examined the body yet. He decided to keep quiet.

Three hours later, seven badly burned teeth were recovered. Dr. Templeton examined each tooth, rendered them diagnostic, and attempted to explain his findings. He held the x-ray strip up to the sunlight, and pointed to an area of the film with the end of his pencil. "This is a gold crown from a lower right first molar area—this is one that was retrieved from the wreckage. And can you see where that white blob is? That is the x-ray of this tooth."

The sheriff nodded as if he understood, barely hiding his hesitation. Even if what Dr. Templeton said seemed upside down and backward to him, he thought it better to defer to the professionals.

"Yep. This is definitely Clint Logan. We'll call Medical Transport and have them bring everything in. I'll check just to make sure and see if we can come up with any other helpful information."

Within three days, Dr. Templeton had faxed his final report to Sheriff Castleman.

The victim, a twenty-nine-year-old white male, was Clint Alton Logan. He made this confirmation based on the "positive dental identification achieved from Tooth Number 31." The forensic autopsy report explained that the victim died of 100 percent total body surface area with fourth degree burns and smoke inhalation." Dr. Templeton also stated on his official autopsy report that "black soot was found in the victim's trachea" and that the official cause of death was "burns and smoke inhalation."

37

CHRISTINE BEGAN her morning with the traditional walk to her local post office. It was a beautiful day, sunny and breezy.

"Hey, Melvin, how's it going? Brought your paper in for you."

Melvin beamed as he watched Christine strut over to the counter where he sold stamps. She smiled warmly at her buddy as she dropped a wrapped copy of *USA Today* onto his counter. They had developed a daily ritual that both seemed to enjoy.

"Hey gal! Bingo! Your lucky day. You got something. Postcard. Just put it up."

"Oh, Melvin! Are you kidding?"

Christine rushed to her mailbox, opened the door with childish excitement. She reached inside to retrieve a glossy postcard with the state of Texas on its cover. She turned it over and squealed with delight. Her hands were trembling so much the card slipped through them and fell onto the floor.

"Oh Melvin. I'm so nervous I can't even hold this postcard."

Melvin laughed understandingly and shook his head. "Settle down there, gal. Just enjoy the moment."

Christine smiled at Melvin and clutched the card toward her chest.

Melvin chuckled at her enthusiasm. "Aren't you even gonna read it?"

"Yes, in a minute. Right now I want to just hold onto this moment."

She finally looked down, and when she did, a teardrop fell onto the freshly buffed floor. Suddenly she felt awkward in front of Melvin. After several dabs at the streams of tears now freely escaping down her cheeks, she felt composed enough to read her card. The dark blue ink had smeared a little in transit, but it was still easy to read:

Dear Sweetie...

Met 2 guys outside of town going to Nashville. Can you believe it? They say I can take the whole ride with them. Will call after I get situated. And, babe, I look at your gorgeous pic in my billfold about 5 times a day. Miss and love you.

Your Sweetie

Christine cried all the way home. But this time the tears were for a different reason.

38

CLINT AND J.D. TOOK SHIFTS sitting up with Amy all night. Concerns mounted as they both realized that her fall from fainting and the lick on her head, she should be becoming alert by now. They rotated on two hours shifts. There were times when her body motion became restless and agitated. Clint responded quickly by trying to talk to her.

"Amy, hey honey, it's Clint. We're home and everything's ok. All that other stuff is just a big mistake." He thought he saw Amy raise her eyebrow and then, the corner of her mouth. J.D.'s thoughts centered with improving her patient care. I'm not suggesting necessarily that we leave her, it's just that...."

"If you think I'm gonna leave Amy, YOUR wife, in this house while we run out on her, you are nuts. She may die if she doesn't get medical treatment, and quick. I don't know; I'm no doctor."

Clint ignored the parts he didn't want to hear. "Well, if either of us take her to the emergency room, they're gonna already know about our car wreck in Dickson. You could take her I suppose, or you could call 911, stay with her since you're supposedly just back from Dallas, and I could split. If we both left her, then who knows what kinda story she would tell folks about what she saw or dreamed last night."

"Like I said, you can forget both of us leaving her. That's out. I don't mind a bit if you wanna split. Head on down the road Clint. Get you a new name now, can't give you any cash, but an open door, 'cause I think that's what you wanna do anyway. Go on, get out. Do it."

"Don't start that crap. If you think I'm leaving town before my own funeral, you're crazy."

"Clint, it sounds like you're the one that's crazy! I mean just listen to the words that are coming out of your mouth right now. You've lost it, man!" There. He said it. He had wanted to say it for a long time. It sure felt good getting that off his chest.

Clint stared at disbelief. He said nothing, because, deep inside, he knew J.D. was right. He just couldn't confess to it.

39

THE SUN WAS RISING when the two hour shift break rotated. J.D. begin his vigil just as the first rays of sun shown through their living room window, casting direct light on the swollen face of Amy Logan. In spite of ice packs, bluish yellow bruising was becoming noticeable just around her right temple area, extending around to include a black eye that was partially swollen shut.

J.D. noticed a sudden movement. Just as a ray of sunshine touched the corner of Amy's eye, a frown appeared on her face.

"Amy. Hey, it's J.D. Can you hear me? We're back here. Everything's ok.

He noticed Amy's brow frown again.

Seeing this encouragement, he stood up, leaned down to hold her cold hand while he whispered words of encouragement. He leaned up to catch any facial expression when he saw a faint smile appear on her face, followed by another frown. Then, in slow deliberate moves, she rolled her head over toward J.D. and gradually opened her eyes. She stared briefly as her eyes would not focus quickly.

"Amy, it's J.D."

Amy smiled again. She managed a meager whisper. "Where

am I J.D.? Is this really you or your ghost?"

J.D. squeezed her hand tightly. "Amy this is the real me. I don't have a ghost! Clint and I are back here at the house. You met us at the back door late last night and we scared you pretty bad. You fainted, we think, and cut your head on that kitchen table. The blow just knocked you outta your senses, I reckon. You gotta headache?"

"It's awful. Worse than the worse hangover you could ever imagine. Can you get me some aspirin or something?"

J.D. delivered her meds after notifying Clint that Amy seemed to be coming around. Clint awoke and sleepily wandered in to speak to his wife. "Hey Amy, glad you're back to join us. I think we freaked you out last night, and then you freaked us out. So we're even!"

She tried weakly to sit up on the sofa, but her energy was inadequate. Her neck twisted around as far as her head would take it to get a panorama of the room. Her brain was taking a few minutes to restore her original network configuration. She squinted as she tried to refocus on her newly discovered surroundings. Slowly, she began to remember bits and pieces of the night before.

"So this is really you and Clint and not a ghost?" She still wasn't convinced. "I'm confused as to what is a real ghost and what is just real."

"There are no ghosts here. Just bad timing on our part last night in scaring you and then your fall...." J.D. was trying to make excuses for the senseless fright they caused Amy last night.

"I just remember someone on the back porch in a bloody tee shirt coming at me last night. He looked just like Clint. That's all I remember. But boy, do I have a thumper this morning!"

Clint edged toward the corner of the sofa where Amy's head

was. "I'm sorry to scare you so baby, but we didn't really have a good chance to call you since this all happened on our way back. But when we got back last night, and saw all the cars in the driveway, we knew we had gotten to you too late. I am so sorry for all this, with scaring you and all, your cut on your head with the fall."

Amy took in every word but was expressionless. She shook her head from side to side in a futile attempt to shake the cobwebs out. She winced, as it exaggerated her already pounding headache. "The sheriff told me yesterday morning they found your body burned up over in Dickson County. I feel like I'm losing my mind, sitting here having a conversation with a dead man!"

"Yeah, baby. I know. But you gotta let me explain. Then, it'll all make sense to you. You see, J.D. and I got this plan on the way back from Vegas to find some hitchhiker, worthless kind of guy, and then knock him off. To the cops it looks like me, and we can cash that $250,000 life insurance policy and we'll all be sittin' pretty. Don't you see what a good idea that is?"

Amy had a puzzled look on her face. "Wait a minute. Are you telling me you two have killed a man?"

"Killed? Well, sorta."

"Sorta? Sorta?!?!?!"

"It was just a hitchhiker."

"So that makes it OK to murder him?! 'Cause he's a hitchhiker? I don't get it. Just because you think nobody knows who he is?" J.D. thought Amy made a lot of sense, especially for someone whose mind was fuzzy.

Clint paused a moment.

"Well…. yeah." Clint looked down at the floor with a blank stare. He had not rehearsed this part of their scheme. Clint glanced over to J.D., expecting at least some contribution. J.D.

quickly looked away, giving full display of nonsupport.

"I tried telling him," J.D. said.

Clint shot him a look, and then continued to try to win her over.

"Don't you see, baby? It'll make life easy for us. You can quit work, we can move somewhere else and start all over. I'll get a fake ID and get a job. You can stay home; we'll start a family. Doesn't all that seem pretty nice?"

Amy was still slurring her words slightly, and she spoke slowly. Nice? I'll tell you what it sounds like to me. It sounds like murder! I've seen enough of those TV shows. Your plan won't work. You're telling me that this body that was found in our burned up car in Dickson was the guy you killed? And now you want me to file a claim on that life insurance policy I have on you from my job? Is that your big plan?"

"Yeah, pretty much."

"Well, count me out!"

40

CLINT ALREADY DECIDED he had given Amy too much information too quickly. They left her alone for a while and she was fast asleep. The boys went down in the basement, the ESPN room, where they would discuss their plans.

"Well, since it looks like she's gonna make it, the first thing I gotta do, is to convince her to stay in our camp. Basically she has to go along with us, or turn us in for murder. She's not as receptive as I thought, but I don't think she would voluntarily turn us in either.

"When she comes back around, I think we have to coach her into calling her mom and the funeral home this morning. I heard her tell her mother on the porch last night that she would pick her up around ten this morning to go over the arrangements with her. It's nine now. We better see if we can get her to postpone it. She can't go out looking like this."

Clint got down close to her ear, and whispered like a child wanting another cookie. "Darling, we need to explain later those details on all our plan, but the bottom line, is we need you to call your mom and the funeral home to let them know you want to postpone making funeral arrangements for a day or so. Tell them that you're not feeling well. Tell them the nerve pills they gave you made you faint last night and hit your head and now you've got a black eye. They'll understand. Basically, you're in the driver's seat. Of course, be sure and not mention that we are both here with you. I know you still have questions about this, but at least for now, just please pretend that last night never happened.

"Just let your mom know that you don't need her help today; otherwise, we have to split. Do you think you can do that sweetie? That will give us time to explain this to you in greater detail when you don't have a throbbing headache.

Suddenly, there was a knock at the door. J.D. and Clint dashed down the basement stairs. Clint stayed up on the top of the downstairs looking out but hidden by the door.

"Yes. Who is it? I'm on the sofa and can't get up right now." Her voice was so weak that it was difficult for the visitor to hear. An unfamiliar voice answer through the front door.

"It's just DeKalb florist with a potted plant for your home. From your friends at work expressing sympathy. I'll just leave this at the front door. I'm sure I'll be back today with some more for you, ma'am. I won't bother you, ma'am, but it breaks my heart to hear about your husband's death. I'm Betty and work for the florist. We met once a while back down at the flea market. May God bless you, child, at this most difficult time."

"Thank you so much. I'll get the plant later. Thanks again for those kind words." She glanced over to the basement door, where Clint had been propped up on his elbows to hear the exchange. He smiled as he took in the words of sorrow.

When the floral van left, Clint prepped Amy for her two phone calls. Of course, Amy was reluctant at first. "I'm not saying I'm going along with this, but, if I do, then when would I tell her I will meet her?"

"Just tell her the meds made you sleepy and you fell and hit your head, have a headache and black eye, and would like them to hold the remains for a couple of days 'til you make your decisions and you get to feeling better. They should understand completely. It's not like it's gonna hurt anything if the service is postponed for a few days." Amy was starting to realize that she had more decisions to make than seemed on the surface.

Amy agreed to call her mom since her arrival time was getting close. Clint dialed the number and handed the phone to Amy. "Hey mom. Those sleeping pills the doc wrote for me made me so dizzy. I got up in the middle of the night to go to the bathroom and fell and hit my head on the bathroom sink. Knocked me senseless. I feel okay now, but look like a train wreck, black eye and everything to go with it. I think I'll call the funeral home and see if I can put this off a day or two."

She paused a moment to get some unsolicited advice from her mother. "Yes, I know mama. Uh, huh. Yes ma'am. No, ma'am, I'm fine here by myself. Well, why don't I call you back later and let you know what the funeral home folks have to say. I may want you to take me to the doctor to have this bump looked at. Let me see how the morning goes. But for now, we're canceling making funeral arrangements."

The call to the funeral home was much less dramatic. She briefly explained her situation and indicated they would call tomorrow and see about making another appointment in a day or two.

Clint was eager to resume the plans but Amy didn't feel like having any discussions about anything. "Clint, why don't you and J.D. let me take a nap and see if this aspirin will take hold. Right now, I'm fuzzy headed, headache and still nauseated from last night. I gotta catch up before I can even talk with you about the rest of that mess."

He and J.D. would watch TV downstairs with Clint counting the hours before she would wake up.

"I think I'm gonna go back over to see my folks. I'll just tell 'em I just got in from the bus station from Dallas, and act like I haven't even heard that you died in a crash. This is gettin' too complicated!"

"Are you sure you feel comfortable enough with that story not to raise any red flags with your folks?" Clint doubted it.

"Of course I am. When I get them calmed down and they see I'm not dead, I'm sure they'll expect me to come back over and check on Amy, since she's grieving and all that."

With that J.D. began his five mile walk to the Scott's residence. He actually looked forward to the solitude of the walk. The intense drama was about to get the best of him.

Clint kept himself occupied by watching sports down in his basement hideaway. He certainly enjoyed what a hot shower and fresh clothes felt like, and, at least for now, he could relax and ponder which chapter of the plan would unfold next.

Three hours later, Amy began to slowly awake from her nap. Her headache was still there, but had subsided. Clint heard her get up to go to the bathroom, and was right by the sofa when she returned. "How you feelin' babe?" He tried to sound genuinely interested in her well being.

"Better, I think."

"You feel like talking about our plan, the one you call our scheme?"

"Not really."

"Well, I guess you saw the bruising in the bathroom mirror. You probably don't want to go out for anything 'til that settles down some. That may take another three or four days or longer. We just need to use that time to come to an agreement on how to carry our plan out."

41

THE LAST FEW DAYS had been difficult for Amy, but not for traditional reasons. She had argued continuously with Clint regarding the logistics of his scheme. After much deliberation, she had decided to go along with his plan, since her only other recourse was to report her husband for murder.

Amy had bought two new dresses: one for the visitation, really more of a sexy cocktail dress since it would be in the evening, and one for the funeral, a conservative black sleeveless silk dress that would help her look every bit the part of the grieving, but still beautiful and shapely, wife.

J.D. returned to his parents' house, explaining about the lies he had told them and McCord's Market. Feeling guilty about their betrayal, he was further worried because he could not tell them anything but his bus ride home from Dallas, Texas, after he and Clint had gotten into an argument. His parents had disapproved significantly, but rejoiced in the fact that their missing son had not been involved in the crash.

Clint, on the other hand, was very much alive, barking out orders, writing everything he wanted for his funeral down to the last detail. Amy had two full days of simulated activities including multiple visits to the funeral home, and planning the details of the service, visitation and burial. She took his childhood Bible to the undertaker to bury with the body. She put several "family" photos together in a collage arrangement.

It was difficult for Amy to get into the appropriate mindset for the visitation because she was feeling a little shaky. And nervous. She had the leading role in a drama she hadn't signed up for. Amy was about to go on stage to perform as she had never performed before, and she was terrified. Clint was breathing down her neck literally and figuratively as she was trying to fasten a string of pearls.

"You're not acting like any dead man I ever saw," she scolded him, as he giggled and kissed her on the shoulder.

"I swear, if you don't leave me alone, I ain't never gonna get outta here on time. Talk about bein' late for your own funeral. Clinton Logan, you're makin' me late for yours!"

Clint began to worry about who might and might not be at visitation to pay their respects. "That Bucky Reynolds had better show up," he growled.

"You want me to take roll? And anyway, they'll have a visitation book for people to sign. Just hang on, and you can read it later."

"Okay, cool."

"No! It's not cool! They're not signing your high school yearbook, ya know!" Amy scowled at Clint, who was quickly getting on her last nerve. Again.

Clint ignored her and continued. "And Roger Griggs better be there, too. He owes me money and was always talkin' about how he and Barbara wanted to take us out to eat. Of course, he never did. And now I'm dead and it's too late. Jerk's probably glad he won't have to buy me a steak."

"Will you *listen* to yourself?" Amy looked in the mirror at her husband's reflection. You know, Clint, you are unreal! Just leave me alone while I try to get out of this tangled spider web you've woven.

"I'll be home by nine-thirty, and I'll tell you who all was there." Once again, Amy rolled her eyes at her faux-dead husband. "You won't miss a thing!" With that, she got in her car.

Clint's curious eyes peered through the blinds and carefully watched Amy drive away. He then closed the kitchen curtains, turned off all the lights, stuck some Hot Pockets in their microwave, and downed his fourth beer.

"So this is what you do when you're dead?" He laughed at himself, his hands arranged over his protruding gut, pretty much in the same position as that body at Whitehaven Funeral Home. Of course, the casket would be closed. Clint grinned to himself. It felt great to pull one over on so many people.

Within five minutes, Clint was a ball of nervous energy. The short line of meth he snorted revved his motor even higher. Who could he call? J.D.? If his parents answered, he would just hang up, he figured. J.D. was still in the doghouse with his mom and dad, since they'd found out about that "trip" to Panama City Beach.

As expected, J.D. lost his job at the Market. His boss never did buy his original tale. But now he was determined to try to win his job back, even if it took some time and effort.

The phone rang. "Hello?" It was J.D.

"Hey, can you talk?"

"Just a few minutes. My folks are already gone to the funeral home. I'm supposed to meet them there in a few minutes. What's up?"

"You serious? They went to pay respects to me?"

"Yeah. Mom cried and everything when she heard. Guess she did like you after all. Or maybe, it's cause of Amy."

"Are you sure you're going to be able to pull this off?"

"Pull what off?"

"My funeral, dumb ass!" Clint knew as soon as he said it that he shouldn't have. "Sorry, man. What I mean is, are you going to be able to act like you're really sad that I'm dead? We have a lot of the same friends. And I bet you've already almost let it slip once or twice to your parents. All it takes is one loose lip and our whole cover is blown."

"You saying you think I'm the weak link?"

"Just reminding you how important it is."

"I got it covered I said," J.D. grunted in a monotone.

Clint wasn't convinced.

"I just wouldn't want either one of us messing things up."

"But mainly me?"

"Mainly either one of us."

"But *me*." J.D. said, his terseness coming through loud and clear. "That's what you meant, Clint. Me."

Clint didn't admit or deny it. But his silence said it all. It was going to be a long night.

42

DeKalb funeral home in Smithville was Amy's choice for the services. She arrived with nervous energy abounding. She had managed to get a Valium from her friend Becky Thornton. She never had been one to take pills, just the opposite of her husband. But tonight was different. Amy was getting lots of sympathy from her coworkers. But she needed more to make it feel genuine. She opened the little pillbox her grandmother had given her, then eyeing the small baby blue pill as it sat lonely in the bottom, she smiled.

Normally, at times like this, she reckoned people took these to help smooth out their grief. So if she seemed a little sedated at the visitation tonight, everyone would certainly understand and assume she was "medicated." Understandably medicated. She stuck the tiny tablet as far down her throat as she could and chased it with a shot of Mountain Dew.

Walking up the sidewalk, Amy imagined herself getting in character for her theatrics. She took a deep breath and greeted Mr. Whitson, the owner, with a weak smile. He had spent several hours with Amy the day before, helping her purchase just the right casket, grave plot, and stone marker.

"Hi, Mr. Whitson," Amy murmured in the meekest of meek voices.

"Good evening, Ms. Logan. Again, we are so sorry for your loss. We have a full team of staff here for you this evening to help you take care of any felt need. Just know that we are here to support you in any way. You have already received some beautiful flowers from your friends and coworkers."

Amy thanked Mr. Whitson for his thoughtful care.

Her first stop was in the ladies' restroom. She began to psych herself up in front of the restroom mirror, conjuring up painful images. Strangely enough, none of them involved her husband Clint in any way.

The director in her head called "Action!" and Amy thrust open the bathroom door, wads of Kleenex gripped in her hand. She marched strongly to the front of the visitation room, mascara running like black rivers down her cheeks.

"Poor thing."

"Bless her heart."

"We'll pray for you, darlin'."

Amy heard a steady stream of heartfelt condolences for two hours. Her parents were there to stand with her by a closed bronze casket, fully adorned with Clint's eight-by-ten glossy, an American flag, and two-dozen red roses. With a population of just over 4,500, Smithville was a small community and just about everybody knew everybody else. There were over fifty members of Amy's high school graduating class living in the DeKalb County area, and most of them stopped by. At several points, there were as many as ten people in line waiting to pay their respects.

Sally Williams had been one of Amy's best friends since graduating from DeKalb County High School in 1987 and their friendship had remained solid. Sally was a flight attendant for

Southwest Airlines and had been out on a seven day trip. Still wearing her Southwest Airlines uniform of khaki shorts and royal blue golf shirt, white socks, and white tennis shoes, Sally had stopped at the WalMart SuperCenter for groceries when Donny Sutton told her about Clint's accident and death.

"Yeah, Sally, I'm pretty sure they said the visitation is tonight 'til eight over at DeKalb funeral home. I was gonna try and go by, but have to go in to work."

"Clint Logan? Oh, my gosh! Thank you, Donnie." Tears suddenly filled her eyes.

Sally went straight from Walmart to DeKalb Funeral Home. She covered her mouth in shock as she paused a moment to read the sign 'Visitation for the Logan family.' Her eyes were instantly flooded with tears as the tragedy became real in her mind.

"Oh Clint, noooo, Clint!" she said as she wept beside the handsome bronze casket. Then Sally went directly to Amy and shared her uncontrollable tears with Clint's widow.

"Oh, Amy! Oh my God, Amy! I just got in town! Oh my God, Amy! I am so so sorry! What on earth happened, honey?"

"Car wreck," Amy sniffled. Sally was Amy's best friend. Amy knew she should have expected her to be there, but never thought she'd need to prepare a statement of sorts for her best friend. Why couldn't Sally just accept her grief at face value? Why all the questions? Then, Amy wondered to herself, if Sally thought she might not be grieving enough? What is the proper amount anyway? I mean, she knows me inside and out.

"Oh Sally. This is all just like a bad dream! I'm sorry you didn't know about it sooner. I knew you were out on a long flight." Sally instinctively released her hug after a few seconds, but noticed that Amy would not let go.

"Sal, thanks so much for coming; your friendship means

everything to me." Amy paused for a short moment, then pulled Sally's ear down to whisper, "I need to talk to you soon! Must be confidential! Please! Can you meet me day after tomorrow at Mimi's Diner at noon? I can't talk on the phone and I'll be surrounded by too many people 'til then."

"Sure! Noon. Day after tomorrow. Mimi's." Sally hugged Amy again, "I'll see you tomorrow at the service."

As Sally buckled her seat belt and placed the key in her ignition, she paused and stared in the rear view mirror. She spoke out loud to herself. "What in the world is going on? This is so not Amy. I know Clint is dead, but there's more to this puzzle. A lot more."

She continued to look at herself in the mirror, as if waiting for her own response. She shook her head, twisted the key and backed out of the space.

Amy just finished telling another school chum in the receiving line how much she appreciated her presence. She reached for a fresh tissue when she looked up to see none other than Jimmy Dale. J.D. sincerely hugged Amy with both arms, and Amy couldn't help but think that this portion of the rehearsal was going off perfectly.

"You know, Amy," he said in a low voice. "A lot of our friends are telling me they wished Clint and I had made up before he was killed. I don't hardly know what to say when they say stuff like that. I feel terrible."

Amy thought she saw real tears in J.D.'s eyes. She smiled and winked at J.D. and made sure he saw the wink. "Jimmy Dale, you are precious. I am just grateful to know that you were the last one of us to actually see him alive. For that, you will always be a special friend. I think you gotta just tell those nosy people that Clint knew you loved and cared for him. No argument could've ever changed that. You were two childhood friends going through life together." Amy let out a long widow's sigh. "By the way, would you be willing to be one of the pallbearers at the service tomorrow?"

"Sure. You'll have to tell me exactly what I have to do."

"Just wear a suit. That black one of yours. The one you bought for court."

"I like that one."

"It's my favorite."

"It's the only one I have."

"I know." Amy smiled at J.D.

J.D. smiled back at her as he exited the receiving line.

43

THE FOLLOWING MORNING, Clint woke up early. It was still dark outside when he glanced at their clock radio on his nightstand. 5:45 a.m. In fifteen minutes his widow Amy would wake up to face the day of her beloved husband's funeral. Clint derived a weird sort of pleasure from these circumstances. He reached over with his right hand. With slow and deliberate effort, he gently rubbed Amy's thigh. Gently, he let his fingers trail up her body until he was fondling her breasts.

Gradually Amy awoke to the sensual massage. A soft groan escaped her lips.

Clint needed very little encouragement. "Hey baby, you awake? How'd you like to screw a dead man?"

Amy rubbed both eyes, still half asleep before realizing exactly what Clint had said. "Clint, you are so disgusting! Don't you lay a finger on me! I swear if you touch me, you'll never get fifty cents of that money! I make all the ground rules now and you have no say so in the matter. You drug my ass into this, and we're handling it the rest of the way with *my* plan. You understand me?" That served as Amy's alarm clock, as she angrily swatted the snooze alarm on her clock radio. Her feet hit the floor; she was ready to get this day over with.

Amy's mindset was typical for a normal workday. She was annoyed at her delays in getting ready since Clint was clinging to her like a flea on a puppy, trying to make sure he didn't forget some particular request he had for his 'special' day. He had to make sure his portable tape recorder was positioned in the outside pocket of Amy's purse, perfectly positioned to catch every sniff, every crying wail that the crowd had to offer.

She finally nodded for the last time, and headed out their front door. As the door latch clicked, she paused and enjoyed the tranquility. No questions or comments for at least a couple of hours. That would be nice.

A few minutes after Amy left for his funeral, Clint couldn't stand the suspense. He had Super Bowl reruns queued up to make time go by faster, but he was pretty sure that wouldn't get his mind off what was taking place. Clint had insisted on hearing every word during the service.

But even if he couldn't sneak inside the church, he *could* go hide in a comfortable resting place and enjoy box seats for his own graveside service and burial. Not many folks out there could make that statement. That would be the next best thing to actually attending the services live.

Clint smeared some of Amy's dark bronze gel makeup on his face and neck, zipped up his black leather jacket, donned his helmet with a tinted face shield, and climbed on his old motorcycle.

He made his way by the back roads to Mount Holly Cemetery, the site of his planned graveside services. It was located on the west side of Smithville just off highway 70. He rode his cycle back and forth through the asphalt paths inside the cemetery where people usually drive their cars to attend graveside burial services. As he passed a marker identifying the next section as: Memorial

Hill, he saw a green canvas awning erected, with a grave already dug under the awning. Three rows of six seats each allowed the mourners some refuge from the elements. Grass-green artificial carpeting had been rolled out, completing the esthetics of the burial site. A mound of dirt was piled off to one side, and covered by a tattered green piece of canvas sheathing. Since there was only one service set up, Clint assumed that this was his grave, and that his was the only one on the docket today. He felt special.

Looking over each shoulder to make sure he had no eye witnesses, Clint dismounted his bike and walked under the green awning. He walked up to the steel rollers that adorned each side and end of the empty grave, and peeked his head down. There is where people thought Clint's final resting place would be in just a few hours.

He surveyed the surrounding area for the best seat in the house. He spotted a massive oak tree, which gave him an aerial view of his burial plot. He parked his bike behind a nearby row of hedges. With his helmet as a disguise and field binoculars pressed to his face shield, he looked like a child's drawing of a housefly as he perched in the tree waiting for the funeral procession to arrive.

The weather was spectacular. Sunny and seventy-two degrees with low humidity. Gentle breezes lightly teased American flags that dotted the rolling cemetery. As Clint surveyed rows of granite markers housing the remains of those gone before, he momentarily relaxed into peaceful serenity.

An hour after his arrival, there was still no sign of the anticipated throngs of mourners driving behind the hearse. His butt was numb and his legs cramped from being precariously propped on a narrow limb for such a long time.

Perhaps the long lines of his devastated friends just couldn't get through the parlor for their final goodbye. That had to be it.

The idea that his friends were standing in line waiting to get into a tiny little funeral chapel gave him the energy to wait.

Thirty minutes later, a black hearse appeared. Only one limo with two cars following behind, headlights on and funeral flags flying from its front fenders. The short procession made its way around the curve into the cemetery and pulled alongside a dark green tent covering Clint Logan's final resting place.

Clint looked down at his watch. More cars would be coming any minute now, Clint was sure of it. Amy climbed from the limo, adjusting her specially purchased funeral dress and reaching under the veil on her black hat to dab her eyes. Funeral home personnel helped her mom and dad, along with Sally Williams, and seated them under the tent. Other cars were directed to park along a path nearby. One car belonged to Jimmy Dale, who had brought his mom and dad. The other mourner was the human resources lady from work who had always been nice.

"This can't be all there is," Clint thought. These couldn't be the only people who thought enough of him to come with his widow to his graveside. He knew that lots of folks bypassed burial services these days, but this turnout was disappointing.

As Clint craned his head around the heavy limbs and thick green leaves to watch on the horizon for more cars, his helmet caught a twig. He reached up to free himself, lost his balance, dropped his binoculars, falling from the tree, landing in boxwoods below, spraining his wrist, and hitting his head on the tree trunk. He would have been knocked out cold if not for his helmet. His hard landing had cracked the dark plastic shield hiding his face, and his badly bruised hip matched what was left of his ego.

He limped to his motorcycle and looked back one more time at the pitiful sight for which he had risked everything; a lonely widow accompanied by her parents who hated him, and four other people—whose feelings toward him were questionable at best. That was it!

This day could only be worse if Amy found out he had been there. It took several painful attempts to get the old cycle kick-started with a sprained wrist and bruised hip, but the motor finally turned over and Clint sped away. Back to his self-imposed cellblock with his microwave, canned chili con carne, and reruns of *Murder, She Wrote*.

Clint would have to get details of his memorial service from Amy who had, from what he could see through the binoculars, quite brilliantly held up her part of the deal with genuine emotion. And she sure looked good.

Fortunately, Clint made it home just in time to beat Amy.

"Well…?"

"Well, what?"

"My funeral. How'd it go?"

"Oh, yeah. Well, J.D. did really well. He really misses you. It was quite heartbreaking, really. But the day was exhausting. I never realized how much energy it takes out of you just to lie."

44

CHRISTINE RAN ON STEAM from that single postcard for several weeks. Only after about a month did she start to wonder when another would arrive. She knew she could expect another card with instructions on how she and Cody could call each other by payphones. That was their agreement when he left. Christine knew he would never break his promise except in an emergency and without getting word to her somehow.

And yet, she seemed less depressed than before. Melvin at first attributed this to the postcard, but he knew that if that were her sole morale booster, then Christine would have some long days ahead.

Melvin and his wife, Kathy, had taken Christine under their wing as she suffered through this acute phase of lovesick blues. They were both fifteen years older than Christine, but had been drawn to the genuine sweetness of this true New Mexico cowgirl. With their encouragement, she began to come out of her shell. Kathy had fixed her some home-cooked meals, and she enjoyed interacting with the couple.

Then, more than a month after the postcard arrived, while

Christine was sitting on the porch with Kathy, rocking on their swing, she confided in Kathy. She had been having some periodic nausea and had gotten a little pudgy in her tummy. She had actually missed her last two periods.

She told Kathy what had happened on that beautiful Sunday she shared with Cody before he left—the intimacy they had enjoyed and how special it had been to both of them.

"Well, Christine, have you been with another man recently, before or after Cody?"

"That was my first time, and then it was four times in one day. Then four more times the rest of that week. Kathy, it was just heaven. I can't tell you how much I love that man. Having his baby would be the next biggest blessing I could ever receive."

Kathy took Christine to purchase an EPT kit. The strip tested positive.

Kathy proved to be a true friend to Christine, loving, nurturing, and supporting her through what would be a very difficult, yet thrilling time in her life. She helped Christine struggle with all the questions she had, the primary one being, "What could have happened to Cody that would cause him to send only one card— and then nothing?"

Christine had even resorted to subscribing to *The Nashville Scene,* a weekly entertainment rag in Nashville just to see if, by chance, Cody had been photographed on stage there. She had the names and addresses of all the country music venues in Nashville doing live music, and she sent letters to each of them requesting help in locating him.

All sources led to a dead end.

The only thing Christine could do was wait. But she had come to a peace in her heart—she felt certain that she and Cody were in one united spirit before he left and that her mission was to raise their child. She was thrilled to have been blessed with the opportunity and the responsibility of having his baby. Wherever he was, she and Cody had something special together that nobody on earth could ever take away. All she needed to do was hang on until the three of them could be together.

45

Mimi's was surprisingly busy for a Tuesday lunch. Amy arrived a few minutes early to ensure they could have a private corner table. These words would not need to fall on the wrong ears. Sally made eye contact as soon as she walked in. Amy stood as Sally approached and welcomed her with open arms and a broad smile.

"Oh, my little friend, I have prayed for you, cried for you, wanted to talk to you. Honey, you look worn out, but, of course. My God, look what you've been through."

A tired looking Amy responded, "Yeah, Sal, I am worn out. But it's not for what you think."

A puzzled look appeared on Sally's face as she cocked her head to one side in curiosity. "Well, now, please don't make me have to guess."

She looked from side to side in an almost paranoid state. "I can't talk about this but in a whisper. I have to be very careful not to be in a situation where someone could overhear us. So let's chit chat a few minutes so they can take our order, then they'll probably leave us alone. Thanks so much for coming to meet me.

I have so wanted to talk to you, but I knew you were on that trip you'd told me about and..."

"Don't be silly," Sally reassured her. Sally was eager to know what this sinister meeting was all about. "Well, whatever you need to talk about, it can't possibly be as bad as losing Clint."

Amy sat up straight and looked suspiciously from side to side. "And that, my dear, is exactly what I need to talk to you about." She whispered so softly that Sally could barely hear her voice.

Juanita, the waitress was back at their table within seconds "Whatchu gals gonna have today? Country fried steak looks fantastic. And that buttered squash!"

Amy and Sally immediately ordered a chef's salad, hoping Juanita would take a hint and give them some privacy. Juanita evidently did not get her intended message.

"Amy I jest wanted ya to know how sorry me and Ben are for you losing Clint. Don't hardly know what to say. We're keeping you'ens in our thoughts and prayers. I'll get your order right out."

"You know her?" Sally asked.

Amy nodded. "Clint and I came in here quite a bit."

"She just didn't get it, did she?" Sally seemed as nervous as Amy. "We may have to go outside for a walk to have privacy. I know it's something important and can't be discussed by phone. Must be pretty top secret!"

"Well, here's the deal." Amy lowered her voice to a barely audible whisper and leaned in toward Sally.

Juanita stuck her head around the corner and shouted, "Gosh, forgot if you wanted sweet or unsweet tea!"

"Sweet." Amy said.

"Unsweet." Sally added.

Both girls stared in frustration. Amy looked at her watch. "I'm gonna run outta time, I know I am."

Amy took a deep breath, trying to decide where to begin. She looked up and saw Juanita heading toward them with two tall glasses of iced tea.

"Oh, no," Amy said. "Here she comes again."

Once the drinks were delivered, Sally suggested, "Let's just wait a couple more minutes 'til Juanita gets our orders. Salads shouldn't take very long. Then, we'll get some privacy. In the meantime, what did you think about the funeral service? I know it sounds kinda weird asking a question like that, but I think you know what I mean."

Sally was running on instinct now. She was saying anything to kill time and try and put Amy at ease.

"Hope I don't have to go through one of those again for a long time." Amy's voice was soft, steady and matter of fact. "The doctor has put me on some medication that's got me a little goofy. Says it's just a temporary thing that a lot people need when they go through a lot of stress."

"Are you kidding me? You are doing amazingly well... considering. My brother's wife had a close death in her family recently and it about tore that family up."

Both girls instinctively sat up as Juanita brought their salads

"I'll leave you'ens be but if you need sump'n else, just holler. And here's the check, but of course, there's no rush."

Amy smiled and looked at her watch. "I can't hurry this, but I have to talk to you about something very personal. So please be patient with me. You are the only other woman that knows this." Amy bent down, so Sally obliged and leaned forward too. Amy whispered, "Well, it all started when..."

"Hey gals! Good to see you!" a man stepped closer until both girls recognized him. It was Craig James. Voted Best Looking in their high school class.

Amy and Sally glanced down at the two open seats next to them. Two that were soon to be one. Craig James was too good of a friend to not offer him a seat.

Amy's special secret was going to have to be put on hold. At least for now.

46

IT TOOK A FEW DAYS after Clint's funeral for Amy to realize that having her husband under her feet 24/7 was going to get old really fast. Neither had stopped to think about the price of "free money."

Before the ill-fated trip to Las Vegas, Amy had been on Clint constantly about finding another job. Now, of course, that was not an option. Amy was trapped with Clint and his untidy housekeeping habits, which were sorely magnified when she came back from a hard day's work. She had kept her job to avoid suspicion, but she was disgruntled with working while Clint was at home lying around in his pajamas.

Clint was beginning to doubt Jimmy Dale's ability to keep his lips sealed about their plan. He had managed to do a good job at the funeral visitation. Clint knew that one absent-minded remark to the wrong person might cause a cascading fiasco from which they could not recover.

About the only thing Amy and Clint had agreed upon lately was that it would be a good thing for J.D. to move in their house. J.D. had hinted to his parents that he might be ready to look for a place for himself, and moving into Amy's house would allow him to keep his best friend's widow company.

After he moved in, J.D. also managed to convince his boss at the Market to take him back, but he was demoted from produce manager to grocery sacker. Amy was pretty sure the store manager took him back just because he felt sorry for J.D. since he'd lost his best friend in such a horrible car accident. Whatever it was, it helped J.D.'s finances until the insurance check could arrive.

After about three months, the check finally arrived. Amy skipped into the house, singing and dancing. She ran down the stairs to the basement, where the two men were perched in their perpetual position.

"Hey guys, look what I got! We're in the money!" She proudly held out the check from Pioneer Life, made payable to Amy Lynn Logan. It had been the only time in six months that she managed a smile for Clint.

"You kidding me?! That's fantastic!" Clint reached up from the beanbag he had buried himself in. "Let me see it!" His face turned sour when he examined the details of the instrument.

Clint scowled. "It's made out just to you, Amy."

Amy was flabbergasted by his ignorance. "You thought they were gonna make it out to *you*? How can a dead man spend any money? Why would they pay it to you?"

"So you gonna cash it and pay us our share?"

"I'll put it in the bank, but it's too soon to start going on a spending frenzy."

"Well, that's why I say we need to get out of town, Amy. I've been telling you since this whole thing started."

"Clint," Amy shot back, "*I've* been telling *you* forever: I'm not quitting my job and moving to another city or state just because you came up with some kind of lame-brain scheme to commit insurance fraud and murder a guy. You should have checked with me before you pulled that bungee cord out."

Clint didn't like the smart mouth on Amy, but he knew that he didn't have a leg to stand on in light of the circumstances. There were so many things that were now unfolding that he had not computed in his original plan.

"What if Amy isn't willing to put this money in a joint checking account?" he wondered to himself. As soon as the thought materialized, he caught himself. "Wait a minute . . . you can't have a joint checking account with a dead man!"

J.D. had never owned a checking account in his life, and a deposit for a sizeable amount like he was owed in the deal would only bring suspicion, especially for a new account. For the first time since Cody's death, Clint was starting to realize that they were now at the total and complete mercy of Amy.

47

Days turned into weeks, which turned into months, and Clint was developing a serious case of cabin fever. Amy kept her job, and J.D. kept sacking groceries. Clint was growing more and more bored. He watched every rerun on television, becoming increasingly irritated at his incarceration with every passing commercial break. This was just like being in prison. Somehow, he had never thought it would end up like this.

After becoming reasonably proficient on the home computer, Clint found a website that sold counterfeit driver's licenses. Grasping desperately at straws, he saw this as his best chance to regain his lost freedom. He was soon the proud owner of a new license and a new identity: Clyde Thomas Lincoln. He had even figured out how to upload a recent picture of himself, which he had superimposed on the worthless document so that it now displayed his 'new' look, slick bald head and long red beard. He hated the beard, thought it made him look like he came right out of *Deliverance*, but Amy insisted that it was a necessary evil. Since he was now risking her reputation, she figured she had some say in the matter.

Amy and J.D. were at work, and Clint was watching TV, hypnotized by a luscious advertisement of the double-decker hamburgers at the world-famous Sonic Drive-In. It was more than he could handle.

"Dammit! I've had enough of this!" he yelled. Clint had become well versed in conversations with himself. He had even picked up the skill of answering his own questions. "No way anybody could recognize me if I just went down to the Sonic for a couple cheeseburgers. I could eat in the car, get a little sunshine, and be back home before J.D. or Amy even know I left."

During the last months, Clint had ridden with J.D. and Amy several times, but usually at night and always in the backseat. Now, he was determined to steal back a little of his freedom.

Clint nervously cranked the engine of his antique Pontiac Firebird. It sputtered, smoke billowing out of the tailpipe. He knew it was fortunate that the car even started.

"There's no way I'm going to live like this for the rest of my life," he said again.

Once outside, Clint felt liberated. The January air was sharp and cold, but the midday sun shone brightly. He had a rare need for sunglasses—a welcome and unexpected treat. For a moment, he remembered everything that he had taken for granted before his self-inflicted imprisonment—like the mere ability to drive down to the local market or drive-through. He deliberately stayed five to seven miles per hour under the speed limit, being careful not to attract attention. He waved sociably at some children playing on skateboards. They paid no attention to him.

Never in his life could he remember when he had so much pleasure eating cheeseburgers and fries. He had the radio on, listening to classic rock and letting his mind wander.

Had he and J.D. done the right thing? Sure, he had regrets—

but it was too late to undo them now. His main goal would be to continue to persuade Amy to relocate, but that seemed like an uphill battle. What options did he have if Amy wouldn't move? He knew one thing—to live like this for the rest of his life was *not* an option. He felt as if he had "earned" that $250,000, and now everyone else was enjoying it!

The disc jockey on the radio reminded Clint that it was 4:45 p.m. He had been daydreaming at the Sonic for well over an hour. The ice in his Diet Coke had melted, even in the crisp winter air. He decided he'd better head back home before Amy got there at five thirty.

"Quit being paranoid," he told himself. "You have to get used to this. This is going to be a regular event."

His right turn onto Highway 70 was uneventful, and he carefully migrated into the left lane, anticipating a turn just a mile ahead. Five minutes, and he would be safe and secure, back in front of ESPN.

Their driveway was empty. Clint sighed in relief. He had just beat Amy and J.D. back home. If he could do this a couple times a week, maybe he could handle this dilemma.

What he didn't realize was that the dilemma would continue to get more and more complicated with each passing day.

48

TWO DAYS LATER, Clint got the urge to venture out again. He had experienced just enough freedom from his Sonic experience that he decided that today would be a good day to take a stroll through DeKalb County. After all, almost a year had passed, and he wanted to see what changes had been going on in Smithville. The sunshine on his left arm felt good as it comfortably hung out the window of his Firebird. He stopped by Sligo Marina, as well as Four Seasons, winding up at Hurricane Mills. All those places were old stomping grounds for Clint. It looked to Clint like some new boats had appeared at these marinas since he had last been there. He sat in his car, and checked each new boat out through his trusty field binoculars.

On his way back home, his eye caught a road sign that sparked his interest. Right off highway 70, the bottle green sign read, "DeKalb Cemetery 3 miles." "Hmmm", he muttered out loud. Looking at his watch, he thought he did have a few more minutes to visit his 'old resting place'. He hadn't ever seen his tombstone, since Amy had it placed over six months ago. He did remember visiting the gravesite after it was dug, but before the service. The curiosity that had been an ever present nuisance in his character rose to the top, and he swung the car to the left.

One little peek shouldn't take but a few minutes. All he had seen was a photo of his resting place, and J.D. had taken that for him. It had been blurry and Clint couldn't make out the details of something that would feed his morbid curiosity.

Within minutes he arrived at DeKalb Cemetery. Following the same 'parade route' that the meager funeral procession had followed, Clint replayed in his mind what it must have been like that day when everyone had been grieving for the sudden loss of one of Smithville's finest citizens. He had forgotten already that the funeral procession consisted of less than five cars.

His point of reference for finding his own gravesite would forever be the now famous oak tree. Clint was sure he cracked a couple of ribs in that fall on the day of his burial. Once locating the tree, it would be easy to locate his tombstone. He had already decided it was time to personally visit where his bones were supposed to be resting.

Small one lane roadways allowed cars to drive through the extensive cemetery, so Clint was able to drive right up to his plot, switch off the ignition and enjoy a few moments of solitude as he wondered how many of his friends still thought of him on a regular basis. He was sure that there were many.

His eyes focused on the professionally inscribed lettering perfectly formed in the mirror-like polish of the marble headstone, depicting the pertinent dates of Clint's life and death. He chuckled with delight as he studied each word Amy had inscribed on his life's tribute. He walked completely around the stone, examining it from all angles. His mind wandered aimlessly as he thought about what it was like to have your body lying in a casket for the rest of eternity. He stood motionless on top of where the grave had been dug. Just six feet below is where everyone in DeKalb County thought his final resting place was.

His trance was suddenly broken when he heard the engine of a local pickup. Wheeling around, he noticed a maintenance vehicle heading out to work. They were on another section of the property, and were of no concern to Clint.

Clint looked at his watch. It read 4:45. If he was to beat his wife and buddy back home, he'd better save some reminiscing for another day. As the Firebird cranked right up; he slipped it into gear, and with a smirky grin on his face, he headed back to Highway 70 and back home. He was starting to enjoy this newfound fun.

49

Amy was cooking a Saturday morning breakfast for all three. Both she and J.D. were off and she didn't mind cooking up an old fashioned country breakfast, complete with homemade biscuits and buttermilk gravy. It made life feel normal again, at least for a while.

Clint stared at his eggs, and moved them around his plate randomly, as if contemplating something important. "Amy, have you thought about how we would distribute my share of the money? I mean, it's really our 2/3rds share, isn't it?"

"Gosh, Clint, it's been four whole days since you brought it up!" Almost every sentence from Amy's mouth seemed to have a sarcastic overtone. "Didn't you think about that before you killed Cody?"

"Not really. But I do think I would have a better chance at starting over if we moved away from here. I'd even be willing to go to upper east Tennessee where we could be closer to your parents. Wouldn't that be a good idea?'

"Clint, you just wanna move 'cause now you don't like your living conditions. You can't go and come as you please. Suddenly, ESPN and Bud Lite are boring and you want to go back like it was six months ago. Ain't happening, Clint. I have no interest in moving to east Tennessee. I like my job and my friends here in Smithville, and I'm not picking up stakes and moving to another place just so you can get out and exercise. You should've thought about all this crap before you came up with your lame-ass murder plan."

"But if I can't get out, how am I gonna spend my third of the money?"

"That's your problem, not mine. I'll get your money out as quickly and reasonably as I can without raising any red flags. As far as I'm concerned, J.D. comes first. He still has his normal life to live, and shouldn't be penalized because you're not comfortable."

J.D. comes first? He was seething inside and Amy could tell it. She also couldn't care less.

Jimmy Dale had decided that he would spend the afternoon at Handlebar's pool hall in Smithville. Amy had already announced that she was going shopping in Nashville "Clint, you want me to bring you back something for dinner in case Amy isn't back in time?" J.D. said, trying to smooth things over between them.

"I guess. Amy, what time you gonna be back?"

"No idea." With that, she grabbed her keys and purse. "J.D., have fun at the pool hall. Tell the boys hey." No goodbyes for Clint. He noticed that also.

With both of them gone, Clint was confined to an empty house with just himself and his television. It happened every day. Seven days a week.

As J.D. was backing out, Amy stopped him before he could pull away. "Hey, J.D., hang on a minute." J.D. rolled down the window and silenced the radio. Amy rested her elbow on the window sill. She had a look of despair. "Let's get together for a while, away from the house, and talk about all this mess. This whole ordeal is about to get the best of me. I mean it's been nearly eighteen months, and I feel tortured. I can't even talk about this to my closest friends. It's just me and you, J.D."

"Sure, where you wanna go? Maybe we should talk about it. I get kinda tired of lying all the time, too. Sometimes I catch myself, and I can't remember which lie I told to which buddy."

"Okay. I tell you what. Let's just meet at Handlebar's and we'll sit and talk for a spell."

J.D. fidgeted awkwardly for a minute. He felt his face get red like a bashful teenager. "Well, I don't suppose there would be anything wrong with that."

"That's fine," Amy said. "But the least said about anything the better. We'll get a table over in the corner where we can talk by ourselves. You and I are the only ones who can even have this conversation. It's so frustrating! We've got to figure out a way to unravel all this mess."

Neither of them noticed the two haunting eyes that peered out between the blinds of the upstairs bathroom. Eyes that quickly disappeared as soon as Amy turned around and headed to her car.

50

HANDLEBAR'S WAS ONE OF Smithville's finest. Good food, clean place, lots of pool tournaments, and the best cheeseburger and Bud Lite in DeKalb County. Beer was all the law would allow in Smithville, and some of the locals didn't even care for the taverns. Many of its residents had strongly opposed the referendum which passed allowing beer sales in grocery stores just a few years earlier.

J.D. got there first and pulled his truck up to a nearly empty parking lot. Not quite time yet for the afternoon pool tourney to start. Roger Gaskins, the sole bar tender, greeted J.D. with a friendly smile. "Whassup, Jimmy D.? You havin' a Bud Lite?"

"Sure, why not? Amy Logan's meeting me over here. We might get a burger in a while. She's really havin' a hard time, gettin' out and just livin', ya know?" J.D. was so sick of passing these lines out, sometimes six and eight a day.

"Yea, I bet she is. Well I knew you and Clint had been buds since grade school, so at least she's got you to kinda get her through this mess. Been over a year now, hasn't it?"

"Yeah. Man she just stays bummed out all the time. I mean I miss what used to be my best friend, but I wasn't married to the guy." J.D. was looking forward to the day where he could just be himself and not have to put on this charade.

Amy came in just as J.D. and Roger were talking about her grieving. She seemed a bit more spirited than just an hour ago when she was around Clint and cleaning up the dishes. "Hey Rog. How ya doin'?"

"Good Amy. Good to see you. Jimmy D. was just telling me he was making you get out a little more these days. It'll be good for you. What can I get for you? Got twenty-five flavors on tap!"

"I'll have a Blue Moon, no pun intended." She managed a weak smile, but at least it was an effort.

Their beers were delivered, and Roger went into the back to restock some supplies before the lunch crowd arrived. Amy welcomed privacy that she had hoped they would experience at least for a while.

"J.D., I don't know about you, but I can't stand this situation much longer. Clint just isn't the same guy he was five years ago. I mean when you guys took off for Vegas, with my savings, by the way, I don't know if you even knew about that. Anyway, he hasn't hit a lick at a snake since you guys got out of your little hitch in the pen year before last. I'm so sick of bein' the only one workin'. And now, with all this mess, he'll never ever get another job. I'm done."

"I know what you mean. He don't even seem like the same guy. Especially since we done that terrible thing to that singer. That trip back from Vegas was the worst part of my life. Seems like he tries to trick me into doin' his shitwork for him, and I just now started to figure it out."

"Well, before you guys nearly scared me to death on the back porch of our house, I mean, what was your plan on how you, or we, were gonna handle all this?"

"I swear to you, Amy, we never discussed it. He just kept saying all along that you'd go along with it. First we would split the money fifty-fifty. Then, he changed it and said we were gonna chop it three ways. I know I'm not the sharpest nail head, but anybody can figure out that ain't the same. And that bastard, no offense, was the one that talked me into the bungee cord to begin with. I could kick my ass for lettin' him talk me into that."

Amy sat up, leaning forward with interest. She needed to vent so badly, that this was precious time for her to experience. "Of course it's not the same. He doesn't care about me, he doesn't care about you. All he cares about is the money. He thinks you can throw a twenty dollar bill at anything and fix it."

"Well, Amy, you may think I'm crazy. But at this point, I could care less about one red cent of that damn money. It just goes to prove that doin' the wrong thing just gets you in deeper and deeper. If you gave me every penny of it right now, I don't know what I'd do with it. My conscious has been aching over what I done for over a year now. If I got the money, I'd feel even worse. Does that make any sense?"

"Yes it does Jimmy. It shows that you really are a decent guy. Somebody who just got drug into this by Clint. The only thing I would say to your face is that if you don't quit that meth, and quit feeding him his supply, it's gonna end up bad news for you both."

J.D. hung his head low. He stared at the ring of water that had formed on the tablecloth around his once full Bud Lite. "I swear I'm done with it today. Never did it anyway as much as Clint. I think he's hooked on that shit."

"I know he is."

Roger shouted from behind the bar. "You guys okay on your beers? Don't want to interfere; seems like you're in deep conversation.

"No problem, man. We'll have another one."

It was obvious that Amy was absorbed by their conversation. Her first beer was still nearly full. "I tell you what I think I'll do. See what you think about this." She looked secretively over one shoulder and then the other; no one could hear this. "I think I will tell Clint to get out; give him ten grand of the money, and tell him to get out of town. When he can prove to me that he's moved out of state, changed his name and got a job, I'll send him $115,000. You can have what you want and I don't really care either. I just want him out of my life, forever."

"That sounds like a plan. Do you think he'll go for it?"

"What choice does he have? He's got to be just as miserable as we are—or more."

"Well, Amy, I'm behind you all the way. I just want to sack groceries, shoot a little pool, play a little cards, and live without having to lie to no body."

"Sounds like a plan."

Having seemed to have made some progress in their situation, both decided it was time to eat a cheeseburger. The regulars were filing in by now, as the tournament was about to begin.

While waiting for the food to arrive, Amy fidgeted nervously with her napkin as she looked for the proper words. "Be honest with me now J.D. In the last year and a half, have you told anyone, I mean anyone about this scheme?"

"No. I swear on my mother's life. No one. How 'bout you?"

"Not a soul. If one person, the wrong person got wind of it, it would blow us up. I keep reliving every detail of eighteen months ago and it's driving me crazy. One other thing." She continued her nervous energy by tearing the napkin into tiny little pieces as she stared at the tablecloth, not able to maintain eye contact with J.D. "I think Clint is jealous of you."

"What?" The puzzled look on his face showed massive confusion. "What do you mean?"

Amy's face turned bright red, and she couldn't hide a sheepish grin, like a teenager. "He thinks I'm sweet on you?"

"Get outta here!"

"I know it's crazy! I didn't say it made any sense. He just has been firing these barbs at me constantly about how he has suspected that something has been going on between you and me behind his back while he was in his house prison."

"Holy shit! I need to move out right away."

"Not so fast, buddy. I think we need each other. He's like a loose cannon. Even though we don't have to hide, we've got to both keep one eye on him. I don't trust him a bit. I need your help!"

J.D. agreed he should continue to stay at the house and the two of them finally relaxed a little. The cheeseburger was great and Amy even managed to laugh a little as several of her old friends came over to their table and said hello. J.D. entered the tournament, Amy watched, and actually had a good time seeing some of her friends she had not seen since the funeral.

51

To avoid unwanted questioning, Amy decided to go home before the pool tournament was over. For some reason, Amy wasn't concerned about approaching Clint or his mood when she got back home. She had gained some renewed confidence in her ability to get this situation resolved. She gave one word answers, volunteering no extra conversation. She went upstairs, took a shower, washed her hair and put on her flannel pajamas for an early night.

She sat down on the couch while Clint sat in his recliner pretending to watch television. He had an emotionless stare. "You know, Amy. I know you are still sideways about our scheme. But the whole thing has worked out pretty good, with the money and all. I just want to know how long you and I are gonna have this type of relationship."

"What type of relationship are you talking about, Clint?"

"We both can hardly stand to be in the same room with one another. I don't think you were happy before J.D. and I even went to Vegas."

"You're right. I wasn't then and I'm still not. I got tired of your not being willing to find a job a long time ago. I've told you a dozen times! You got six months in jail for your brilliant drug idea two years ago. So now you're a convicted felon. What do you think you'll be if they get wind of this murder? It just seems like I'm married to some lazy prick who always is looking for some cheap way out to beat the system. I mean why couldn't you have put your pants on and gone to work every day like the rest of the world?"

"I can do that now. I've always just needed a break. I got one now."

"That was your break? It's too late, Clint. You're doomed to a life of hiding. I'm sick of it, and I'm sick of you!"

Clint knew Amy was right, but couldn't think of a good comeback. "Well, you wanna just split up then? You stay here and I go my way?"

"Probably." Amy was expressionless. That wasn't an answer Clint was expecting.

"Fine, then. Give me my $83,000 and I'll get out."

"I knew it would come back to the money. I don't trust you, Clint. At least with me controlling the money, I know there won't be any irresponsibility. With you, I never know what to expect. I'll tell you what I will do. I'll get you out ten thousand dollars, and you take the Firebird and hit the road. Since you're already dead, there's no need for a divorce. You already got your fake driver's license. Don't know how long that'll work. Get you a mobile phone, find a new place to live. Fill out some job applications, get a job and start all over. Send me a paycheck stub, a voided check from your new checking account showing your address, and I'll send you the other $73,000. How does that sound?"

Clint's face turned red. He resented Amy trying to plan his entire future out for him like he was some kind of clown.

"You're the one that's the gold diggin' bitch, and I'm tired of you holding this over my head! And by the way, what were you talking to J.D. about this morning out in the driveway?"

"I don't know what you're talking about. That meth just makes you plumb paranoid."

"You lying whore!" Reaching back to gather momentum, Clint swung at her, striking a glancing blow across her left cheek; blood flew from her face and splattered on the sofa. Amy groaned with pain.

"You insane monster! I'll call the police and turn this whole thing upside down in a heartbeat!" Amy reached for the first object she could find, which was a table lamp that was sitting beside the sofa. Yanking the plug loose, she hurled it the short distance in Clint's direction, its base landing across the top of his head, gushing blood down his face.

"Go ahead and call 'em, you slut. They'll put your ass in the slammer as quick as they would me. You're in this just as deep as me, whether you like it or not!" Clint laughed with a sadistic maniacal rant. He glared at Amy as if he were cutting a laser directly through her heart.

"Maybe, maybe not. I didn't choke anybody to death with a bungee cord. So I like my odds a lot better than yours."

"Then make the call."

Amy hesitated. "You make me sick, you disgusting excuse for a human." She picked up the brass candlestick holder sitting on the coffee table and hurled it at him with all her strength. The candlestick caught Clint on the left side of his head knocking him totally unconscious. His body collapsed to the floor, blood rushing from both wounds.

J.D. opened the door. He paused in disbelief. "What's going on, man? You okay, Amy?"

Amy was so distraught, so frightened and enraged, that she could barely catch her breath to make a sentence. Tears were streaming down her face, mixing with blood gushing from her gash. "The bastard tried to kill me! Look what he did!" Blood was gushing down her face, already staining the top part of her blouse.

"You better stay here 'til he wakes up. I caught him pretty good with that candlestick holder. See if you can help me with this cut on my face. There's a first aid kit in the trunk of my car. I better go with you in case he wakes up while you're gone."

J.D. took a closer look. The gash was just below her right eye, almost two inches long with its edges considerably spread open.

"You may have to go to the hospital for stitches."

"It'll be fine."

"Man, I don't like this a bit, especially after our talk this afternoon. You sure…?"

"Shhhh!' Amy replied with a scowl on her face as she glanced over at the still unconscious Clint. "I'm gonna be ok. I'm just glad you're here now."

The two walked outside and retrieved the first aid kit out of the Toyota. J.D. stopped her. "Amy, listen, if he lays another hand on you, I promise you I'll kill that sonuvabitch! I've already killed Cody, and won't think twice about taking him out! He's already supposed to be dead, anyway, so if I kill him again, who the hell is gonna know about it?"

"J.D., please don't talk like that. It will get us nowhere!"

"Amy, I'm tellin' you, I won't put up with it. What was this argument about?"

"I think I was just too honest with him. Told him I wanted him out and wasn't sure I was gonna give him any of the money. Told him he could leave, and that's when he went off. Wouldn't surprise me if he hadn't been doin' some meth this afternoon. He seemed pretty cranked up."

"Ok, look. I'll stay in this and referee the argument, but if he gets weird, I'll shoot him dead in three seconds. I swear to God, I will. I've got a .38 in my drawer. He is no longer my friend. Regardless of what happens. To hell with the money! I was happy before without it and I'm really happy now, and haven't even spent any of it.'

Amy broke down and sobbed, as J.D. held her in a consoling embrace. Neither would have any way of knowing that the same two eyes were peering at them through the same bathroom window.

52

J.D. HELD THE DOOR OPEN for Amy, holding a bloody cloth over the cut on her cheek. At that same moment, Clint came out of the bathroom with a similar bloody rag on top of his head.

"Brought your food, Clint. What the hell's going on here?"

"Just a little misunderstanding, that's all. It's ok." Clint dabbed at the gash on top of his head which was still streaming with blood. He stumbled as he tried to walk over to the chair to have a seat.

Amy found her way into the kitchen and sat down. He washed his hands at the kitchen sink and attended to her wound with the kit. After cleansing the wound and applying ice to the gash, J.D. thought it would be better to have a doctor look at it to see if it needed suturing. "You know I'm getting' pretty good at this. Last time you did it to yourself when you passed out. This time's a little different.

"That's fine, J.D., but who am I gonna say beat me? You are the first one that they're gonna look at. I'm not gonna drag you into this mess."

"What do ya mean? He's already in this mess!" Amy and J.D. both were startled. Staggering into the doorway was a Clint who could now barely stand up. His hands were covered with his own blood, and it was difficult for him to maintain his grip on the door jamb. They slowly slipped down the door frame, leaving red bloody streaks showing palm and fingerprints smudged all the way down the sides of the door facing. His knees buckled underneath his weight.

He was either suffering from a severe concussion, or he was stoned, or both. He glared at J.D. and Amy with an evil determination in his eyes that made the hair on J.D.'s neck stand up. He seemed almost demon possessed. Amy screamed. She was frightened beyond words.

"Get outa here! Don't you dare come near me!"

"I'll do as I please!"

"You're gonna leave her alone, Clint!" J.D. glared back at Clint. "You double crossing bastard!"

Clint staggered back into the living room. "We can say you got in a fight at the pool hall. Maybe you just fell down and cut your face. I don't have to go with you. I just want to take care of you."

"I think you've been doing a pretty good job of takin' care of her all afternoon!" Clint's voice shouted in a slurred almost inaudible voice from the living room.

J.D. ignored his implication. "Clint. Big mistake here, buddy! Beatin' up your wife? Come on!"

Clint collapsed in the recliner. He was out.

J.D. and Amy exchanged glances. The two decided that J.D. would drive Amy to the Smithville emergency room and have a doctor look at it. One thing they knew for sure was that Clint wasn't going anywhere in his condition. Clint's self-imposed 'house arrest' made some things more convenient than they ever expected. And if Clint did have a concussion and he needed medical attention, well, that was the least of their concern.

Three hours later, Amy and J.D. returned to the house. The visit to the emergency room had proven to be a wise idea, as the doctor placed six facial sutures. Fortunately, she saw no one in the hospital she knew.

As the two opened the front door, they saw Clint slumped in the same chair, as motionless as he had been three hours ago.

"You think he's dead?" Amy asked.

"We couldn't be so lucky," said J. D. "Come on, follow me." He grabbed Amy's hand and led her down the stairs. He reached into his drawer, sifted through his underwear and tee shirts, and retrieved a .38 revolver. He placed it securely in his front pocket. "This will give you a little piece of mind."

By the time they began their trip up the stairs, they saw two eyes peering through the crack in the door looking down at them. "Whatchu guys doing now?" Clint cackled in a perverted tone, as if he had just caught them in the middle of some forbidden act. The maniacal voice startled both of them, causing J.D. to pull his revolver immediately. He pointed it straight up the stairs, warning Clint to freeze.

"Whoa now, J.D." Clint slurred, "Just asking what you're doing with my wife." He had a "Charles Manson" look as he glared down the steps with one hand behind him and the door partially cracked. J.D. and Amy were frozen at the foot of the stairs.

J.D. shouted, "Open the damn door and hold both hands out or I'll blow your head off, Clint! You've seen me do it once before and you know I'll do it again!"

"Shit man! Talk about overreaction! Where's the J.D. I used to know? Things kinda change when you start screwin' with my wife, don't they?"

Amy had all she could stand, "Oh shut up, Clint. You're so messed up right now you don't know where you are!"

"I'll give you to three to open that door!" J.D. pulled the hammer back on the revolver. "I can't miss from this range, you pervert, and nobody on this earth would ever miss you. Remember, your ass is dead already. I kill you now and get a free pass. Pretty easy to figure out, even for me. Remember, I'm the dumb ass! Well guess what, bastard, I'm not the dumb ass you think."

Amy was trembling with fear, tears streaming from her swollen eyes. "One, two…I'm telling you… Ok, three…" J.D. squeezed the trigger. Amy screamed. Fire and smoke streamed from the end of the revolver, as a large half inch hole appeared in the door within four inches of Clint's head. Clint was startled by the splintering of the wood and instinctively jumped back.

"By the way, bastard, that miss was on purpose. Just to get your attention. I won't miss next time. The next one winds up square between your eyes!"

Amy was inconsolable. "J.D., please don't! We can all work this out! Clint, please, for God's sake, open the door and back away. Show both your hands."

"Ok, ok! Hell, you guys take everything too seriously!" He opened the door slowly, backed away from the threshold, and brought the other hand from around his back. J.D.'s sight was trained on Clint's forehead.

Slowly, Clint brought out an empty hand. J.D. wasn't so convinced. "Clint, get back in that chair. Right now, damnit! I mean it I'm tired of screwin' with you!"

"Ok, ok! Jeez!" Clint stumbled back to the chair and collapsed. When Amy and J.D. reached the top of the stairs, the pair walked around Clint's chair trying to stay as far away as possible. They both sat down on the sofa.

J.D. was boiling, Amy was sobbing, and Clint was mostly

incoherent. The gun remained trained on Clint, with J.D. looking for any reason to pull the trigger.

Amy and J.D. exchanged glances while Clint seemed to drift in and out of consciousness. J.D. reassured her that Clint's behavior was probably a combination of a concussion and the meth working on him. "I think what we have to do now is just sit here and wait it out. The meth will be out of his system by morning. If he's still acting weird, then we'll know it has something to do with the fight ya'll had."

And so the vigil began. The pair took turns dozing, while the one on duty kept the revolver. At one point, Amy asked J.D., "I think he has a pistol somewhere, but I haven't seen it in ages. You know where he keeps it?"

"No. We didn't even take this one when we went to Vegas. Besides, if we keep this on him, he has little choice on what to do or where to go."

After a lengthy discussion, the two decided on an action plan. If and when Clint finally came to his senses, they were going to tell him that J.D. was moving back in with his parents, and Amy would stay temporarily with Sarah Porter, one of her single girlfriends at work. That would give them some peace of mind away from him. As far as his health goes, they both agreed not to take him for any medical care, regardless of the situation since it would jeopardize their own freedom.

J.D. made some coffee for whoever was trying to stay awake at the time, Amy seemed to become more settled. They were able to verify that the gash on his head had stopped bleeding, even though closer examination showed that it was deep and potentially serious. Meanwhile, J.D.'s aim stayed constantly on Clint's head. He was looking for a reason, any reason, to pull the trigger.

53

SUNDAY MORNING BROUGHT a change in behavior from Clint exactly as J.D. had predicted. He had done enough meth with Clint to know how long it would usually take for a meth binge to wear off. Amy fixed the two of them breakfast while J.D. continued to hold Clint at gunpoint. By noon, he started to show signs of more consistent awareness.

"My head's killing me!" he groaned. "And what's been going on around here anyway? J.D., what are you doing with a gun pointed at me?" Clint acted as if he had no recollection of the night before; J.D. suspected otherwise.

"Dude, how much of last night don't you remember? You almost got yourself killed a bunch of times. We didn't know if you'd come back around or not."

Amy walked into the living room when she heard the conversation.

"Hey, Amy, what happened to your face?"

Amy smirked with no hint of any compassionate feelings. "Sure, like you don't remember anything about last night. Nice try, but I'm not buying one bit of that."

Clint shrugged indifferently. "So, what are we doing today? What *is* today anyway?"

"It's Sunday, and *we* are not doing the same thing *you* are doing," Amy said. "*We* are moving out. J.D. is moving back in with his mom, and I am going to stay with Sarah Porter from work. Neither of us is going to live in conditions like this anymore!"

"Conditions like what? If you guys leave, how are we gonna chop the money up?"

Amy laughed sarcastically. "You know, you continue to amaze me. We actually haven't given the money a moment's thought during all this. But that's all you seem to be concerned about. Let's just say that we'll bring you some food and supplies until we can decide what each of us is going to do. I made you an offer last night, you didn't like it, and went off on this maniacal rampage. I am totally done with you, for good and forever."

"Oh, so you guys are running out on me, huh? I'm the captive one; have no way to protect myself or my interest, and you're both going to leave me here like a damn dog in a kennel! Where's my water bowl? Well, that really sucks!"

"Dude, I don't mean to get in the business of you and your wife, but you were pretty far out last night. I've never seen you act like that. Scary, man. Like some kind of demon inside your head. As long as I've known you, I've never seen you treat Amy like that. Man, you beat the hell out of her. That kinda shit last night is not worth $250 million to me, much less $250,000."

From the blank stare that Clint returned, it was difficult to read any reaction. J.D. didn't care whether he took any of his belongings or not. He just wanted out. He had his revolver, and his pickup, and the rest didn't really matter. Amy grabbed what she thought was a month's worth of clothes and loaded them into the back of her Toyota.

"I still think there something goin' on you're not telling me about," Clint said. "Don't seem fair 'cause I can't do a damn thing about it."

"You dug your own hole, Clint. Now see if you can get yourself out." With that, she walked out the front door, leaving both of the men behind. J.D. looked down at the floor, "Man, I didn't ever think it would come to this, but nobody can trust being around you anymore, Clint. I'm outta here, too." With that, he walked out the door.

Dusk was fast approaching on that crisp fall Sunday afternoon. Amy was rearranging some of her things in her back seat, stalling a bit in order to give J.D. time to close out his relationship with Clint.

Amy and J.D. stood out in the driveway, recapping the last few days.

"So, are you really going back to your folk's house?" Amy asked.

"Probably. I'm just tired of all the questions from my folks. I think they wonder if somethin' strange is goin' on, but I ain't said. Are you really going to stay with Sarah Porter?'

"I think so. There might be a few more things for us to discuss, since all this has come crashing down so quick. I may just get a hotel room for a day or two. Hate to just spring in on her with no notice."

"I think I might do that too. My daddy has been asking me a lot of questions lately. Catching me off guard with all this stuff going on. He's been asking me a lot about you, and how you're doing."

Amy paused. "Well, I think the Lake Motel over on highway 70 might be a decent place to stay, and it's cheap. Why don't we see if we can get a couple rooms over there, and we can hash this out a little more."

"Sounds good. I'll just follow you over there."

They both looked back up at the house which now had only a few lights on, but there was no sign of Clint. "This whole thing is really turning out terrible." Amy shook her head in disgust. She reached up and gave J.D. a big hug. "See you over there then. We gotta hang in here together."

In spite of their unawareness, that same pair of sinister eyes had seen it all. Clint closed the blinds, fumed to himself for a few minutes, and began to formulate his own plans on how to end this madness.

54

AMY ARRIVED FIRST at the Lake Motel, a modest but clean strip of rooms carved right out of the fifties. A young blonde in her late teens welcomed her at the registration desk. "Hi, I'm Amy Logan. You got a couple of rooms for a night or two? We're locals but are having some problems at our house."

"Hi. I'm Darla. Sure thing. How many rooms, how many folks?"

"Two rooms, single for each. Just put it all on one ticket; I'll take care of both of them. Put the rooms close together, if it's available."

"Sure thing. No problem."

Amy was just finishing with their paperwork for both rooms, when J.D. arrived. "Darla, this is J.D."

"Welcome J.D. Glad to have you here. You're in room 7 and Amy, you're in room 8. Here's your keys and paperwork. Let us know if you need anything. We have cable TV now."

"Great, Darla. Thanks a lot."

Amy and J.D. were looking forward to escaping the drama that had totally consumed their lives. They had intended to discuss their future plans, but decided that sleep would serve them better, and then, they could have a more meaningful discussion after work the next day. As each weary guest took their belongings into their separate rooms, they agreed to meet in the parking lot at 6:30 and get breakfast at Angie's.

Back at the Logan household, Clint tried to sleep, but he was too angry. He was convinced his wife had begun a torrid love affair with his lifelong best friend. The thought made his blood boil. He paced the house like a caged leopard. Some meth, that's what he needed. His head was still splitting and that would help. The blood scattered throughout the house resembled a mass murder scene. The thought of a mass murder sounded intriguing to him.

He had to find a way to get even. Even with both of them. He had been manipulated like a puppet. They made a fool out of him for the last time. Trying to hold out on his money. If it weren't for his ingenuity, no one would have *any* cash. And now, he was left holding the bag.

He'd show them, but first, he had to find the meth. It wasn't where he thought he'd hidden it. Was it in the bottom drawer of his chest of drawers in a plastic baggie in the very back? Or was that the previous place for his stash? He had played games with Amy for so long and with so many hiding places that he couldn't remember.

Or maybe he had used it all up last night in his tirade. Like a madman on a rampage, he began a haphazard ransacking of their house. Pulling open every drawer, dumping its contents on the bed, in the floor, in the bathtub. The meth was nowhere to be found. Then he started on Amy's drawers. Flinging clothes like darts on a dartboard, he cussed and fumed as each new searching point proved fruitless.

Next came the bathroom drawers; out came the toiletries Amy had left. He knew it was not likely, but he would turn the house upside down if that's what it took to find the meth. Now that J.D., who was his sole source for the powder, had deserted and betrayed him, he had nowhere to turn. He finally collapsed on the living room floor near the sofa. He would rest for a few minutes before resuming the hunt.

Both Amy and J.D. would have given their life savings for a sleeping pill that night. Getting a few miles away from Clint, even though he was confined, was not enough to bring peacefulness to allow her to sleep. She wondered if J.D. was having the same problem. She looked at the red LED lights on the bedside alarm clock. It was 2:30 a.m. This night would never end. She tried counting sheep, but then sheep turned into dragons.

Just as J.D. was about to get relaxed, there was a loud knock on his door.

J.D.'s heart pounded. "Who is it?" Surely Clint would not have ventured out and found them. He went to the door, put the chain on, and gave the door a crack.

"Yeah, who is it? What's going on?"

"You got an orange pick-up truck?" The voice didn't sound familiar.

"Yeah, why?" J.D. asked.

"Sorry to wake you up, but you left your interior light on in your vehicle. Battery will be dead by morning. Hated to wake you up, but was trying to save you some grief by morning. I'd turn 'em off, but the cab is locked."

"Ok, thanks. I'll be out in a minute." He peered out from behind the drapes; the interior truck light was on indeed.

The next morning, they both agreed that it was the longest night of their lives. Black coffee was all they could handle at Angie's Diner. Neither had an appetite. They said their goodbyes and prayed for a clearer head after a good day's work. They would discuss their options over dinner and then decide their future plans.

Neither could have imagined in their wildest dreams exactly what the future would look like, even as soon as the very next day.

55

Amy's day at the bottling plant in Smithville was rather routine. Two co-workers had called in sick so they were shorthanded. That made the day go by quickly, and she actually looked forward to seeing J.D. after work. At least now, she had a confidant, someone to share in misery. She couldn't remember how long it had been since she looked forward to seeing Clint after work.

J.D., on the other hand, had a mini-confession at work. He had decided to tell everyone at work that police had discovered something very suspicious about Clint's death, and it had to do with him. He said that's all he could say for now, but asked some of his coworkers to pray for him during this very difficult period. He wasn't sure why he had opened up to someone. But it felt right. He would discuss that with Amy later. After work, both he and Amy pulled into their parking spots immediately in front of their rooms, within five minutes of each other.

"Well Jimmy Dale, how was your day?" Amy had a look of concern.

"It was okay. I'm gonna take a shower, then we can go to Hillcrest Diner and talk. Gimme about thirty minutes."

"Great, just knock on my door. I'm liable to be napping."

Meanwhile, Clint awoke from a few hours in the living room floor. His head was pounding. He reached up to feel the top wound, which hurt more. Painful wincing produced a few expletives as his hand pulled off some crimson brown scabby residue from his scalp. Meth. That's what he was looking for when he stopped for a snooze. Now he must resume his search.

Every upstairs room looked like it had been looted by robbers looking for gems. As each previous hiding place proved fruitless, his anger increased. By 3:00 p.m., the only room left in relative order was the kitchen. Clint hadn't searched there yet. He fixed some coffee and then began to look in drawers, cupboards, and their kitchen pantry. When he got to one drawer, he found three years' worth of water and light bills, and underneath that stack, discovered a shiny Smith and Wesson .38.

"Well hello baby…" he smiled to himself.

Out of habit, he rolled its cylinder to confirm the gun was actually loaded, then he stuck it in his pants' waistband. Then came the magic drawer! Underneath a two year old yellow pages, he found a small zip-lock baggie with two or three good lines of meth remaining.

"Hot damn! I knew I'd find it!"

Within thirty seconds, he had one line organized, and it was already up his nostrils. Within four minutes, he could see through steel. After fifteen minutes, there was nothing on the planet he couldn't do. Clint lost complete control of his mind and rationality. He vowed to get rid of anything and anyone that caused him misery. He had himself convinced that J.D. had encouraged the idea of their 'Cody' project in the first place. And now he was screwing his wife. Almost before his very eyes.

He taunted himself as he pulled in the last of the lines, "To hell with the money, I'm going after the sonuvabitch right this minute, and that slut wife of mine sleeping with him! Revenge is sweet!!" With the tirade of a madman, he pulled out the .38, and fired a shot into the floor in a bitter rampage.

It was 4:00 p.m. by the time Clint located his counterfeit driver's license. With Smith and Wesson in hand, he set out on his motorcycle, the same motorcycle that took him to watch his own graveside burial service. He would hunt them down, knock off both of them, and be back to the house soon after dark. Who would ever suspect Clint Logan, after all? He was six feet under. To Clint, this seemed kinda cool.

The Kawasaki cranked on the third kick. The deed itself would be one of the sweetest revenges he could ever imagine. The more he dwelled on it, the more excited he got. He would cover every square inch of DeKalb County to stalk his prey. His black motorcycle helmet, with gray skull and crossbones on the back, was particularly appropriate for his task at hand.

As he stopped at the first stop sign, he reached to his rear to confirm the presence of the all-important piece. It was there, ready and loaded.

He began by cruising by all the local motels. He wasn't falling for their lies. There weren't that many in the county, and that's where his instinct told him they would be. He looked at his watch; it was exactly 4:30 p.m. They should both be getting off work about now.

First, he swung by the Scott's house; there was no sign of J.D.'s truck there. He really wasn't expecting it to be there.

Center Hill Motel showed nothing but out of county trucks; he was looking for Amy's Toyota and/or J.D.'s orange rusted pick up. Either one would be a find. A few miles down the road was the Center Hill Motel. Lots of trucks with fishing boats, but no sign of Amy or J.D.'s vehicles. His third stop was the Lakeside Motel. He drove by and mentally froze in his tracks. This was too easy. Right there, in front of room 7, were both Amy and J.D.'s vehicles. He took a slow pass on the street again, checking for anything suspicious. It could be a trap.

He chuckled to himself. This would be like shooting fish in a barrel he thought. The meth had enhanced some senses and suppressed others. His face felt hot with envy as he mentally considered every detail of the double murder. His perverted and demented mind had assumed a rage with no control. He began to imagine what was going on behind the door of room 7. Down to the last detail. They were probably screwing right now. Laughing that they cheated him out of his take of the money. The motorcycle cruised by again, slowly, deliberately. He planned his attack. Go down the road a mile or so. Turn around and slowly drive back to the parking spot next to J.D.'s truck. Leave the motorcycle running. Get off. One swoop. Kick the door in. Fire two shots. Right between their eyes. Or in the back of their heads. But before he pulled each trigger, they must see him, so he could relish the panic in their eyes right before each took their last breath.

He'd be back on the bike in 10 seconds. They, and all his problems, would be gone forever.

His heart rate climbed as he executed the U-turn of his plan. He double checked the piece's position again. Everything was a go. Lakeside Motel was only one hundred yards away. It would all be over soon. Two gone. He'd be back at the house soon, relishing the bloodshed of his two victims. He placed the turn signal on to pull into the Lake's parking lot and downshifted as he approached J.D.'s truck. He kept his helmet on, pulled out the .38, left the engine running, and approached the dark green door with the gold number '7' painted on the door. He paused for a moment. His right thumb slowly pulled the hammer back into the cocked position of the revolver. He drew his right foot back to give the kick of his life.

56

His attention was suddenly diverted by a blue flash. The distraction stopped him in his tracks and caused him to turn around. Immediately behind him with blue lights flashing was one of DeKalb County's finest. The officer used his loudspeaker to announce, "Remain with your vehicle, please. This is a routine traffic stop. Please remain with your vehicle."

Clint froze. J.D. looked out of the curtain of Room 7 to see the commotion. There was Clint standing right there six feet away from J.D., separated only by a sheet of glass, outside his hotel door with a .38 waving in the air. Their eyes met in a blank stare.

Amy peered out of the window of Room 8. She gasped in horror.

The officer announced on his speaker from inside the patrol car. "Sir, I have just stopped you to inform you of a burned out tail light on your motorcycle. But I see you're carrying a .38. I'm gonna need you to show your carry permit and driver's license. But first, place your weapon on the ground and raise your hands over your head."

The officer got out of his patrol car, his weapon already displayed and aimed on Clint. He cautiously approached Clint, who had already laid down his weapon. Clint's hands were high above his head. He was now having trouble maintaining his balance. In trying to comply with the officer's request, he reached in his pocket for identification.

"Officer, here's my license," Clint said, handing the officer the phony license. "I don't have my permit on me, but I'd like to explain," Clint said. "See, my wife's in that hotel room screwing my ex-best friend!"

The arresting officer studied the license carefully "Is that so, Mr., uh, Lincoln? I don't know what your real name is, but it's not Lincoln. This might be the sorriest counterfeit license I've ever seen! Try to remember your real name while you're riding to the station. You're under arrest. Sir, there's no law against adultery but carrying a gun with no permit with a fake ID, now that'll get your ass lit up a little." The officer carefully latched handcuffs tightly around Clint's wrists, and escorted him to the patrol car. Clint asked that he stop a minute.

"Before we go, sir. I have to ask you a question. Aren't you going to get J.D. outta that motel room with my wife?'

The officer replied in a soft but very forceful voice. "Sir, as I mentioned before, there is no law against adultery." His demeanor with Clint was both stern and rigid.

"Well, how 'bout murder then? He's the one that killed Cody, not me! You gonna let him get away with murder?"

The officer stopped suddenly, a stunned look showered his face. "Murder? Did you say murder? Who murdered who?"

"J.D. killed him, not me! I swear to God!"

"Sir, you might as well save the rest of this story 'til we get down to the station. Better turn your motorcycle off, you're not going to be driving it."

As J.D. and Amy watched Clint being handcuffed and placed in the patrol car, they could hear voices, but got no details. Blue lights stayed on as the patrol car left the hotel parking lot. Both curtains went back and forth with curiosity until the flashing lights disappeared. They both opened their respective doors within seconds.

"Holy smoke! That bastard was coming to kill us both." Amy's hands were shaking along with her voice.

"You said he was jealous of me but I never thought of this."

"Well, guess we all knew this day was coming. Surprised it didn't come sooner. I couldn't hear exactly what was said, but I think I did hear something about his wife screwing his ex-best friend. We can still go to dinner, but, to tell you the truth, I've lost my appetite."

"I also heard something about 'not killing anybody.' Sounds like to me he's thrown himself and both of us totally under the bus."

"Same here. Why don't we go back to the house and see what he's done to that. We won't have to worry about him following us there. But you gotta know they're gonna come looking for both of us soon. No since runnin' or hidin'. His mouth will be like an open book. You can count on that!"

J.D. nodded in agreement. "I'm gonna stop by my folks first and try to warn them about this trouble. They're getting on there in age, and this will kill my folks. I'll stop by your house, or call you in a couple hours. They both left in their separate vehicles. The parking lot of the Lake Motel was now empty. Except for a lone motorcycle.

57

THE INTERROGATING OFFICER, Sergeant Ronnie Townsend, booked Clint into their system, under his real name, Clint Logan. A quick check of the state system showed that Clint Logan had never owned a carry permit. He was put in a holding cell and given a new pair of jailbird stripes. The prison doctor was called and arrangements were immediately made to seek adequate wound care for his head.

Sergeant Townsend began the questioning. "OK, Mr. Logan, I understand your last name is Logan, not Lincoln. I also understand you were just stopped for a burned out tail light. Is that correct?"

"Yes sir. That would be correct."

"And when the officer questioned you about the validity of your license, you caved and admitted to having been a part of a murder for insurance fraud, is that correct?"

"Yes, sir, that is correct." Clint answers were stoic.

"And why, may I ask, would you confess so quickly to this conspiracy that has been so successful for almost two years? Doesn't make sense."

"No sir, it doesn't. But it's the right thing to do. Besides, it wouldn't have taken one day for you to piece my last two years together. I just saved you a little time." Clint didn't know how successful he was in selling the officers on his sincerity, but he had little to lose.

What Clint had decided to do was to implicate both Amy and J.D. as masterminds of the entire scheme, perhaps allowing him to cut a plea deal. But what the officer didn't tell Clint was that both J.D. and Amy were also being brought in for questioning. All parties in the investigation were carefully separated to make sure they had no opportunity to collaborate on their stories. In the meantime, Clint did not realize that his entire version of the story was being filmed by closed circuit television and would be replayed for courts, the investigating team, and the forensic doctors before this case would solved.

58

An HOUR AFTER Clint's interrogation began, Monty Taylor, one of DeKalb County's most senior deputy sheriffs, approached the Scott's house. A sharp knock produced Mrs. Scott, J.D.'s mother.

"Ma'am, is there a Jimmy Dale Scott at this house?"

"Why yes, he stopped by for the evening. Is there a problem?" J.D.'s mother was not only naïve, but also a Christian woman who had led a quiet and conservative life. Any insinuation of criminal activity or suggested wrongdoing by anyone in her family would produce a violent shock and horror. J.D.'s father was cut from the same cloth.

"If you don't mind, ma'am…if I could just come in and speak with Jimmy Dale, you'll hear the details." His wife's best friend knew the family quite well, as they attended Rocky Hill Baptist Church together, and had been close friends for years.

"Certainly, Officer. Please come in." She held the door open, but maintained a look of horror, as if she anticipated that something very wrong was about to unfold. Deputy Taylor politely thanked her, crossing the threshold and entering the living room. By now, J.D.'s father was standing behind his wife, eager to learn the cause of this unexpected visit.

"Roger, the law needs to speak with Jimmy Dale." Mrs. Scott said.

Jimmy Roger Scott's initial reaction was defensiveness. "What seems to be the problem, sir? We're law-abiding citizens around here."

"Sir, I am well aware of that. I'm sorry to have to present you folks with this matter this evening, but there are some facts about J.D. that you may not be aware of. Is he here now? It's important that I speak with him."

J.D. had heard voices and was already coming down the hall and into the living room. "I'm here, mom." Jimmy Dale hung his head in shame. "I came by here to talk to you folks about a little trouble, but I can't make myself do it."

Mr. Scott's stern voice resonated. "J.D., what is this all about?"

J.D.'s eyes froze when he saw the uniformed officer standing in his parents' living room beside Mrs. Scott, who was already sobbing into several clenched tissues in her shaking hands. Without giving the deputy a chance to greet J.D., she asked, "J.D., they say there's some kind of problem. What is it, son?"

J.D.'s eyes passed briefly over each person in the room, but he said nothing. Deputy Taylor broke the awkward silence hanging heavily over them. "Sir, is your name Jimmy Dale Scott?"

"Yes, sir." J.D. was as expressionless as a man in a trance.

"Mr. Scott, I have here a warrant for your arrest. You are being charged with the murder of a John Doe, whose first name may be Cody. You have the right to remain silent. You have the right to obtain counsel. If you cannot afford an attorney, the court will appoint one for you. Please turn around, face the wall, and allow me to place the handcuffs on you."

Mrs. Scott's sobbing turned immediately into uncontrollable wailing. "J.D.! Oh, dear Jesus, tell me what this is all about! There has to be some kind of mistake!"

J.D. said nothing, but obeyed the officer by turning around to face the front wall of the living room. As Officer Taylor handcuffed him, he maintained a blank stare into the oil portrait of Jesus, framed over the living room sofa. By this time, Mrs. Scott had collapsed onto a side chair. Mr. Scott had no choice but to attend to her.

"I'm sorry, Mama. It's a big mistake. Clint done it. He just had me along for the ride." Somehow J.D.'s meager explanation did nothing but add fuel to the fire.

"J.D., what are you talking about? What's going on, son? What in heaven's name is going on? Does this have something to do with Clint's death?"

Deputy Taylor interrupted politely. "I'm sorry folks, but the rest of this conversation needs to take place down at the station. You are certainly welcome to come along, but you will not be allowed in the interrogation room."

The deputy's statement further solidified the graveness of the charges and produced another wave of wails, as Mrs. Scott clutched at a pillow in agony. Mr. Scott only glared at J.D. in anger and disgust. Neither of them knew in that moment that this would be their last exchange.

Two days later, Jimmy Roger Scott, J.D.'s dad, died of a massive heart attack.

59

AMY SLIPPED HER KEY into the front door; it clicked obligingly. She entered their living room and quickly locked the door behind her. She gasped in horror at what looked like a bloody crime scene. She assumed correctly that Clint had gone off on one of his meth induced rampages.

She carefully toured each room, looking over her shoulder as if someone or something might be following her. After completing a survey of each room, Amy returned to the living room. She then collapsed on the sofa breaking down in an uncontrollable sob.

Where was her life going? What could she do to undo any of this? It was all like a bad dream that would not end. Suddenly, there was a knock at her front door. Amy jumped like she had been shot. Her first instinct was to run, but she had nowhere to run. She ran instinctively to her bedroom, tripping over clothes, dresser drawers strewn about the room. She peeked through the bedroom blinds to identify her visitor.

She froze in fear when she saw the black and white sheriff's car parked outside. The last time a uniformed officer appeared on her front porch was almost two years ago. Her mind instantly flashed back to that horrific day.

Amy slowly opened the door, hands shaking and sweat beading under her nose. She opened it wide enough to allow her to greet her visitor.

"Yes, deputy? Can I help you?"

"Good day, ma'am. I'm Deputy Halsey. Are you Mrs. Amy Logan?"

"Yes, sir, I am." Amy answered in a halting voice.

"Ma'am, could I come in a minute? I need to ask you some questions."

"Well, uh, I guess so, but, uh . . . I just got in from work. Uh, is there something wrong?"

"I need you to come down to the station and answer a few questions. I'm sorry, but it's important."

"Well, can you tell me what this is about?" The palms of Amy's hands were wet. She could feel sweat as it dripped from under her arms, leaving dark circles of green highlighted around the seams of her light green blouse. Her mind raced as she attempted to sort out what to say or do. It was like *déjà vu* of that morning two summers ago, when this whole nightmare began.

"Yes ma'am. It's about your husband Clint Logan. I'm here to tell you that he's alive. He's in custody. Charged with murder one."

Amy's voice shrank to a whisper. "Come in. Let me get my things."

60

THE TENNESSEE BUREAU of Investigation assigned the case to two of its most seasoned veterans, with more than fifty years of homicide and crime scene investigation experience. Not only did Special Agents Wayne Hartley and Bruce Akers have the task of gathering enough evidence to put the suspects away, they had to figure out who was buried in Clint Logan's grave.

Both Akers and Hartley conducted their preliminary investigation of Amy Logan within hours of Clint's arrest outside the Lake Motel. She was escorted into one of the interrogation rooms. Amy looked haggard, mentally exhausted and frightened.

"Good evening, Mrs. Logan. My name is Agent Hartley and this is my partner Agent Akers. Local authorities have just arrested your husband, who was originally thought to be dead, outside the Lake Motel. Were you aware of this?"

"Yes sir, I was." Amy hung her head in shame and began sobbing. She looked around the room for something to dry her eyes. Hartley passed her a box of tissue.

"And how were you made aware of this arrest?"

"I was in the Lake Motel with his friend J.D. Scott, and we heard the commotion outside in the parking lot. I know he was coming to kill us; we saw him waving a pistol around in front of the arresting officer as he got off his motorcycle. J.D. and I were hiding from him, and he had been hiding in our house for the last eighteen months or so."

"You and J.D. were hiding from your husband in a motel room? Is that your statement?"

"Yes, sir. We were staying there temporarily, in two rooms. J.D. is like my big brother, and my husband's best friend. The thing about it is that Clint has turned maniacal in the last few months, and I have truly lived in fear of my life."

"Tell us please about your involvement in this murder that Clint has admitted to. There seems to be some controversy about exactly who committed the murder, but both men admit involvement. They both also claim to not know who it is that they killed. Can you help us with that part?"

"Sir, all I know is that they said his name was Cody. Didn't know his last name. Picked him up hitchhiking out in New Mexico on their way back from a busted trip to Vegas. My stupid ass husband stole all my money I had put back in my keepsake drawer, and then lost it all gambling. Sir, I honestly had no idea about any of this scheme until after the murder had been committed."

Both agents sat up with special interest. "Go on."

"Sheriff Roswell came by one morning about two years ago to tell me that my husband had died in a car crash near Dickson the night before. Our marriage had been on the skids for some time, but when you get shocking news like that, it still hits you pretty hard. Supposedly they were able to positively identify him by dental records that I got from our family dentist. So the next night, some people at work, church and all our friends started to come by the house to comfort me and to offer condolences. I had an appointment to plan the funeral the next morning. Two hours later, those two show up on my back door step and scare the hell out of me!"

"What happened after that?"

"The whole thing shocked me so much that I must have fainted. I hit my head and was really out of it for several days. I had already made appointments for funeral arrangements to be done the next morning. Obviously, those plans had to be changed. After a few days for me to come back to my senses, we began a conversation about where to go from here.

"Well, my husband told me what they had done, and that he or we were going to cash in the life insurance policy I had taken out on him through the group plan where I work. I basically had a choice to make. Either go along with Clint's idea and become an accessory to the crime with life insurance fraud, or turn my husband in for murdering a guy that nobody even knows who he is."

Hartley looked at Akers. They both shook their heads. It seemed that they each believed Amy's story, bizarre as it was. "So what did you do at that point to get involved? It's obvious that you chose a path not to turn in your husband."

Amy sobbed again as she completed wrapping up her story.

"Sirs, I know I've done wrong. But please try for a minute to put yourself in my shoes. I had no good choices. Clint has been on crystal meth for over two years, and his behavior is so erratic that sometimes it's violent. I have become afraid of him. So I chose to go along with the plan. It seemed like the least of the two evils."

"So after the next few days had passed, after everyone had come over to console me, I assumed a new role. I went to the funeral home that morning to plan a fake, but real funeral. It was the hardest thing I've ever done in my life. This is not who I am and does not accurately define my values in life. I know I'm in big trouble, but just hope that you will take this statement into consideration when you decide what to do with me."

"So when they left your house two years ago, you actually thought Clint and J.D. were just driving out to Vegas for a boy's trip. Is that your statement?"

"I didn't know they were going. Just one of those 'guys trips' he would pull off frequently. No notice. Nothing. Just a note on the kitchen table when I came home from work saying they had decided to go to Vegas for a while. He called me once they got out there. I've heard so many stories, I don't know what to believe. After they lost all their money, they moved onto their next scheme which was evidently to pick up a hitchhiker or a drifter, kill him, burn the car to make it look like Clint. Apparently, whoever got killed was misidentified and was buried in what was supposed to be Clint's casket. That's where I got involved, I guess. After we got Clint's death certificate, I filed a claim for the $250,000 life insurance claim. We got the money. Have already spent some, but not much. It's in a saving's account at DeKalb County National Bank.

"But I was so worn out with being the only one working in our household. I've never even had a speeding ticket, and that worthless husband of mine spends all his time trying to figure out an angle to everything. Trying to get free money, trying to hoodwink somebody. To be honest, I was glad to see him go to Vegas; get him outta my hair for a while. I never could get him to work, and now that he's supposed to be dead, he can't work, and all he's doing is sucking the life out of me.

"To tell you the truth, I'm kinda relieved that this whole scam is over. I told both guys from the start that this scheme would blow up in their faces sooner or later."

"Mrs. Logan, are you willing to submit to a polygraph test? Lie detector?"

"Absolutely. I'd be happy to take it right now."

"Please give us a minute. We'll be right back." Both Akers and Hartley left the interrogation room and stepped into an adjacent conference room.

"Holy shit! Now, I've seen it all! What do you think, Ake?" Hartley wanted his partner's opinion before he offered his.

"I think she's completely above board. I'm buying the story. Let's run the polygraph, just to be sure. To tell you the truth, I feel bad for the situation she was in. How 'bout you?"

"Completely agree." They both paused to observe Amy's behavior now that she was alone on the concealed television. She had her face buried in her hands, sobbing uncontrollably.

"Let's get Jennings to run one on her this evening; I just saw him come in. If she passes, then let's call DeKalb and Dickson County DA's and ask for a plea out. May need to contact the U.S. Attorney's office, since the feds may want in on this one. Transporting a dead body across state lines. I think she might have more info that could help us crack what's left of this circus. Unless we come across anything else in their stories, I vote for complete immunity in exchange for testimony."

"I'm all over that."

Both men went back to Amy who was still sobbing and shaking her head. Her pile of tissues had become substantial. "Mrs. Logan, I'll tell you what we're gonna do. We're gonna run a polygraph on you as soon as we can get it set up.

"You know we have both men isolated. They will have no opportunity to talk with you or each other. We both think you can help us with tying up loose ends on this. We're gonna try and get the DA to give you immunity from prosecution for accessory to murder in exchange for testimony. I think we can talk him in to it; he may insist on some probation or paying back some money to avoid insurance fraud."

Amy sobbed openly. "Sirs, I have had this weight on my shoulders for two years. I was not raised to ever be a part of this type of life style and will do anything, I mean *anything* to help. I am so sorry for my part in this tangled mess."

"We'll prepare a gag order for you to sign. It will also outline conditions for an agreement. You will not be incarcerated, but will be confined to this county until trial, and must report physically and daily with a parole officer. In exchange for this immunity, you do agree to be an ally of the State and help us completely and to whatever extent we ask you, to determine any other pertinent details. Are you willing to do this?"

"Absolutely," Amy agreed, and then breathed a sigh of relief. "I just want all this to come out. I'm so worn out with living under this black cloud."

"We're gonna have to ask you to remain here until we can get this approved. Should be able to get this paperwork done in a couple of hours."

Amy's results on her polygraph showed authorities her answer to every question was consistent and truthful. After about three hours, the paperwork was approved. Amy was released to go home.

"Now ma'am, let me tell you about a gag order. If you breach any part of the agreement, everything becomes null and void, you will be immediately arrested. Do you completely understand?"

"Yes sir, I completely understand. You will have total cooperation from me."

61

ONCE THEY WERE SURE Amy would cooperate, Agents Hartley and Akers interrogated Clint Logan and Jimmy Dale Scott separately.

Agent Hartley made Clint squirm with his first question.

"It's my understanding, Mr. Logan, that you admit to participating in an event that resulted in the death of an unnamed hitchhiker you and Jimmy Dale Scott picked up outside of Albuquerque, New Mexico, some two years ago. Is that correct?"

"Yes, sir," Clint replied in a low voice. "But I didn't kill him."

"And, Mr. Logan, you also acknowledge that you and Mr. Scott simulated your death by placing the hitchhiker's body in your car, setting the vehicle on fire, and crashing it into a tree?"

"Yes, sir, but Jimmy Dale killed him. He choked him with a bungee cord while I was driving. I had nothing to do with him getting killed. There was no pre-meditation."

"How, then, Mr. Logan, were you going to fake your own death if you didn't *plan* to have a dead body to substitute for you at the scene of the accident?"

Clint stared at the wall. He had no idea how he was going to respond.

"Is it also true, Mr. Logan, that you and your wife Amy Logan have collected $250,000 in life insurance money from the Pioneer Life Insurance Company because they think you, sir, are . . . dead?"

"Yes . . . sir."

"Mr. Logan, what is the name of the man who was killed?"

"All I can remember is . . . he said they called him Cody."

"No last name, Mr. Logan?"

"No sir. He was a guy coming to Nashville to sing country music."

Agent Bruce Akers waited for Jimmy Dale Scott to be brought into another interrogation room. After hitting so many dead ends, he was hoping to get something from this suspect that would fill in the blanks.

Jimmy Dale shuffled his shackled feet as he was escorted, wearing a bright orange jumpsuit, his hands cuffed to chains around his waist. He took a seat at the small table and gulped a cup of water as Agent Akers began.

"Mr. Scott, is it true that you participated in a scheme with Clint Logan to kill an individual and stage Logan's death, and to receive a share of $250,000 in life insurance benefits?" Akers asked.

"The whole thing was Clint's idea," Jimmy Dale answered. "I was just going along with his plan . . . We were both broke and. . ."

"Mr. Scott," Akers interrupted, "isn't it also true that you were riding in the backseat of a Honda in Texas and strangled a hitchhiker with a bungee cord as he rode in the front seat?"

"No sir. I was driving, and Clint choked him, not me. He planned the whole thing out."

"And, Mr. Scott, what is the name of the man who was killed?"

"Cody," Jimmy Dale answered, looking at the floor.

"Cody who?"

Jimmy Dale wrung his cuffed hands and began to sob.

"All I know is . . . Cody. He wrote a song . . . sang it to me . . . I know he was warning me that he would be back again after he died. I can't get it outta my mind."

According to the guards, Jimmy Dale was inconsolable that night as he prayed and cried alone in his cell.

62

THREE DAYS AFTER Clint's arrest, the DeKalb County District Attorney's Office obtained a court order to exhume the body alleged to be Clint Logan. Smithville had not experienced this type of drama, murder and conspiracy since anyone could remember.

There were many questions to be answered. Whether the decedent's name was really Cody—or whether this was just another lie two drugged out losers had concocted. The Associated Press picked up on the story and joined in speculation, and a short segment had been broadcast on NBC's *Today Show*.

Unfortunately, there were quite a few misconceptions surfacing in public conversation regarding forensic identification. Many newspaper articles covering the much-anticipated exhumation led readers to believe that just digging up the casket and examining the body would uncover the identity of the "mystery man". Later, they would all realize that nothing could be further from the truth.

Dr. Stanley Gowen, of the University of Tennessee Department of Forensic Anthropology, was called to investigate the project.

His research facility, called the Body Farm, had already reached world notoriety from previous cases.

Forensic anthropology is the science that deals with the study of human bones, the effort to determine "who is it." Forensic anthropologists can make determinations regarding the race, sex, height, weight, and sometimes nationality and creed of a deceased individual, based on the composition of the skeleton.

On Monday morning, January 25, 1999, it was announced that the exhumation would take place that afternoon. Only a short notice was released to the media in the hopes of cutting down mounting frenzy. That logic was unsuccessful.

By noon, media trucks with towering satellite dishes, positioned themselves strategically for coverage. Ironically, the trucks were parked within a hundred yards of the oak tree that Clint Logan had climbed to witness his own burial about twenty-four months earlier.

This time the crowd surrounding the grave was much larger, but still no one was there to represent the decedent's family. No one was there to grieve for his death, or lay his remains to rest with proper respect and dignity. The media had a field day reiterating these tragic realities.

Various news reporters surrounded the headstone. It read:

Clint Alton Logan

Born March 3, 1969

Died July 14, 1997

His God fearing soul is now with Jesus

One of the television reporters couldn't resist the temptation to ask the cemetery manager an obvious question.

"What will you do with this headstone, casket, and vault now that it won't be needed anymore? Is there a market for such a product?"

"I have no idea. Never been asked that question. I suppose we will store it for law enforcement officials in case they need it in their investigation."

The cemetery employed its own people to open and close graves. Usually, they opened a grave the day of the burial and closed it immediately following the family's departure. The cemetery manager had never before been asked to return to a grave and re-open it.

A small backhoe was brought in, and Clint Logan's headstone was removed and set aside. The backhoe driver then began removing dirt. He placed aside about five feet of rich, black topsoil, exposing the concrete vault housing the casket. A heavy chain was used to attach to lead eyelets to retrieve its contents.

When all were secure, the backhoe slowly pulled the casket and vault out of the ground. Its boom swung around and gently lowered its contents on a cemetery truck.

The next step was a full anthropological and dental examination by the University of Tennessee Department of Forensic Anthropology in Knoxville. The truck transported the body to Knoxville, accompanied by two Tennessee Highway Patrol officers.

As the truck drove off with the unidentified contents of the casket, reporters were left scratching their heads over a story so puzzling they couldn't quite figure out how to cover it.

63

Dr. Gowen led Dr. Walsh and Lana downstairs to the forensic examination laboratory in the basement of the University of Tennessee Medical Center. Unlocking a large white door, he led them into a cavernous, stark area with concrete floors, block walls, florescent lighting, and laboratory benches. They donned scrubs, rubber gloves, and surgical masks, and followed Dr. Gowen.

In the corner, a dirty casket was sitting atop a steel gurney. Neither Drs. Gowen nor Walsh expected that they would have much to work with. Gowen explained while working. "This is a really weird case. Homicide with a staged death. Somebody trying to collect some life insurance money. It was supposed to be a Clint Logan from Smithville, but he's turned up, so we know it's not him. Wonder how the misidentification happened. You ever work this case, Chris?"

"No. Dr. Templeton did this ID on his own. Really don't know why either. I did all his ID's for years, but not lately since he lost his job. I am glad to be able to work with you though, since I've been asked many questions since this case has been in the news. There are lots of folks that think I might have made a really terrible mistake."

Using a special tool to release the coffin pins, Dr. Gowen worked with the corroded metal until the seal released with a hissing sound. A putrid odor filled the room, leaving all three scrambling to put their masks over their noses.

"Sorry, guys. I wasn't expecting such an odor with so little soft tissue."

Inside the coffin, a thick, black vinyl body bag held the remains. On top lay a moldy, dusty black book. Dr. Walsh reached in to pick up the book and dusted it off carefully with one finger. The tiny book was inscribed "New Testament Bible" with "Clint Logan" inscribed in gold leaf on its cover.

"Here," Dr. Walsh said, handing the Bible to Lana. "We can send this to Logan in the state pen. From the looks of things, he could stand to re-read it." Lana rolled her eyes and placed the book on the dissecting tray.

"Take a look at this, Chris," Dr. Gowen said, pulling a document from the case file lying beside the casket. "Bet you've never seen one of these before!"

It was Clint Logan's death certificate. Walsh grabbed the document in fascination. "How about that? Can't say that I ever saw a living man's death certificate. That's pretty creepy!" All three examiners shook their heads in disbelief.

Dr. Walsh stood over the recently exhumed body, curled into a fetal position. It was badly marred by fire, and what little soft tissue remained was partially decomposed. The fingers and toes of the corpse were burned off, leaving only charred, gnarled nubs. The body had been interred for nearly two years, after having been incinerated in a motor vehicle accident. It was now difficult or impossible to determine the sex, age, or any vital details of the individual at the time of death.

Dr. Walsh put one gloved finger to the body's taut, blackened upper arm. His fingertip came away with a thin, white substance, like talc, coating it.

"That's formaldehyde powder," Dr. Gowen explained. "Undertakers use that when there isn't enough soft tissue left to embalm. It's supposed to cut down on odors, but after two years, nothing is going to work."

The rib cage was open, like that of a field dressed deer. Some of the organs were missing. Clearly, this was not the first autopsy this corpse had undergone.

Walsh grabbed a #15 surgical scalpel blade making a lateral incision at each corner of what was left of the mouth extending toward the ear. The soft tissue was minimal, and somewhat mummified, making the cutting of the tissue much like cutting dried leather with a pair of dull scissors. When the incisions were complete, Walsh was able to gain access to the burned oral cavity; revealing only seven human teeth.

There were numerous sockets open, some with shattered, burned bone around the top rim of the socket. "This is where these teeth got knocked out just before the fire. You can see that the bone is burned, but you can see the alveolar crest is shattered. The jaws broke just before the fire erupted. Must have been pretty forceful, as it knocked out multiple teeth."

Gowen nodded with interest as he was beginning his anthropological workup with a tape measure. "That's pretty interesting stuff. What is the clinical condition of the remaining seven teeth?"

"Seem to be pretty good. As you know, the enamel on human teeth remains is the hardest and most durable substance in our body. This enamel is stronger than human bone and is usually well preserved even in human remains that are thousands of years old. I've never seen a tooth completely burn up, that is in a petroleum based fire. Now, in a crematory, that's a different matter.

"You can see also that the seven remaining are the posterior teeth. They did not get subjected to the same trauma that knocked out the anteriors. Also, being further back, they were shielded somewhat, at least for a while." Walsh thought now might be a good time to give Lana a brief orientation in forensic odontology.

"In most areas of Western civilization, medical and dental technology have developed many materials for repairing broken, decayed, or destroyed teeth. Pure gold has been used for centuries for ornamentation and as a very durable reconstruction material. Its bright yellow color, while cosmetically objectionable to some, is considered desirable for the rich and famous in some cultures.

"In the early part of the twentieth century, silver fillings were developed as a less expensive way to restore damaged teeth. Amalgam fillings came next, a combination of various metals including silver, mercury, tin, zinc, and copper. Amalgam and gold fillings are particularly strong because of their melting points above a thousand degrees Fahrenheit. But in the 1930s, a tooth-colored restorative material called composite resin was developed. It has a lower melting point, but because of its more pleasing appearance it is now widely used, especially in the restoration of front teeth.

"Any of these materials will show up on a dentist's X-ray as a distinct spot on the tooth. A typical human being has thirty-two teeth—counting the ever-popular wisdom teeth. Forensic dental exams consist initially of charting the presence—or absence—of all of these thirty-two teeth. The teeth are numbered 1 through 32, beginning with the upper right wisdom tooth in the back of the upper arch. If there are any teeth missing, then detailed notes are made to document exactly if that tooth has been replaced, and if so, whether with a bridge, partial, or an implant.

"Each tooth is then evaluated to learn if there is an existing filling, and if so, what material it is made of and which specific surface it covers. There are five surfaces or sides on each tooth. Statisticians tell us that five to the 32nd power is a number greater than the number of all people that have ever lived on planet Earth. The probability of any two people having matching dental records is practically zero."

Once Dr. Walsh and Lana had completed a chart of the seven teeth remaining, they compared their notes to a bitewing dental X-ray of Clint Logan's mouth, taken from his dental records. The first notation Dr. Walsh saw on the X-ray showed that Logan had a gold crown on tooth number 18. Dr. Walsh turned to the chart Lana had just made of the exhumed corpse's remaining teeth. A quick examination revealed that number 18 was a virgin tooth, no presence of dental decay or previously existing restoration— totally inconsistent with Logan's X-ray.

Their very first point of comparison confirmed what they had known all along; Dr. Templeton's investigation had yielded an incorrect conclusion. Clint Logan's teeth were unmistakably different from those of this body

"Hey, this is interesting. Look…" Walsh's attention was directed to the neck area. "Don't know how this part survived the fire, but this is a little segment of the trachea that somehow didn't get burned too badly."

With his scalpel blade, Dr. Walsh peeled back a portion of the windpipe, exposing its inside lining. Filleting the inside of the trachea, he exposed a cherry-red fragment of soft tissue that had been spared from the intense heat.

"Clean as can be!" Dr. Walsh said, looking up from his work and shaking his head. There was no trace of black soot inside the trachea, indicating that the individual could not have been breathing at the time of the fire. "This man didn't die of smoke inhalation," Walsh murmured. "He was dead before that car ever burned."

Dr. Gowen appeared further intrigued with another adjacent finding. "And check this out, Doc. Little anthropology lesson for the both of you. See that little bone near the windpipe? That's called the hyoid bone. It is unique in that this bone is totally supported by muscles and ligaments. Not attached to any other bones. Look at the distal periphery. See the end of it is broken? That is almost a hundred percent diagnostic of strangulation. It's nearly impossible to fracture unless a victim is being strangled. That's your cause of death right there. No mention of that on the autopsy report. We'll definitely have to get another pathologist to look at this."

There was such a small amount of soft tissue remaining on the corpse that the doctors were able to remove the skull with very little effort. The doctors also were able to resect the jaws for closer inspection. They placed it on the lab worktable and began scrubbing with a steel brush and warm, soapy water. Dr. Gowen returned to the gurney to continue examining. He had a tape measure out, and was attempting to get some overall dimensions. Height determination would be difficult in this case, especially since the extremities had been burned so badly. Dr. Walsh studied the skull with the help of Lana.

"Lana, so far all we know for sure is that this guy is not Clint Logan. Our next step is to find out exactly who he is. We may have to get another forensic pathologist to give an opinion about cause and manner of death. The soot free trachea and fractured hyoid bone are two critical pieces of data that could change opinions. It certainly looks like it could have been foul play instead of a routine motor vehicle accident. Sometimes that's easier said than done, but that's what makes this such a worthwhile mission."

Walsh, Gowen, and Lana stood in silence for a moment, looking at the exhumed body that had for two years lain buried under a headstone bearing the wrong name. The weirdness of that concept gave Lana chill bumps and made her skin crawl, but it also excited her. This is what she thrived on.

"All we know is that authorities claimed his name was Cody. We have absolutely no other clues," Gowen explained. "And we can't even be sure of that. I mean, the suspects are hardly reputable types. They probably wouldn't think twice about lying about a victim's first name, just to throw us off and cover their tails."

Dr. Walsh had no way of knowing that moment, but finding the corpse's identity and what had happened would become his challenge, even his obsession. It would haunt him every day for the next decade.

64

THREE MONTHS AFTER Cody left for Nashville, Christine was seriously worried. A single postcard had left her emotionally charged for days. Her daily post office walk became a ritual. Every morning she returned, hoping against hope to receive another word from Cody. It never came.

Melvin had grown close to Christine, and every day his heart broke as she opened her empty box. Even then, she would summon all her strength to wave goodbye to him, never failing to return the next day.

Christine's pregnancy lifted her spirits. She didn't know where Cody was or why he wasn't writing, but she did know she would soon bear his child. That gave her comfort.

One sunny October afternoon, she was sitting on Melvin and Kathy's porch swing, drinking a cup of tea and chatting with Kathy when Cody's name came up again.

"Don't you think we should contact the police?" she asked. "I mean it's been over three months now, and I just know something's wrong."

"Remember, Melvin and I didn't know Cody very well," Kathy said patiently. "We only met him once. And I know in my heart

243

that you truly believe he was sincere. But you know the first thing the police are gonna do is roll their eyes when you're not looking. Another cowboy leaves his girlfriend in Albuquerque and seeks his fortune in Nashville, then disappears. I'm not saying I think that's what happened, but from the outside looking in, I'm sure you've got some doubters out there. Those that don't know the depth of your relationship."

"Yes," Christine replied. "But Kathy, you have to believe me. Cody's not like that. We knew each other two years at the Blueroom Cafe. At first it was just a simple friendship. Then things began to blossom. I think he had an eye for me after about six months. I'd had an eye for him after six days!"

Both girls laughed at the silliness of love and the mysterious ways in which it worked. They felt like they were back in sixth grade, gossiping about boys they had crushes on.

"Tell me how it started," Kathy said softly. "Paint the picture for me, so I know Cody the way you do."

Christine nodded, bliss spreading across her face at his memory. "He sang six nights a week and I tended bar. We went in about five and closed around two, or whenever the last drunk stumbled out. We were off on Sundays. After about six months, we started doing a few things after work. Just friendship type of things—talking about stuff, about life. You know what I mean. Neither of us had brothers or sisters, and we both had lost our parents. Cody's dad was killed in a car wreck when he was ten. His mom died from breast cancer. My mom was an alcoholic, so we'd never been close. And my dad died year before last."

Kathy reached out and touched her arm. "I'm so sorry, Christine."

"It's okay. He was gone on out-of-town jobs so much when I was growing up—or so my mama told me. I hardly knew him.

"Anyway, when Sweetie and I got to know each other, it was kinda weird at first discovering similarities between us. We both like music a lot, especially country music. I never met a person so driven and determined to make it big in country music. He has a beautiful voice, and he's so handsome—he could sing all night long and I'd never get tired of his songs. Sometimes I'd get caught up in listening to his golden voice, and it made me forget about taking care of my customers. I had to keep reminding myself that I was at work!"

Kathy gave an encouraging nod, and Christine went on.

"It was eight and a half months from the time I met Cody before he finally kissed me. It swept me off my feet. I had a few boyfriends in high school, but nothing serious. Most of them spent more time getting into mischief than trying to get a girlfriend. Cody's mom had bought him a ukulele when he was young, and he spent half his childhood playing. He graduated from high school but playing music is the only serious thing he ever did in his life. It was like he was destined to be a guitar player and singer. Nothing was going to get in the way of his dream." She paused. "Not even me."

Kathy listened intently. This was the first time Christine had really opened up about the details of her relationship with Cody.

"Well, honey," she said. "That's a good thing. Not everybody knows what their life's calling is. And plenty of people would give their right arm to be able to know for sure what they're supposed to do. So tell me, how did this relationship develop after that first kiss?"

"I might have rushed things a little bit, but I just couldn't help it. I told him I had never felt like this with anybody else. He said it was the same for him. Since we both worked nights and had to sleep in most days, our regular day didn't start till noon or so.

Then we'd have to get back to work around five. We would spend maybe two or three afternoons a week together doing fun things for that first year and a half. It really didn't make any difference to us what it was we were doing, we just loved being together.

"It was one year to the day that he told me he loved me. I remember it like yesterday. We were sitting out in the driveway in my VW. He leaned over and kissed me. And this time it was a real kiss. I'd never felt anything like it. He said, 'Sweetie, I'll love you forever.' And what do you think I did? I cried like a big doofus!" Christine laughed out loud, but the memory made her voice quiver.

"Then there was the issue of sex. Believe it or not, we talked about it, a lot, as a matter of fact. But that's all we did, talk about it. I wanted him so bad I didn't think I could control myself. Cody said he wanted me just as much, but he felt that it would make things more difficult when he left. For both of us. Damn, if he didn't have self-discipline!"

"About the sex?" Kathy asked. "Or about leaving town?"

Christine laughed. "Both. You see, he'd had his trip to Nashville planned for over a year. So we never had sex until the last week before he left town. And even then I kinda felt like I tricked him. I mean, I told him since he was leaving in a few days, I was giving him a proper send-off whether he liked it or not. I suppose he could have turned me down, but he didn't. Then after that first time, oh my gosh, we just didn't do much else those days before he left. And my, oh my, we got plenty of that done! No regrets. None at all. I replay those days over and over when I lie in bed at night. That was the best week of my life.

"But even then I could tell he was holding something back. I think he was worried things between us would get too serious. That he wouldn't be able to go out and live his dreams. And that if he got too involved with me—if he really let himself fall head over heels—we would go ahead and get married, have kids, and then twenty years from now, he'd still be singin' at the Blueroom Cafe. And I'd still be tending bar. He felt like he had to get outta Albuquerque if he was serious about his career. And I think he felt like our relationship might prevent that from happening.

"I didn't want to press things too far. I didn't want that to happen. So I just chilled. Or tried to, anyway. I brought up the future several times, and he always seemed optimistic. He said he'd never been in love with anyone else but me, and he knew our relationship was genuine. He even said he'd send me a plane ticket to Nashville as soon as he got settled and had some steady work. I know in the deepest part of my heart he truly meant that."

Christine leaned forward on the porch swing. "That's why I know something's happened. I wish now that I had pushed a little harder. I could have gone on to Nashville with him right off the bat. Hindsight is 20/20."

The two women sat in silence for a moment. Then Christine spoke up.

"You know, Cody told me about this wise proverb he learned from his grandfather. 'If it's meant to be, you can't stop it. If it's not meant to be, you can't make it happen.' He was a pretty strong Christian, and tried to live his life like he was taught in church. His folks were good people. Once his dad died, his mother worked her fingers to the bone to keep him in clean clothes and food on the table. Then she got cancer."

Kathy nodded sympathetically. "You know, from what you tell me, he sounds like quite an impressive young man. Very few people his age, in that business, have the emotional maturity and stability to be able to plan their life in such a manner. He loved you, Christine. That much is obvious. And I think he *did* intend on bringing you to Nashville. No way was he just saying that to pacify you."

Her friend's reassurance put a warm glow in Christine's growing belly. She had not given up and she never would. And this baby was God's most precious gift; it had given her the strength and courage to go on.

"I think you're right," Kathy was saying. "I think we should go down to the police department and file a missing person's report. Do you know if he has any living relatives?"

"Not a one. That's what's so bizarre. Same for me. We're both only children, and none of our parents had any siblings that we know of. So we have no relatives at all."

"Let's try one thing before we go to the police. Let's use our local resources first. How about we start making a list of people that we both know from church and the post office, and see about printing out some handbills and flyers? We'll get the word out. Who knows? We might turn up some clues on where he is and what's going on. Might even get the local TV stations to pick it up and give some regional coverage."

"I would have done that already, Kath, but I've been so hung up about this baby. I'm starting to show now, and I'm paranoid or self-conscious. I'm afraid how this will look to everybody else. Here we have a young gal who just turned up PG, and her boyfriend has left town hitchhiking, and now the poor thing's trying to track him down. I'm afraid it'll look like I'm chasing down child support. I know I have a hang-up about it, but it's really getting to me."

"I completely understand," Kathy said. "But just stop and think for a minute. You can't and you mustn't let what people think affect what you know in your heart you must do. And that is to find Cody. It's way more important to find your sweetie than to worry about what someone else thinks."

Christine nodded. "Kath, you're exactly right. You always know the right thing to say and do. Let's get a list going. I don't want to wait another minute."

65

WITHIN A DAY OR TWO, Kathy and Christine had fifty volunteers lined up for a Saturday search. They printed up fliers at the Quick Copy print shop with Cody's picture on them.

MISSING
CODY BRITTON. LAST SEEN JULY 11.
IF YOU KNOW ANYTHING ABOUT HIS WHERABOUTS,
PLEASE CALL OUR HOTLINE AT 505-555-1000.
REWARD OFFERED.

The girls hadn't thought about the details of the reward. They figured they would cross that bridge when they came to it.

A lot of the regulars from the Blueroom Cafe showed up at nine o'clock that Saturday morning. Christine recognized many of them, most by name. She felt a little self-conscious with her poochy tummy, but Kathy kept reminding her that it simply didn't matter. Even so, it was difficult to wrap her head around all the implications.

Chet Fisher, one of the oldest regulars at the Blueroom, broke the ice by asking the obvious.

"Christine, I didn't know you and Cody really had a thing going, but—" His eyes dropped to her belly. "Guess so, huh? That's crazy how he just disappeared on you. I haven't kept up with what's goin' on since Roddy closed his doors."

Christine looked at Kathy. This was the very thing she had feared. If she was going to set the record straight, the time was now or never.

Christine turned around and looked Chet straight in the eyes.

"Chet, let's get one thing straight. Cody didn't run out on me. When Roddy decided to shut the Blueroom down, Cody had already made his plans. He left for Nashville, to make music in Music City and live out his dream. Yes, we had a close relationship, and I was going to move there with him as soon as he got settled. I heard from him once, but now I have good reason to believe that something bad has happened. Before we start to tear Nashville apart, we thought we'd comb this area and make sure we didn't leave any stones uncovered. Now are you in or are you out?"

"I'm in," Chet said, a little sheepishly. "I'm here today to help in any way I can. I thought a lot of Cody, and I'll do anything I can to help you."

"Thanks, Chet. We're gonna do this every Saturday this month and if nothing turns up, we'll contact the police. We'd love it if you help spread the word. The more people we have looking, the better our chances."

Christine breathed a sigh of relief as she glanced over at Kathy. That hadn't been so bad. She saw Kathy smile and mouth the words, "I told you so." Christine's self-confidence soared.

Kathy was the group spokesperson. She first thanked the crowd for showing up and gave a brief overview of their goal. Many in the group were totally unaware that Cody had even left town. Since the Blueroom closed, many of the regulars had migrated to Dovies several miles down the road, where a jukebox made a poor substitute for live music. There were a few who immediately offered words of encouragement to Christine.

"Listen, Christine. There's a real good chance he got hammered with interest and is running in circles trying to get his feet planted on the ground. I bet he'll be sending for you any day."

Kathy was sure those words felt good to Christine, but Kathy still wanted to protect her. "Well, that certainly is a possibility," Kathy said, "but we're trying not to get false hopes up. Christine did get one card from him in Texas, so we know he's not around here. It was postmarked from Amarillo. Just thought we'd pass out these fliers all over the county and see if we can dig up any info that someone might have about who picked him up from here or where they were going."

Kathy had an organized system in place for the canvassing. Each member of the search party left armed with a stack of fliers and a staple gun, with specific instructions on what part of town they were to cover. By day's end, they had put up two thousand notices all over metro Albuquerque. Every time a question was asked about the handbill, each volunteer had the opportunity to spread the word about Cody Britton.

Christine and Kathy took the establishments located near all I-40 exits for fifty miles east of town. Truck stops, restaurants, gas stations, and markets were their primary targets. Both girls thought this was their best chance at picking up clues, so they spent time at each location speaking with people. They got no useful information. By dusk, Kathy was exhausted and Christine was dejected.

"Now honey, you listen to me," Kathy said. "What was your hope and intent today? It wasn't like we were expecting to find him having coffee with a truck driver at a gas station. You know how much territory we covered today? We hit twenty-two interstate exits! I'll bet you somebody calls that hotline in the next week to let us know they recognized his face. We'll just have to wait on our clues. Sometimes things don't happen at the time you want them to."

Christine knew Kathy was right, but she needed to hear that message over and over in the coming days. These were fragile times. Cody was constantly on her mind, and sometimes the hopelessness of their mission sank her into a deep depression. It was better during the week when she had things to keep her busy, like the job she'd started working at Red River Hardware.

"Sometimes I don't want to get out of bed," she confided to Kathy, who reminded her it was a completely normal response.

"Anyone in your situation would react this way, honey."

For the next three Saturdays, the poster group gradually grew in numbers, and yet no one produced any viable leads. They'd had several calls to the hotline, but it was just people having seen the number, calling to express concern and to see if any useful information had surfaced.

Then, toward the end of the third Saturday, the hotline received a call from Action 7 News, one of the local television stations in Albuquerque. They were interested in doing an interview with the organizing group looking for Cody. Christine scheduled the interview for the following day.

66

SHARON GILLESPIE KNOCKED on Christine's door promptly at 7 p.m. Kathy was there to answer. "Christine? Hi, I'm Sharon Gillespie from Action 7 News."

"I'm Kathy, actually. A friend of Christine's. Please come in."

Kathy ushered Sharon into the living room where Christine stood to greet her. "Hi, Sharon. I'm Christine Browning. I spoke with you yesterday. It's so good to meet you."

Sharon went through her normal routine of gathering the facts regarding Cody Britton's disappearance three months before. As luck would have it, Sharon had been to the Blueroom Cafe right before it closed with a couple of girlfriends, and she remembered Cody's velvet voice. "Oh yes. Do I ever remember him?"

Sharon soon realized that neither girl was optimistic about Cody's whereabouts.

"I'm already the lucky girl," Christine said. "We were going to get married. I hope and pray each day that we can find out what's happened to him and that he can be with me when his baby is born."

This was heavier than Sharon had expected. She quickly redirected the tone of the interview to strike a more serious and somber note. "So his last known whereabouts were in Amarillo, Texas—he sent you a card in the mail that was postmarked from there, correct? And he had confirmed on that he was hitchhiking with two guys heading back to their home in Nashville, right?"

"Yes, that's right. No contact with him since then and it's been over three months. We've started by blanketing the area in case someone saw him or has heard from him. It's not likely, but we thought it was the first place to start. He has no next of kin, so we haven't reported him to police as officially missing yet. The whole thing is a little weird since we weren't married. He doesn't even know I'm pregnant."

Christine cringed inside as she thought how this must sound to someone who didn't know all the facts of the situation.

"I see." Sharon looked up from the notes she was taking on her legal pad. "But he was going to send for you as soon as he got situated in Nashville, right?"

"Yes, that's correct."

"Do you have any contacts in Nashville who could help you follow there?"

"I don't even know anyone who has *been* to Nashville. All I've done is subscribe to a weekly paper called *The Scene*. It's supposed to be the latest on what's happening in Nashville and who is playing where and when. I comb each page weekly to see if there's a guy named Britt playing. He said that was going to be his stage name. But so far, nothing."

"Has his picture been circulated? Anywhere besides the telephone poles and local business establishments?"

"No. I've wondered what would be the best way to proceed. We had a very serious relationship for two years, and the public doesn't realize that."

"Who cares what anyone thinks. We have a man who has gone

missing in Albuquerque and that requires police notification and media coverage. That's the only way to find out what's going on. Let's get this story running!"

Sharon snapped her legal pad closed. "I'll have this on the news tomorrow. I'll also have someone from APD call. If you're okay with it, I'll be back tomorrow with a camera crew and we'll shoot some footage. Now don't worry, we don't have to say a word about anybody being pregnant unless you want to."

Christine thanked Sharon and walked her to the door. Both she and Kathy had a good feeling about the situation. At last, they were going to get some professional help in trying to locate Cody. Christine couldn't have been more pleased.

Time dragged by slowly at Red River Hardware the following day, as each hour was a step closer to the first media coverage of Cody's disappearance. It had been scheduled for the six o'clock news. Following that would be a video interview and fact-finding session with a detective from Albuquerque's Missing Persons Bureau. Christine insisted that Kathy be present. Christine had spent more time with Kathy than Melvin had over the last month, and she was grateful her friend's husband was so understanding. Fortunately, Melvin's post office position kept him occupied most of the time, and sports on ESPN filled up the rest of his day. He also struggled with a chronic heart problem, which meant he couldn't participate in much outdoor activity anyway. Kathy said the sports channels were good for him. "Adult pacifiers," she called them. "If my baby can't play sports because of his heart, at least he can watch them on TV!"

Kathy and Christine waited anxiously for the six o'clock news. Sharon Gillespie opened the segment with the short blurb on the mysterious disappearance of Cody Britton. All the details that made Christine uneasy were graciously left out of the news piece, as Sharon had assured her they would be.

The viewers were urged to tune in the following day for a more detailed report of the missing man, and what role local police would play in tracking his disappearance.

"Well, Ms. Browning," Kathy said when the segment was finished. "That was quite an impressive, objective account of our problem. Do you feel okay about it?"

"I do. Sharon is great, isn't she? So kind and helpful. It gives me a little more peace about it. But it also gets my hopes up, and I know you reminded me to be careful about letting that happen."

"Well, we're all just human. Just handle it the best you can. You and I can talk about this anytime you want. I'm here for you. Melvin is, too. It's probably easier to talk to me, though." She laughed. "You know men!"

Both girls giggled. "You better get ready for the interview," Kathy said, squeezing her arm. Within the hour, Sharon was back over at Christine's apartment. Kathy thanked her for her gracious and sensitive coverage of this unusual situation. Sharon acknowledged its importance.

Within fifteen minutes, the interview was complete and Christine felt good about it. "You were great," Sharon said. "I think Detective Clay Newman will be here in about thirty minutes. I'm supposed to call him now that we're finished. Can I use your phone?"

"I'm sorry. I don't have a phone. I think it's time I get one though. Couldn't really afford one before."

Sharon nodded. "That'd be a good idea. I know Cody won't have the number, but you do need to be able to be reached easily. If I were you, I'd just get a mobile phone. They're not that expensive."

Christine liked the idea of referring to Cody in the present tense. It made her feel like others still held out hope that he was alive. She just wasn't so sure herself. No one knew Cody like she did. It was totally impossible, from her point of view, for him not to get in touch with her for ninety days . . . unless something bad had happened to him.

Christine took Sharon's advice. By noon the next day, she was sporting her first Motorola mobile phone. Every day she prayed it would ring and Cody would be on the other end, although she knew it was impossible. Even if he were miraculously unharmed, how would he have her number?

In the meantime, her tummy was getting larger by the day. The excitement of her baby kept her going.

Several months went by and Christine's little pooch was turning into a watermelon. She continued with her regular exercise programs, got good reports from her doctor, and barely gained fifteen pounds.

It didn't take Christine long to stop worrying about how her pastor and a few friends might react to her pregnancy. In fact, the entire community was overwhelmingly supportive. She received an outpouring of love; a number of people from the church even promised to use their regional influence in the search for Cody, assuring her they would do everything they could to help Christine with the case.

The next few months were some of the most pleasurable moments in her life. She enjoyed her job at Red River Hardware, and she was lucky to have very few pregnancy side effects. Kathy had become her soul mate and thanked Melvin every day for sharing her with Christine.

"Kathy, I've been thinking for a long time about what to name this baby," Christine said one day. "You know, if it's a boy, I think we name him after his dad, like 'Junior.' Only we'll call him Britt. That's what Cody said he wanted to be called when he made it big in Nashville. If it's a girl, I think we'll name her Brittany."

Kathy stretched sleepily as she repositioned herself on Christine's sofa. Kathy mothered her like a hen. She was practically old enough to be Christine's mother then she might as well act like it.

"I think that's a wonderful idea. The one thing I learned in raising my three was this: the only person you have to please in picking out names is the mama and daddy. In your case, the mama. Personally, I love those names, but as long as you are happy with them, nothing else matters. And I think Cody would like them."

"I'm so lucky to have you, Kath. You're the mom I never had, at least in a long time. Will you go with me when it's time to go to the hospital?"

"Will I go? Is that what you said, *will* I go?" Kathy asked. "You're not having that baby without me, young lady! Deal?"

Christine grinned. "Deal."

67

CHRISTINE'S WATER BROKE three days before her projected delivery date. As she groped for the Motorola on her bedside dresser, she said a quick prayer, thanking God that she'd listened to Sharon and bought a mobile phone. Kathy was the first person she called.

"Kath. Oh Kath. My water just broke. I'm a little spooked right now. Can you come over?"

"On my way."

One quick look at her bed sheets let Kathy know it was time to head for the Hospital. "Hey, we're gonna get to use this little overnight bag we packed a few weeks ago just a little sooner than I thought."

"What would I do without you, Kath?" Christine laughed and tottered slowly to the door. No sense in getting dressed, since they'd just put her in a hospital gown.

The ten-minute ride to the hospital was uneventful. Kathy helped with the paperwork at admissions and got her a bed assignment. Christine's preliminary exam showed her at eight and one half centimeters. "Girl, you're not wasting any time, are you? Good thing you got that mobile phone!"

"No kidding!" Christine was so glad to have Kathy there for support.

Like a prince announcing his most dramatic arrival, Mr. Cody Jay Britton, Jr. weighed in at eight pounds one ounce, and was nineteen inches long. Kathy was the midwife, for all practical purposes.

On the third day, mom and baby boy were discharged and happily situated at home with Kathy serving as a full-time nurse. Kathy and Melvin had raised three boys, but never had any grandchildren. For Kathy this was the perfect opportunity to nurture the grandbaby she'd never had. From day one they were practically inseparable.

Britt was a wonderfully cooperative baby. He slept through the night by week four. Christine spent hours in a rocking chair by the baby bed, just staring at her present from God. Sometimes she put her trusty old cassette player in her lap and played the tape of Cody singing *"I Will Return."* She must have played it five thousand times, and the quality was becoming poor. But it was precious music to her ears. *"I Will Return"* was not only the last song Cody ever recorded—it was the last one he ever sang. For the next decade, it would be Christine and Little Britt's national anthem. Their promise for the future. Because in their heart of hearts, each of them hoped that Cody and Daddy would return.

Christine's love for Cody was so strong that even though she hadn't heard a word from him since the first postcard, she still held out hope he would send for her. The unknown nagged at her, but it was better, at that point in her life, to live in uncertainty than to receive the final news of what had truly happened to her love.

She had three special pieces framed, matted, and hung over Britt's bed. First was the postcard from Amarillo, a handwritten lyric Cody had copied down from his songwriting book and given to her the night he left, the words to *"I Will Return."* and a beautiful oil portrait Christine had composed from a photograph back when Cody sang at the Blueroom.

These three mementos would provide Christine a comfort she would lean on for the rest of her life.

By the time Britt was four months old, Christine was ready to reenter civilization. She had thought about going back to work at Red River, and she knew Kathy would love to serve as chief nanny. One day the subject arose naturally, and it was actually Kathy who brought it up.

"Have you given any thought to going back to work?"

"As a matter of fact, I have. I was just going to talk to you about that."

"Well, before you say another word: I want to be the nanny or babysitter or whatever you want to call me. I'm not trying to push you back to work too fast, but I'm just going on record as saying I want to apply for the position. And by the way, my pay rate is zero dollars per hour. Doubt you'll get any offers to beat that rate. Slightly below union scale, ma'am, but I really want the job!"

"Very funny!" Christine teased. "You knew you had it in the bag. You didn't even have to apply!"

"I've got something for Mr. Britt," she said, and pulled out a most unusual baby gift: a high-quality video camera.

"Oh my gosh," Christine said. "Kathy! You shouldn't have. This is too much."

"Nonsense. How else are you going to record Britt's life?"

Christine's eyes filled with tears at the thought that someday, Cody would come back, and when he did he would be able to watch a video anthology of his son's early years. She tried not to set herself up for ultimate disappointment, but now that the bliss of the pregnancy was over, she found herself increasingly depressed about Cody's disappearance.

Kathy and Melvin had come along at a critical time in Christine's life. The age difference turned out to be perfect: Kathy truly was her mother or big sister Christine never had. And now God had blessed her with yet another gift: the knowledge that her precious son would be well cared for by her best friend.

"Thank you," she said softly.

"Of course!" Kathy replied, thinking she meant the video camera when really it was Kathy's friendship that Christine was most grateful for.

Within two weeks, Christine was back at Red River Hardware. The first few days felt liberating. It was her first contact with civilization since Britt had been born. In four short months, a lot of things looked different. For starters, she hadn't driven her VW and had almost forgotten the gearshift pattern. The old Beetle had been one of Cody's favorite toys to tinker with, and she would never sell it. It always reminded her of Cody. It was in this very car that Cody had kissed her for the very first time. But then everything reminded her of Cody.

68

DURING HER FIRST WEEK BACK, Christine called Kathy every hour. Kathy was amused at her instant motherly instinct that had kicked in the moment Christine gave birth. She'd never seen this side of her friend before. But then, Christine had never been a mother before.

After Christine mentioned that Red River had a bowling team, Kathy convinced her to go to the Thursday night social gatherings at the alley.

"I don't want my nanny to feel like I'm taking advantage of her!" Christine cried.

Kathy just smiled. "Nanny is for keeps, remember? I won't even charge time and a half!"

Both girls agreed it was good for Christine to get out, so she began her weekly trips to Double Strike Bowling Center. The camaraderie with other people her age was healthy, especially at that point in her life.

Before anyone realized where time was going, Britt celebrated his first birthday. Kathy organized everything, made a personalized cake and invited four or five of their friends from church and work. Two others brought their toddlers, but mostly it was adults celebrating. Britt was starting to develop his motor skills, giving him limitless access to all the rooms.

Soon Kathy started taking him to the church daycare one day a week. She really didn't want to give up her full-time nanny position, but she also realized that little Britt needed some interaction with other kids.

The Red River bowling league turned out to be a great idea, one that really helped Christine reconnect with society. One guy on their team, named Jerry Cantrell, worked in the plumbing department. He wanted to sit beside her on bowling nights. The two had been friends back in the day when she worked at the Blueroom, and he was a good friend of Cody's. In the last few months of their bowling league, Christine was pretty sure Jerry was coming on to her. She was trying to figure out whether she should be sad or glad. Mostly she was confused. She was still using all her resources to look for Cody.

Surely Kathy would know what to do.

"Look, darlin'," she said when Christine asked her advice. "Look in the mirror. Can you tell what beautiful looks like? You remember that hit that Sammy Kershaw had a few years back, *She Don't Know She's Beautiful?* That's you. My point is, you shouldn't be surprised. And as far as it being Jerry, who was pretty good friends with Cody? You gotta let that issue go!

"If you're lonesome at the same time he's lonesome and you happen to be around each other at that moment, be willing to take your friendship to the next level. And if nothing happens beyond just being friends, you could still use a friend."

Christine nodded slowly, recognizing the truth in what her friend was saying. She smiled. "Kath, sometimes I think you know me better than I know myself."

The next Thursday Jerry made his move. At the end of the

third game, fifteen minutes before they were wrapping up, he approached Christine.

"Hey there," he said, trying to mask his nervousness. "Would you be interested in having a beer with me? There's something I'd like to ask you."

"Jerry, that's great. Kathy's with Britt tonight so I'm open."

Christine was glad Jerry didn't smoke—it meant they got to sit at the corner of the 11th Frame Bar and Lounge that was a designated No Smoking Section. He ordered a Miller Lite and she ordered a Corona.

"Thanks for meeting me, Christine. This is a little weird, 'cause I don't want to appear presumptuous. But I have looked at you a little differently in the last few months. We've known each other for over ten years. I know it's a little weird since I was pretty tight with Cody. Some would say that's great, and others would say no way. But what I'm trying to say is . . . you are a fun person to be around. And the fact that we've known each other for longer than average?" He grinned. "I feel like a babbling idiot right about now."

"Jerry, I understand. I feel exactly the same way. You have spent several Saturdays helping me get info on Cody. You are a precious friend, and I appreciate that more than you could ever know.

"But I want to be honest. Right now, my full attention is focused on trying to find out what happened to Cody. I don't know what tomorrow holds, but I'm trying hard to trust in God and let him guide my path. I hope you understand that. Let's just see what happens and take one day at a time. Without knowing for sure what happened to Cody, what other choice do we have?"

Albuquerque Police continued to keep Cody Britton as a high priority. It had become universally accepted that Cody was nowhere in the desert southwest. The postcard caused most of the law's attention to be focused on a line from Amarillo, Texas to Nashville, Tennessee. Missing Persons reports were filed in all major cities in between the two.

It had become obvious to Christine that the farther one got away from Albuquerque, the more difficult it was to get help. Other people thought this was just another runaway country singer wannabe. That might not have been the true picture, but since nothing seemed to be happening, it became more and more futile for Christine to try and tell it the way it was.

She had already realized that the chances of solving a Missing Persons case dropped like a rock after the first year. After that, it was reviewed on a "space available only" basis. It broke Christine's heart. The last thing she wanted anyone to do was forget about looking for Cody.

No matter what happened, she knew she never would.

69

AT THE PRELIMINARY HEARING in the murder trial of Cody Doe, two special agents of the Tennessee Bureau of Investigation, Bruce Akers and Wayne Hartley, were questioned by Davidson County District Attorney Dennis Whisnant, and Public Defender George Martin. Jurisdiction was assigned to Davidson County, though the particulars occurred in several counties and states. It would prove to be a difficult and most unusual hearing, since no one knew who it was the defendants had killed.

Both the DA and the Public Defender labored together as they tried to determine what the fairest way to proceed was. Both sides knew it would be a difficult task to find a sympathetic jury, with no grieving relatives in the courtroom. Whisnant was trying to understand how the body of the hitchhiker was misidentified as Clint Logan in the first place.

"Agent Akers," attorney Whisnant asked, "have you heard of a case where a murder occurred and the body was misidentified?"

"No, sir."

"How is it possible that misidentification could occur?"

"It had to be human error, sir."

"Who made this misidentification in this case?"

"Dr. Arthur Templeton, the forensic pathologist that Dickson County used."

"In burn cases, don't investigators use dental records to confirm identity?"

"Yes, sir."

"Does the State of Tennessee have a forensic dentist?"

"Yes, sir. Dr. Chris Walsh."

"Was Dr. Walsh consulted in this case?"

"No, sir, he was not. Dr. Templeton did this portion himself," Agent Akers responded.

"Do you know why Dr. Walsh was not consulted?"

"No, sir, I do not."

The questioning of the special agents went on for three hours, after which Dr. Templeton was called to the stand.

"Dr. Templeton, can you tell the court exactly how you made the determination that the burned body in this case was that of Clint Logan?" Attorney Whisnant asked.

"Through dental records," Dr. Templeton said.

"Are you certain that you have made the correct identification in this matter?"

"Obviously since Clint Logan is alive, he and the decedent must have similar dental records."

"Isn't it true, Dr. Templeton, that dental records are as unique to an individual as fingerprints?"

"That's usually the case, but there is always a chance for duplication. I suspect what happened is Clint Logan extracted one of his own teeth and placed it in the decedent's mouth before blowing up the car."

The D.A.'s jaw dropped. Everyone was shocked by the doctor's statement.

"Sir, let me just confirm to the court, and let the record reflect that your testimony is that Mr. Clint Logan had to have extracted one of his own teeth and placed in the decedent's mouth. Just to reconfirm, sir, is that your testimony?"

With no hesitation in his answer, Templeton said, "That's correct."

"Dr. Templeton, do you usually use a forensic dentist to assist you with identification in cases such as this one?"

"Sometimes I use Dr. Chris Walsh, but it wasn't necessary in this case. It was so cut and dried that I performed the diagnostics myself."

"Did you examine the ante-mortem X-rays of Clint Logan?"

"Yes, I did."

"Did you examine the post-mortem X-rays to compare to Logan's X-rays?"

"No, I did it visually," Dr. Templeton answered.

"Dr. Templeton, is it not the proper standard of care to take X-rays of the body to compare with those you are trying to match?"

"As I said, I did it visually."

"Dr. Templeton, do you own a piece of X-ray equipment in your office?"

"No, I do not."

A few people in the courtroom gasped.

"One final question, Dr. Templeton. Our testimony from both defendants, Logan and Scott, indicates that the victim was killed some two to three days before the car was crashed and set on fire," the DA continued. "Your autopsy report indicates that there was black soot found in the trachea and one of the causes of death was from smoke inhalation. Can you please explain this to the court?"

"They're both lying. The decedent was breathing when the car caught fire."

"No further questions, your honor."

The final questioning brought Dr. Chris Walsh to the stand. The court officer went through the routine formalities of expert witness testimony.

"Dr. Walsh, you are the chief forensic odontologist for the Tennessee State Medical Examiner's Office?"

"Yes, sir, I am."

"And for how long have you held this position, Dr. Walsh?"

"Since 1983."

"Exactly what role did you have in this ID . . . or shall we say 'mis-ID'?"

"Dr. Stanley Gowen, associate forensic anthropologist for the Body Farm, and I have presented programs and worked together on cases for many years. I received a call from Dr. Gowen requesting a forensic dental consult to determine the identity of a Cody Doe they had received from DeKalb County Sheriff's Department.

"I traveled to Knoxville on several occasions for work on this case with anthropology before the body was ultimately retained in Nashville. That happens to be the facility where I work."

"Dr. Walsh, is it true that when you joined on this case, you already knew that the body was not Clint Logan? Then your task has been to find out who it really is, is that correct?"

"That's correct."

"And you had no role in the identification of this body when it was first retrieved approximately eighteen months ago?"

"That is correct, sir."

"And you still have no idea who this person is?"

"That is correct, sir. I've compared lots of possibilities whose families sent records for us to compare to the skeleton's X-rays we took. So far, no match. We know lots of people that it's not, but don't know who it is."

"How many teeth were recovered?"

"Seven."

"And you feel reasonably sure that seven teeth present and twenty-five missing will be enough evidence to make a positive ID? Even though, that is, it seems to have already been done once, albeit incorrectly. Do you agree, Dr. Walsh?"

"Sir, I'd prefer not to editorialize, but I do believe that it is possible for seven teeth to provide enough ID markers to confirm the identity. It depends on the clinical description of the fillings or crowns that are on these seven teeth. It sounds elementary, but if we can find the dental X-rays of this person before he or she died, we can positively correlate it with Cody's X-rays very quickly. We haven't run across that person's X-rays yet!"

"Can you tell us exactly what you mean by 'an ID marker'?"

"An ID marker is a point of comparison on a single tooth whose filling or shape configuration is consistent."

"And how many of those ID markers are necessary to confirm a person's identity?"

Walsh paused a moment. "We try to get as many markers as possible. It just strengthens a case. Sometimes you can get twenty; sometimes only three. The more markers you have, the stronger the evidence.

"What happens frequently in a John Doe ID case," Walsh went on, "is that you are looking for an 'unexplainable discrepancy' which might be a single marker that doesn't match that would eliminate that person from consideration. For example, if Cody has a filling in tooth number 14, and the missing person's X-rays submitted show that in their case tooth number 14 is missing, then that person can be immediately eliminated. A permanent tooth will not grow back once it has been extracted. All it takes is one of those to rule them out."

"One final question, Dr. Walsh. How often is it that you are never able to determine the identity of an unknown person?"

"There are about six bodies each year that get buried in Nashville in a section of the City Cemetery. These bodies all get a proper burial, even though their identity is unknown. Their case numbers are carefully gridded and named either John or Jane Doe. All information about each case is cross referenced and documented to allow easy retrieval if needed."

"That's all I have, your honor."

70

THE NEXT PERSON on the stand was Amy Logan. After swearing in procedures were completed, Amy made herself comfortable for questioning.

Whisnant went first. "Mrs. Logan, is it true that you had no knowledge of this murder for insurance proceeds until after it was committed?"

"Yes sir. That is correct. All I knew was that J.D. and my husband Clint decided to go on a 'boys' trip to Las Vegas. On my money! I had been putting some money back for a rainy day, and Clint stole all of it before he left. He called me later, saying he would repay me, but no mention about murdering somebody. I had already decided I'd had just about enough of his antics. He'd been arrested for selling drugs and served six months. He'd just been laid off at work. I'll admit I'd gotten so frustrated at his not making any effort to make this marriage work.

"Then I get a visit from Sheriff Roswell saying my husband has been killed in a car wreck. The following evening after several friends come to our home to offer their condolences, the boys show up at the back door near midnight. Nearly scared the life out of me! I had already been thinking that one or both of them was dead!"

"Then what happened?"

"Clint starts telling me some about their predicament and how he wants me to partner with them and help with some conspiracy to fake his death and to collect a life insurance policy that I had taken out on him at work."

"So you refused to participate?"

"I knew it was wrong, but honestly, I didn't know which direction to turn. It was either cooperate with his plan, which I didn't want to do, or turn them both in for first degree murder. I couldn't do that either. I've known J.D. all my life and really feel like he got placed into this mess the way I did, just on a different level. I didn't want him going away for life ... or worse."

"Is it true that you have agreed upon immunity in exchange for your testimony, as agreed upon by the Public Defender and District Attorney?"

"Yes, sir."

"Can you tell the court your involvement with the murder?"

"None! Like I said, sir, I had absolutely no involvement with any murder whatsoever! My crime was only the time I spent deciding whether to report my husband and his friend, or help 'em cover it up some way and collect the life insurance money. I know this sounds cold and cruel, but when your husband and his best friend tell you that they killed somebody who has no name, and you know absolutely nothing else about the incident, and don't want to know, it almost seemed like they ran over some animal and were trying to get rid of the blood stains on the fender. But your honor, I do regret lying to the insurance company and getting a cent of that money."

"The $250,000 from the Pioneer Life Insurance Company?"

"Yes."

"Go on..."

"I have never known anything about any of the details, other than what I already said. I heard one of them talk about a bungee cord, but I promise, I do not even have any idea which one committed the murder. Maybe neither one of 'em. Maybe there's more to the story. I don't know."

"That's all we have, your Honor." Whisnant concluded.

"I have nothing more, your Honor." Martin concurred.

71

As AMY WAS BEING escorted from the courtroom, she passed J.D. in the hallway. He was being escorted to the courtroom for questioning. She smiled at him. This was the first time they had seen each other since Clint was arrested outside the Lake Motel. J.D. smiled and then looked down in dejection as he walked awkwardly between metal shackles that restrained his every movement. His hands were cuffed in an elaborate fashion using a metal pipe for reinforcement.

After swearing in was complete, legal dialogue began.

"Mr. Scott, would you please state your complete name for the court?"

"Yes, sir. It is Jimmy Dale Scott."

Whisnant proceeded immediately with his points.

"Is it true, Mr. Scott, that you and Mr. Clint Logan conspired to kill an unnamed and yet to be identified man in exchange for a $250,000 life insurance policy held on the life of a Mr. Clint Logan?"

"No sir. I did not conspire on anything. Clint had mentioned something about collecting life insurance money on his death, but the whole plot to the story was so complicated, I had a hard time following. All I can tell you is that we did kill a man, that is, Clint killed him. We picked him up off I-40 somewhere near Albuquerque, New Mexico. He was headed for Nashville, and Clint thought we could kill him and make him look like Clint. That's where I got lost in the plans, but I did go ahead and follow Clint's idea. I knew we was doin' wrong, but I drove the car while Clint choked him with a bungee cord."

"What would you say if I told you that Clint claims that you killed this hitchhiker, and that he had nothing to do with the idea?"

"Sir, I didn't even know a thing about life insurance 'fore we left for Vegas. I didn't even know anything about gambling in casinos. I couldn't organize a plan like this by myself."

The courtroom was deathly silent. It certainly was a believable statement.

"Did you and Clint have a discussion about who was going to 'take the fall' for this murder?"

"I'm sorry, sir, but I don't know what you mean by 'take the fall.'"

"Who was going to admit to killing the victim?"

"No sir. We never had a conversation about ever getting caught. He just kept telling me to quit worrying about stuff. He just kept saying to follow his orders, and pretty soon, I'd have more money than I could ever spend. I know it was wrong, your Honor. I've already asked God to forgive me, and that poor man. He didn't deserve to die."

"That's all I have, your Honor." Whisnant concluded.

"I have nothing further, your Honor." Martin agreed.

The final interrogation led J.D. right past an escorted Clint who glared stoically at J.D. He saw nothing but J.D.'s head, as it was hung down so low.

After Clint's swearing in was completed, Attorney Whisnant opened with his questioning.

"Please state your full name for the court."

Clint sat up tall cleared his voice, and said, "Sir, my name is Clint Alton Logan."

"Mr. Logan, I'd like to show you a photograph and ask for your explanation. Your Honor, I'd request this be registered as Exhibit 26."

With both sides approving, the color 8x10 was passed to Clint. It was a close-up photo of a tombstone of Clint Alton Logan, complete with flowers, birth date and date of death. Clint studied it briefly, and hung his head in shame.

"Can you please tell the court what this is a picture of, Mr. Logan?"

"It's a picture of my tombstone."

"Whose idea was it to place another human being's body in your grave?"

"I guess mine, sir. But I did not kill Cody. J.D. killed him."

"Who had life insurance to gain if Clint Logan was dead?"

"Me. I mean my wife, Amy."

"Excuse me, Mr. Logan. A man was killed and you don't know who got the money?"

"We got the money; all of us. But I did not kill Cody. J.D. choked him with a bungee cord."

"Who told you his name was 'Cody'?"

"He did. We talked to him for a while as we drove across Texas."

"What was Cody's last name?"

"No idea. He never said."

Clint's questioning was the shortest of anyone that day. Finally, the two attorneys asked the judge for a recess until morning.

The two attorneys sat opposite each other in a conference

room and stared at each other. Usually they were bitter enemies when court was in session, and many people didn't realize that they were best of friends.

"Well, George. This one's a pickle. I gotta be honest with you—I don't know if we can successfully prosecute this at a Murder One level and have a jury issue a true bill. We have no family or friends in the audience. We might both lose this case! This is the damndest thing I've ever seen in my life!" He laughed to himself. "This case has got so many twists to it."

"Dennis, you took the words right out of my mouth. I don't think I can defend either one of them either. This is nuts!"

"George, if I ask for murder one, they may not go for it since we don't have definite proof on either one. We have a confession, but look how many times James Earl Ray recanted his testimony and confession. Wouldn't it be terrible if they found both of 'em 'not guilty' on Murder One; both of these slime balls walk after having confessed to killing this guy?"

"I'm right there with you. Let's go to my office, away from the crowd and kick this around. I've got a new bottle of single malt I'd like to share with you. Sixteen year old Lagavulin."

Dennis nodded with a grin. "Be there in ten minutes."

The private law firm's office gave both men an opportunity to further discuss the particulars of this case. This would be the time where intense negotiation would be critical.

George poured the scotch. It's smoky aroma was like a tulip to Dennis' nose.

"Nothing better than a good single malt!"

"No kidding." George took a light sip, breathed in deeply to absorb all the full aroma.

"What if we got 'em both to plea to second degree with a guaranteed fifteen years to serve? They both would be idiots to turn it down. They think by pointing at the other it will get their sentence lighter."

"I hate to admit it, but right now, it is a plus on their side. We've got to decide if we can get twelve humans to get their arms around killing a ghost. If the ghost had any friends or relatives around, they sure wouldn't go for this, but apparently those people don't exist."

"I agree. Let's go for it!" Both men smiled, toasted their scotch glasses. They knew what they were doing. They also knew that was the quickest they had ever come to an agreement on anything.

"The only thing we have to hope is that Walsh and the new medical examiner can ID this guy soon. It'd be the pits for these guys to get out, and all of us still have no idea who it is that they killed!"

72

Dr. Walsh took Cody's skull back to Nashville. For the next few years, it sat on a shelf in the cooler at the State Medical Examiner's Office. He saw it every week and began to feel like he knew Cody.

Scores of records arrived at the Tennessee Bureau of Investigation offices. The agents made every effort to contact all identification services that exist in the United States and around the world.

Forensic artists were hired to draw facial profiles of Cody based on description's that Clint and Jimmy Dale provided—though it remained unclear whether or not they were being truthful. These artist renderings were nationally distributed to law enforcement offices. A forensic facial reconstructionist used the anatomical landmarks on Cody's skull to compose a sculptor's idea of what his face would have probably looked like.

The work product was stunningly natural. It almost gave a name and soul to Cody's skull.

The specific dental charting showing all the different shapes and sizes of the fillings and crowns in those seven teeth of Cody's were submitted to the newsletter of the Journal of the American

Dental Association, along with a plea to its members to check their files to see if Cody had been their patient.

The TBI also worked closely with a national database in Washington, DC, called the National Crime Information Center. The NCIC instructs law enforcement agencies on how to key code a list of data on missing individuals that might lead to their identification. This data includes unique identifiers such as presence of tattoos, hair color, height, weight, and dental records.

Over the years that followed, Dr. Walsh had many opportunities to compare Cody's teeth with those of hundreds of missing people from all over the world using the NCIC and other databases. None of them matched.

"You know, they called him Cody," they'd say. Cold cases were tough. It was a challenge to the families who grieve daily for their missing loved ones. It was challenging to the investigators who yearned for nothing more than to crack a cold case and finally bring closure to heartbroken families.

They always hoped it would be their man—but each time, it wasn't.

Dr. Walsh looked at dozens of artist renderings from various law enforcement agencies searching for missing people. TBI had employed an aging expert, an artist specializing in projecting what a person might look like ten years later.

"This is an example of what this person looked like; he's missing, and his name was Cody," the investigators would say. Again, no match.

This kind of long haul wasn't atypical. As any investigator who works on cold case files will admit, most of the clues they get are dead ends. To a good investigator who is passionate about their work, handling unsolved cases can be rewarding.

You never know when you're going to get a hit.

73

After more than two years of false leads and disappointments, Special Agent Wayne Hartley received a call that peaked his interest. Out of nowhere, he had some information that truly seemed promising.

"Agent Hartley," a voice on the line said, "my name is Daniel Shelby. My family dentist suggested I call you. It seems that you might be able to help me find my son."

"I certainly hope we can, Mr. Shelby. Tell me what you know."

"Well, my dentist gets a newsletter from the American Dental Association, and last week he clipped a notice in it from your office. It says you've found a body that you can't identify, and that the person was—" Mr. Shelby stopped suddenly. Agent Hartley could hear his breath coming ragged. After a pause, he murmured, "I'm terribly sorry, sir. This is difficult. If we are talking about my son here . . . well, it seems he could have been murdered. This notice says the person you're trying to identify was last seen somewhere in the desert southwest."

"That's correct," Agent Hartley said. "I understand that this is difficult, Mr. Shelby. There's no need to rush. If you can, would you tell me a little about your son, and where he was last seen?"

"He was in medical school at the University of Florida" Mr. Shelby explained, his voice constricted with an odd mixture of pride and pain. "He had just finished his first year, and he had called to tell us he'd packed his car and was on his way home to visit while he had a short break. We're out in western Arizona. He left Florida, where he was in school, on July 10, 1997."

Agent Hartley felt a small surge of adrenaline. The details were starting to add up. "And did you speak to him again after he started his drive?"

Mr. Shelby was silent for a long moment. "No, sir," he said finally. "I'll always regret it."

"Do you know anything about what happened after July 10?" Agent Hartley asked gently.

"I'm afraid I don't. He was driving a light blue Toyota Camry. We've reported it to all law enforcement agencies from Florida to Arizona. No one ever found his car. No one remembers seeing him."

Agent Hartley made a few notes on his legal pad. "Mr. Shelby, I just have one more question for now. What was your son's name?"

"Corey."

Wayne Hartley came bounding into Dr. Walsh's office at his dental practice that afternoon. "Doc!" he exclaimed. "I had to come over here myself. I was too excited to call."

Dr. Walsh looked up and grinned. He was always glad to see Agent Hartley, even if he was starting to get a little less than optimistic about the leads the agents were collecting.

"Whatcha got this time?" Dr. Walsh asked.

"Check this out," Agent Hartley said. He spread a folder with his notes out on Walsh's desk between them and began with details of Corey Shelby's life. "I know you've looked at a million of these, but this one has promise. I swear!" His friendly grin was contagious.

When he was finished, Dr. Walsh leaned back in his chair and rubbed his brows. "You're right," he said. "The timing lines up. The location lines up. Camry, not a Honda, though. May be some reason for that."

"Right," Agent Hartley said. "We've got to do a comparison of dental records. This could be our Cody."

"Did you ask Daniel Shelby to send over his sons records?"

"I did," Agent Hartley said. "But get this. He's convinced this is his missing son. He said this is the closest he's ever come to getting some answers. He wants to fly out here with the records, so he can be here when you do the comparison."

"No." Dr. Walsh said quickly. "Let's just get him to overnight the records like we handle all the other cases. We just can't do that to him. If it turns out it's not a match, it'll be like the poor man is losing his son all over again."

"I agree," Agent Hartley said. "I'll call him back and see if I can convince him to stay there and overnight the records. I'm not sure, though, I can physically prevent him from seeing this through to fruition."

Agent Hartley, unfortunately, was unsuccessful. Mr. Shelby's heart had already been filled with hope, and he couldn't let it go. He wanted to be present so that he could return immediately to Arizona with his son's remains and give him a proper burial.

Two days later, Mr. Shelby arrived at the Tennessee State Medical Examiner's Office with his son's x-rays. "Good afternoon, gentlemen. My name is Daniel Shelby. I'm so happy to meet you." The trio each introduced themselves to the spirited father.

Walsh broke the ice. "We are so sorry that your family has suffered this long with uncertainty. It must be a gnawing that never goes away."

"Thanks for understanding. It has been a rough ride for the

wife and I. Here are all his dental records since birth. I just hope and pray that we can get some closure soon." He handed the manila envelope to Walsh containing radiographs and clinical notes.

Walsh heart sank as he heard the voice of hope in Shelby's voice. "Let's go inside the office and have a look. I have already made notes of the decedent's dental charting. To tell you the truth, we've looked at it so many times in the last few years, we've all three about got them memorized."

Dr. Walsh opened the envelope with anticipation. He had serious doubts about the details that didn't correspond between Corey's and Cody's story, and he was worried that more disappointment would come for Mr. Shelby. At the same time, the man's hope was somewhat contagious. Dr. Walsh paused as he spread the records out, reminding himself to remain clinical and emotionally detached.

Three very specific procedures immediately jumped out to Dr. Walsh. Dr. Jim Radnor, their family dentist, had placed:

1. A silver amalgam on #12 covering the occlusal surface.
2. A silver amalgam on #15 covering the occlusal/lingual surfaces.
3. A silver amalgam on #21 covering the occlusal surface.

Walsh looked down at his notes displaying the clinical markers on the seven teeth from Cody. "Whoa! This could get interesting!" Walsh exclaimed. "So far, three out of three markers are perfect!"

Both detectives sat up straighter in their chairs, their interest heightened by Walsh's comment. Daniel Shelby stood up with excitement. "Dear God, do you think it's him?"

"Hang on guys, there's more here."

Walsh rifled through the rest of the xrays and clinical notes, referring back and forth to 'Cody's' information. "Let's see, let's check out these last two markers."

    4. Root canal with porcelain crown on #13.

    5. Extraction performed on #18.

Dr. Walsh's facial expression sunk. "Oh no! Two snags here."

"What is it Dr. Walsh? Tell me, please!" Shelby's voice was trembling with excitement.

"I'm sorry to say we have two unexplainable inconsistencies. Your son has had a root canal and porcelain crown on tooth #13, and Cody's tooth is virgin, no filling decay or anything."

"On top of that, our specimen Cody's #18 is a virgin tooth, and on your son, Corey, well that tooth is missing. You can't un-fill a root canal or undo a crown, and you can't grow back a tooth that has been extracted."

Mr. Shelby sat back down, scratched his head, and with a slow and deliberate voice, he asked, "So what does that tell you?"

"Sir, unfortunately, that tells us that this is not your son."

Shelby covered his quivering mouth with his shaking hand. "How certain can you be of this?"

"I'm sorry, Mr. Shelby," Dr. Walsh said softly. "This just can't be your son. It is simply impossible. This is what I was afraid of."

Agent Hartley was visibly shaken. His lower lip quivered as he groped for some comforting words. "Mr. Shelby, we really wanted this to be your son, believe me."

Tears welled up instantly in Shelby's eyes. He slowly lowered his head to the conference table and sobbed.

Another false lead for Cody's case, another disappointment for the Shelby family. A heartbroken Mr. Shelby headed back to Arizona to continue the search for his son.

74

By the time Walsh made his drive home, he was feeling completely dejected and disheartened about ever finding Cody. He tried to mask his disappointment from Brandie, but his success was limited. His playful welcome from Mollie and Millie went totally unnoticed. Brandie was reviewing files on the dining room table. She looked up in anticipation as he placed his briefcase in the corner. She also knew about Mr. Shelby coming into town and was just as anxious as Walsh was for answers.

Before he could speak, Brandie cocked her head to the side, her lips lifting in gentle smile. She closed the file folder in one smooth motion, dropped it on the coffee table, and in three steps she had crossed the room and wrapped her arms around Walsh's neck. He didn't need to tell her; she had seen it on his face.

Brandie stood up on the tips of her toes, bringing her petite frame just a little closer to Walsh's height. She placed a soft kiss on both his cheeks, then his lips. Then she took his briefcase from his hand and set it down against the wall. She finished the job of unbuttoning his coat, pulled it off his shoulders, and tossed it over the back of a chair. Taking his hand gently, she led him across the room and sat him down on the couch, sliding in beside him and pulling her bare feet up underneath her. Millie and Mollie, who were never far behind, jumped up on the couch, showering Chris with licks. He managed a slight grin.

"He's not Cody?" she asked simply.

Chris couldn't muster a reply. Brandie knew what that meant.

"It wasn't a match. I had a feeling about it when Mr. Shelby said he wanted to bring his son's records to Nashville himself. I should have called him myself and told him to stay at home and try not to get his hopes up just yet."

"But everything seemed so promising," Brandie said. "How could you have known? They didn't put you on this case because they thought you'd be dry and clinical and matter-of-fact. They put you on it because you *do* care. They put you on it because of your passion."

Walsh shook his head.

Brandie gave him a swat on the knee. "Look at me," she said. "What are you always telling me about cold cases? If anybody thought rationally, they'd never even try to solve them. They're the hopeless causes. They don't get solved with numbers and charts; they get solved with instinct and passion and elbow grease."

"Well, maybe I'm kidding myself," Walsh said. "The numbers and charts are telling us we've got no clue, two years later, who this guy is. When do you cash in your chips?"

She rested her head gently on his shoulder and sighed. "If you don't care about Cody, who will?"

Walsh picked up one of Brandie's hands and interlaced her fingers through his. "You know what I keep wondering?" he asked. He paused for a moment, not sure if he should admit this to his wife. Finally, he asked quietly, "What if it was one of our kids? What if we didn't know where they were or what had happened to them?"

Brandie lifted her head. She was silent, looking into Walsh's eyes. "I've thought the same thing, too. And you know what? If any of our family members disappeared, I'd want a man like you out there looking for them. If I had my choice between some doctor with all the degrees in the world and a man who was going to say to himself, 'This is someone's son or daughter, and I'm going to bring them peace,' you know who I'd pick. I'd pick the man who's not going to think twice about the odds. Instead, he's going to think all day and night about the real person and their family."

Walsh smiled. He put his hand to Brandie's cheek, lifted her face toward his, and kissed her.

"You're right, Brandie," he said. "I know in my gut that Cody's got someone out there wondering where he is, who's just as brokenhearted as Mr. Shelby. If it's humanly possible, I'm going to bring Cody home."

75

D r. WALSH STARED out the window of his office in the Forensic Science Center. The lead-lined, bulletproof glass that protected the State Medical Examiner's Office distorted his view. A beautiful, cloudless day announced summer to Music City, but Walsh barely took note of its crystal-blue sky. His mind sank deeper and deeper into the mystery of this poor soul named Cody.

Walsh had spent so much time comparing dental records to the "Cody" skull that his colleagues were starting to call his office "the Cody Room." On more than one occasion, Walsh had caught himself mid-conversation with the skull, which had become a near constant companion.

"Hey, buddy," he'd say, "if your name isn't Cody, please just give us a hint." His TBI buds even accused him of talking to himself since he became so involved with the 'Cody case'.

Both suspects, Clint and Jimmy Dale were serving prison terms, but the case was far from over. They both had decided to accept the plea agreement which would keep them in prison for fifteen years. If Dr. Walsh believed half their testimony the two men had given in court, not to mention countless interviews they'd given, then it was clear that Cody had one incredible story to tell. But for now, he wasn't talking. Walsh had to be patient, whether he liked it or not.

He sank back in his chair, eying the skull and wishing that he could delve into its secrets as the TBI agents had pried Clint and Jimmy Dale for theirs. It had been a while since Dr. Walsh had to disappoint Daniel Shelby, telling him that Corey Shelby and John Cody Doe were not the same person. He had felt disappointed himself. And now, with each passing day, that frustration and sense of helplessness was needling at him.

Just at that moment, the song *"Who Are You?"* by The Who began playing over the building's overhead sound system. Walsh felt himself smiling wryly.

Walsh rubbed his forehead, his train of thought interrupted by the music. When techs working overtime at the Medical Examiner's Office started piping music through the building to break the monotony, Walsh could just tune it out, or whistle along. But this particular song kept tugging at his consciousness, pulling him out of that present moment.

He hadn't heard this song in a long time. It had become the theme song for the 9/11 benefit concert in Madison Square Garden in New York City.

Dr. Walsh's line of work wasn't about predictability. He could never anticipate when his next case would come, what it would concern, and where it would take him. If someone had told him when Cody's body was first exhumed that he'd still be working on his case three years later, he would never have believed it. And if someone had told him on September 10, 2001 that next month would find him in New York City, working alongside dozens of other forensic specialists to identify the victims of an attack on the United States, he wouldn't have been able to wrap his mind around that news either.

He still couldn't wrap his mind around it, more than half a year later.

Sometimes it seemed like just days ago that he'd temporarily shut down his private practice, put away his case files he was working on, and taken a flight to New York with an open-ended return ticket. The experience had hovered at the edges of his thoughts, sometimes barging in and taking hold. Dr. Walsh wouldn't exactly call these moments *flashbacks*—more like daydreams he couldn't shake himself awake from.

Walsh found himself drifting back to Ground Zero once again. Unconsciously, his gaze floated away from the skull sitting stone silent on his desk.

It was October 17, 2001, his second day as a forensic odontologist for the Office of the Medical Examiner for New York City.

He inhaled slowly and deeply, staring down at his first black body bag. Bold, yellow letters reading NYCOME (New York City Office of the Medical Examiner). Hesitatingly, his hand found the bag's zipper.

"I've done this weekly for over twenty-five years," Dr. Walsh told himself. "What could be so different about this?" He couldn't say exactly how, but this was different. Very different.

The black body bag was unzipped to reveal broken human remains inside, and Walsh's heart sank. An MOS—New York's verbiage for a "man of service." This was someone who had died in the towers while rescuing others.

His skin was well preserved, almost mummified, though not visually recognizable. It had a brownish tint with a leathery consistency. The odor was negligible. The body was mostly intact, a rarity among the nearly one thousand bodies Dr. Walsh and their forensic team in New York would spend more than the next nine months helping to identify. Still another two thousand bodies were unidentifiable, completely vaporized, like all the jet's black boxes.

The body now before Walsh still wore an FDNY jacket with "Brown" stitched above the left breast pocket. A legible emblem reading, "New York City Firefighter #683794," hung from its breast. Walsh carefully placed it inside the personal effects bin, knowing it would be a priceless memento for a heartbroken son or daughter.

The right hand still tightly clutched a fire ax, as if the man's last few moments on this earth had remained frozen in time. He had an oxygen cylinder on his back. The dials read, "0000." He had literally sucked his last breath on earth from that cylinder.

Dr. Walsh blinked and the "Cody" skull came back into focus on the desk before him. And for a moment, he thought he might succeed in staying in the present, but then he once again became aware of that song ringing overhead. "Who are you . . . ?"

76

THE BUZZING SOUND tossed Dr. Walsh right back into his daydream.

"They just uncovered a breezeway down at the pit!" a voice rang out over the intercom. The term "Ground Zero" hadn't yet been coined. "They think it was stairway twelve out of the North Tower. Have about twelve to fifteen bodies coming in from 'the pit'. Several of them are intact. At least one MOS in the group."

For a surreal moment, Dr. Walsh imagined himself at Arlington National Cemetery, watching a changing of the guard at the Tomb of the Unknown Soldier. Around him, every worker had exited the building and stood motionless outside its rear loading dock of the morgue. Slowly, they began a salute as an EMS truck pulled up and several men in coveralls carefully removed an oversized, black body bag draped with an American flag.

The fifty or so medical personnel stood silent for a moment, paying their respects before continuing clinical examinations. They stood like statues. No breeze, no cold, just tears. Five minutes later, it was back to work.

"Okay, Walsh," a voice at Dr. Walsh's elbow interrupted him. He turned to find a colleague from the NYCOME handing him an address scrawled on a slip of paper. "The MOS ante-mortem records are with Sally Reed. Her office is one block east of here.

Would you pick them up, so we can start checking them against what we have here?"

Twenty minutes later, Walsh returned with the records. During his absence, his teammates had been busily logging all personal effects and measuring, weighing, and evaluating all the remains that were enclosed in the body bag. Pounds of twisted rebar, melted glass, and ground-up concrete were thoroughly comingled with the bodies, compounding the team's effort to sort out the body parts for their study.

One of his colleagues reached over and took a folder labeled, 'Brown, Adam'. "Let's get started," he said. "This one's an ante-mortem on a Brown who came out of Fire Hall 7. First name Adam. Let me see what kind of records we have to compare."

The first thing that caught his eye was a family dental record labeled "Adam Brown." Beneath his name was the man's Social Security number, his address, and his FDNY badge number.

683794.

Gently, Dr. Walsh started to turn the page. That's when he saw it. A rumpled sheet of notebook paper had been stapled to an inside flap of the dental record.

The paper was scrawled with a child's penciled handwriting. Some letters were backwards, and some were correct. Dr. Walsh read it silently, then reread it. For a moment, he stood frozen, thinking his heart was going to stop beating.

"Walsh, what is it? What's wrong?"

"Listen to this . . ." Walsh murmured. He read aloud.

Dear Doctors,

Thanks for helping to look for my daddy. He is a firefighter and he is missing. I love him very much and I miss him a lot. I sure hope he isn't dead. Thanks again.

Love,

Alex

Dr. Walsh gently closed the folder and set it down.

"I need to take a break," he said. He hadn't even been on duty three hours.

The other doctors nodded in quiet agreement. They were all seasoned professionals, each one with more than twenty years of experience in forensic identification. They had volunteered for this job willingly. And yet none of them could ever have been prepared for an emotional impact of this magnitude.

Together, they walked outside to get some fresh air and a bite to eat. Each time Dr. Walsh left the morgue at 30th and 3rd, he had to pass a Psychological Debriefing Tent. The temporary facility had been strategically erected where all workers would walk right by. Its gray canvas flap waved lazily in the mild, unseasonably warm breeze that meandered through Manhattan. A simple, white cross on a dark background of the flap of a tent was respectfully displayed. Dr. Walsh couldn't pass it without thinking of old *M*A*S*H* episodes.

When he'd first arrived, counselors had frequently mentioned the Psychological Debriefing Tent during his orientation period. They had told him to expect lingering thoughts about what he saw and heard. They cautioned him to be prepared for his family members to notice certain personality or mood changes upon his arrival back home.

They told Dr. Walsh that they were there to give him suggestions and methods of coping with seemingly insurmountable grief that would be associated with his investigation. That had been the first time Walsh had ever paid attention to the words "Post-Traumatic Stress Disorder." At first, the command post had merely suggested that forensic team members stop by the Debriefing Tent; then they began to require it.

77

"Let's see if you can blow all five candles out at once! Come on now: one, two, three, GO!"

Britt leaned over his birthday cake, took a giant breath, and blew out five flickering candles. His mother burst into applause.

"Good job!" she cried, wrapping him up in a big bear hug. "See, I knew you could do it. That's my big boy!"

Christine was so proud of her Britt. It seemed like only yesterday that she was pregnant with him. As Kathy was always reminding her, "Seize the moment, it won't hang around long." She was beginning to understand.

Christine laughed at the sight of Britt's disheveled friends. No birthday party for five-year-olds would ever be complete without its fair share of messes, including at least half of their outfits wiped out by chocolate ice cream.

Britt was growing into a bright, wonderful boy. He would start kindergarten in the fall, and he couldn't have been more excited about going to "big school." And Red River Hardware had become a permanent home for Christine. Christine received several substantial raises from all her hard work.

And yet, despite all those positive changes, there was still a burning void in Christine's heart. This, she knew, was the consequence of life without Cody.

Jerry was still one of her closest friends, but Christine continued to be in denial about his efforts to take their relationship further. Whatever the future held, he would have to be satisfied to be one of her best buds, and nothing more.

In the fall of 2003, Britt started first grade. He was doing great, but Melvin's heart condition was slowly getting worse. The doctors had diagnosed his condition as cardiomyopathy, a chronic degenerative heart disease, curable only by a heart transplant. He had been placed on the heart transplant list at University Hospital, but Melvin wasn't sure he was up for it. He had taken medical retirement from the post office, which took care of his and Kathy's finances, but a full time dose of ESPN was more than he cared for. He was increasingly unable to exert himself physically; eventually even walking to the mailbox was too much of a strain. By the time Britt was in second grade, Melvin was confined to bed.

One Saturday morning, Kathy and Christine were having coffee. "It's your turn to give me counseling, Ms. Browning. I'm feeling torn for the first time in my life. The guilt of not staying with Melvin 24/7 is becoming heavy. I'm only spending four hours a day with Britt now, but this time is increasingly critical for Melvin."

Christine nodded. "I understand one hundred percent. And I support you completely."

Kathy continued with a grieved look on her face. "You know he has never begrudged one minute I have spent with you and Britt. He considers you and Britt to be our extended family. Our boys live so far away and we see them so infrequently, you and Britt are closer to us than our blood relations."

She sighed before continuing. "The doctors have said he's pretty high on the transplant list, but I don't know what that means. When you try and pin them down on a date they all scatter like rabbits. It seems like Melvin is getting weaker each day. Maybe until he gets his transplant, someone else could pick up Britt after school . . . it breaks my heart sayin' that, but I really think I have to devote all my time to Melvin." Her eyes got misty as she said it.

Kathy's tears made Christine cry, so they cried on each other's shoulders for a while. It was cathartic for both of them. Then they laughed a little bit, joking about the "bad influence" of one weeping woman on another. After that, Christine got serious.

"Kath. I'll look into the after school program they have at the church. It isn't that expensive, and we could do that on a temporary basis, at least until we figure out which direction Melvin's condition is heading."

This arrangement seemed to pacify Kathy, who nodded gratefully although there were still tears in her eyes.

"I've gotta go—I'm going to go check on my hubby now." She hugged Christine goodbye and started home.

As soon as Kathy unlocked her front door, something didn't feel quite right. Quietly she tiptoed so as not to wake Melvin. She peered into his bedroom. Her husband lay motionless in bed, fully covered with sheets and blankets. She walked in a closer to make a more detailed inspection, all the while a bad feeling was growing in her gut.

"Melvin?" she whispered. "Are you okay, honey?" His color was ashen. She reached down to feel his forehead and realized he was ice cold. The realization swept over her like a pail of cold water had been dumped over her head. Her Melvin was gone.

She sat down by his bedside and wept quietly. Even though

she'd known this might be coming, she wouldn't in a million years be ready for it. She prayed silently for his spirit to be joined in heaven with his maker, Cody, and all their previously departed friends and relatives.

Then Kathy picked up the phone and dialed her best friend. In a soft, muffled voice she said, "Christine, Melvin's gone home to be with the Lord."

"Oh no, Kath," Christine said. "We're on our way."

Trying to explain death to a second grader is a hard thing to do, especially when you are trying to get your fifteen-year-old VW to crank. Tears were streaming down Christine's face. Britt sat very still.

Kathy had been such a blessed servant to their family; now it was time for role reversal. Christine used the eight-minute drive to explain to Britt exactly what death was.

"You know, son, when your body gets old and worn out, there comes a time when your life here ends and it's time for you to go and live the rest of your life in heaven. Mr. Melvin, has died. His body got so tired that he's gone to live in Heaven. KK is very sad right now, 'cause none of us can see Melvin again till it's *our* turn to go. That might be soon and it might be a long time."

"Mom, do you think that's where Daddy is? Do you think he has gone to live with Jesus?" Britt had a very solemn look on his face. This idea of death was a hard one for him to grasp. He had such a sweet and precious disposition that he could hardly stand to see a housefly swatted.

"Yes. That's exactly where your daddy is. I've been praying about this for a long time, asking God to help me find strength and wisdom and proper words to explain it. But right now, as certain as the sun will come up tomorrow, Melvin is seeing your daddy."

Britt wasn't finished, even though by now the trusty VW had deposited them in Kathy's driveway. "But Mama. Daddy's body wasn't tired like Melvin's? Daddy wasn't old. What happened to him, Mommy?"

Christine took a deep breath. "You're right, Britt. His body wasn't tired. So it's a very good question. He went on a trip without you and me. We're not completely sure what happened, but he never came back. I think some bad guys may have gotten him, and we're still trying to find out what happened. But I do think it's safe to say that both Melvin and Daddy are having lunch with Jesus today."

"Mama, if you go eat lunch with Jesus today, can you come back down here after you're done?"

Tears rolled freely from Christine's face. She reached across and gently kissed her son's forehead. "No. Once you're there, you really don't want to leave. It's that wonderful of a place. Now, let's go inside now and be strong for KK."

Britt looked up in his mother's eyes and saw the hurt and sadness there. It was the same sadness that was always there, only now Britt felt it in his heart. Before he could stop it, a teardrop fell from his own eyes. It hurt him when his mommy hurt.

"I love you, Mommy."

"I love you, too, Britt."

Christine's heart felt like it was about to burst. Her little boy was growing up.

78

One night in November, 2010, Christine was randomly channel surfing to pass idle time. Britt, now thirteen, was in his room buried in a history book, facing an important exam before the Christmas holidays. Christine's curiosity was aroused when a program caught her eye. America's Most Wanted, a television series dedicated to helping identify and locate missing persons. They showed an interesting trailer that dealt with an unidentified man, whose identity had been a mystery for over a decade. The commercial promised to give complete details.

Christine didn't really want to watch it, but any news piece regarding identification would always catch her eye. Since she had been developing her computer skills, she had kept an effort going to search for her Cody. She had discovered a website called the John Doe Network, which assisted families in locating missing persons. She had also become familiar with the NCIC national database in Washington, D.C. Christine kept the channel on that station, while she looked for other websites on the computer dealing with the location of missing persons.

The TBI had submitted a short video trailer to true crime programs in hopes that television publicity might help solve this very cold case. Tonight was its night to air on America's Most

Wanted. Christine called for Britt to take a break from study and watch the short clip dealing with an unsolved mystery in Nashville, Tennessee. Britt gladly closed his books for a while, and curled up with his mom to watch this newest bit of information.

Christine and Britt had watched lots of programs like this, so this one was just another routine stop on their forensic quest for more knowledge. The viewers were informed of an unknown body that had been exhumed from a middle Tennessee grave, after law enforcement had discovered two men had committed murder and staged a death in a car fire to collect life insurance money.

The two had confessed to a random murder off the interstate in Texas in 1997. A fraudulent life insurance claim appeared to have been the motive. The body had been transferred to Tennessee, falsely buried, and the insurance claim completely paid. The plot was accidentally uncovered when the offender, who was supposed to be dead, was apprehended with a fake Tennessee driver's license. When asked to help identify the unknown victim, the criminals could only remember that he was called Cody. It had been uncertain to law enforcement officials whether this information could be relied upon or not, but all leads were being investigated. It had been over ten years with no successful identification.

Experts explained that there had been a considerable number of dental procedures performed on the victim, so access to pre-existing records would be crucial to an identification. A forensic artist had been used to submit several sketches of a victim known as 'Cody', and a forensic sculptor had used putty and clay to re-simulate the facial profile reported by the confessed killers, including contour and skin texture.

Christine gasped. She stared blankly at the model. It looked eerily like her Cody. Could this be their first real clue in over a decade? She wanted to believe it, but couldn't stand another disappointment. How could the name be the same? Ten years was a long time to hold your breath. She placed the DVR on pause and studied the wax up. His nose had the same little curvature she always noticed when he smiled. The color and texture of the hair was a medium brown, thick and slightly wavy. The lip lines in the mockup gave her goose bumps as she could visualize her Cody's lips pressed against the microphone, singing her a love song. Two tiny tears from each eye followed their way down her cheeks at the same time.

She looked at Britt.

"What's the matter, mom? They're not even sure his name is really Cody. Are you thinking you should call them? We've chased down a million leads and they all seem to turn up dead end streets."

"Sweetie, that looks just like your father! Britt I do believe that is Cody." She sobbed as she leaned her head over Britt's shoulder. He held her closely in his arms. This young man had become mature beyond his years, as he had served both as a biological link from his mom to his dad, and a steadfast rock to comfort her weakened emotions as she continued her quest for Cody's whereabouts.

"I hate to say. I don't want to jinx our luck. I really think this is your father. There are too many things that fit together. I just have this feeling that will not leave me. I know we're on to something now."

Christine wrote down the 800 number that was provided should anyone want to get more information, which would then be funneled directly to the Tennessee Bureau of Investigation. "We've just gotta keep trying."

Britt looked up in his mother's eyes and smiled. "I know, mom. I've got the best mom in the whole wide world. If Dad was here, he would be so proud of you. I know he would." Britt grinned; Christine wept. She had always been proud of him.

79

Cody's case had entered its second decade. Most of Walsh's mysteries were solved in a matter of weeks. Not this one. It would be difficult to follow the details of such a case without developing some sentimental attachment. Walsh began to worry that his attachment to the case might have caused him to overlook some item or detail that could have cracked it.

Walsh had become bitter at J.D. and Clint, two men that he didn't know. He had said countless times that if these two criminals served their time for a capital offense and were released before anyone knew who it was they had killed . . . well, that would be beyond pathetic.

One day, Dr. Walsh got a visit from his two favorite TBI agents, Hartley and Akers. They came to his dental office one Monday morning, promising him an early Christmas present. Walsh was always glad to see his partners in crime solving.

"We know you're gonna laugh at us, but we really think we've got a lead this time that's for real," Agent Akers said.

"What makes this different than the other twenty 'Codys' you've brought me before?" Dr. Walsh laughed.

"Now, hold on, Doc. Listen just a minute," Agent Akers said

with a broad smile.. "There's a lady in Albuquerque, New Mexico named Christine Browning who was watching TV last week when we aired a trailer on *America's Most Wanted* about the Cody case. She called the 800 number and was put through to TBI."

Agent Hartley butted in as if he couldn't wait to share his information. "I talked to her. She had a relationship with a man named Cody Britton in 1997. They worked at the same place outside of Albuquerque called the Blueroom Cafe. She tended bar and he played country music. They supposedly had a relationship going before he left to seek his fortune in Nashville. He was supposed to be hitchhiking on I-40, and it was about the same time that Clint and J.D. were on their rampage.

"He sent her a postcard en route. He mentions being picked up by a couple of really nice guys from Nashville. This is one of these 'Honey, I'll come back and getcha' songs that has been around for years. She swears something bad happened 'cause she's positive he wouldn't just dropped off the map."

"This Christine gal seems really sharp. Has a young teenage boy named Britt who she says is Cody's son. Except she calls Cody 'Sweetie.' Talks in the present tense, like he's coming home any day.

"Supposedly, Christine advised Albuquerque PD years ago, and there has been an all-points bulletin out for quite a while, but it got hung up somewhere and never got sent to the National Crime Information Center in Washington. I've already talked with the Chief there, and he said this has officially been an open missing persons case since 1997. That's thirteen years, just about the time that our two clowns started their science project!

"Christine remembers going with Cody to a dentist in the area to have a few fillings done, and has offered to get dental X-rays sent to us if we can help her get records released. They never were married, so they won't release dental records with this new HIPAA stuff to anyone but that patient.

"I've arranged for a court order to release those X-rays and clinical notes. There was no next of kin listed on his health information form on the dental chart. Laugh if you want to, Doc, but this time I think we might really be onto something."

Agent Hartley grinned from ear to ear. Walsh was already on the edge of his seat. He returned a grin to both as big as Agent Hartley's. "Boys, you may *really* be onto something this time. How soon can I get the records?"

Agent Hartley couldn't help laughing. He reached around his back, and displayed his present. "Here, my good doctor, are Cody Britton's dental X-rays, dated February 14, 1996. Don't let me down, Doc!"

Dr. Walsh looked at his watch. He had already seen his last patient before lunch and had an hour before the first patient of the afternoon.

"I think we better spend lunch finding out as much as we can about this," Walsh said.

"Of course!" Agent Hartley was getting excited. "How many times have we done this? You always say, 'It's like déjà vu, all over again!'"

80

THE THREESOME DROVE down to the State Medical Examiner's Office, entering the building and walls of bulletproof glass that shielded its forensic team from any wayward citizen. The men laughed and joked as they strolled. If the general public heard their levity in the face of death and tragedy, they might get a wrong opinion. But these men truly had a love of mankind that drove them to work tirelessly to solve heinous crimes like this one—and bring relief to families. They had learned from hard experience if they were to conduct their professions all day, every day with doom and gloom on their faces, they would quickly turn their own lives—and those of everyone they came in contact with—into one really long, bad day.

The Forensic Science Center was truly a state of the art facility. It had already become known nationally as an elite facility of its kind. The building combined elegance with modern architecture. It looked to be anything but a typical morgue.

The entire exterior of the building was constructed from gray and tan brick with pleasing architectural lines. Its roof line had interesting angles, and lines to accommodate for multiple multifaceted glass panels like a horticultural greenhouse. Twenty-four-hour video surveillance cameras carefully monitored every inch of its exterior and interior. There were no actual keys for entry; all access was granted by electronic key fobs that were swiped over a sensor. The computer recorded which pre-assigned key fobs was used for entry, so records would show who entered which door at what time. Security levels were prioritized, so that certain key fobs allowed entrance to different sections of the building while others did not.

Upon entering the facility, the centralized waiting area resembled an alcove of a modern hotel. A vaulted glass ceiling overhead allowed ample natural sunlight to brightly illuminate each room. A series of thick, glass blocks added a nice architectural touch, giving class and elegance. An impressive black and gold marble slab adorned the entryway, displaying the mission statement for Forensic Medical, Inc., the parent organization of the facility.

Taceant colloquia. Effugiat risus. Hic locus est ubi mors gaudet succurrere vitae. "Let the laughter flee. This is the place where death rejoices to help the living."

The main autopsy suite held facilities to accommodate six autopsies simultaneously, three on each side of a central water supply system, which helped morgue attendants keep the lab neat and tidy, considering the nature of their business. An impressive grid of skylight panels more than adequately lit each area of the operating suite.

The concrete floors were highly polished. Sand-like particles imbedded within its floor covering provided firm and balanced footing, even on a floor that was often wet from being hosed for cleanliness.

The trio would limit their study to the "decomp room."

A light sensor automatically opened its hydraulically operated sliding door. Inside the decomp room, there was space for only one case. It consisted of a room about twenty by twenty with similar design. The ceiling pitch had been carefully designed to merge the ceiling flow. It was in a wing by itself so that families of decedents could come and view the bodies for positive identification in private.

Since most dental IDs are either decomposed or burned, the decomp room was an easy way to isolate these cases from other forensic autopsies being performed. The smell is quite offensive, and so a special ventilation system in the decomp room eliminated odors within seconds of their detection.

The skull of Cody had been previously removed from the color and lay on the main dissection table.

Dr. Walsh introduced the agents to the new morgue attendant, Gelina, who was finishing her first week. He couldn't pass up a chance to tease a new employee. "Now, Gelina, have you met Cody?"

Gelina giggled with a sheepish grin "Yes, Dr. Walsh, as a matter of fact, I have. I met Cody actually before I met you, on my first day of orientation."

The administrative personnel had already taken the X-rays and notes on the skull and digitized them in a forensic file labeled MEC-00-0123, officially registered to John Cody Doe. They had been collecting a national and international database of individuals that Cody was *not*.

Walsh opened the overnight package, trying unsuccessfully to disguise his enthusiasm. When the binding tape would not release, both agents laughed at his frustration.

The ante-mortem X-rays that Christine Browning had sent were limited to one upper right posterior and one lower right posterior radiograph. No other records existed, and Christine was sure that these X-rays had been taken the only time Cody Britton had ever been to a dentist.

"I'm gonna croak if this turns out not to be Cody." Walsh looked over at Akers and winked. Finally, the package surrendered its contents. He placed the X-rays up for display and evaluation.

Walsh paused a moment, studied some more, then looked down. "Are you serious?! I cannot believe this!"

"What is it, Doc? What do you see?"

"You might guess that those are the teeth that were burned off in the car fire. They have no radiographs of the left posterior, and that's what we have to see. We have nothing to compare. This makes me sick!" Walsh shook his head in disbelief.

"Doc, are you serious?" They were stunned.

Dr. Walsh rolled his eyes back and uttered a few choice words. Without more X-rays or more human body parts, the case would go back on the shelf. They had been so sure that they were on the right track, and it looked like their case was back at square one. "Let me show both of you this X-ray. This is like a bad dream." Walsh retraced his thought process and explained the details in layman's terms, just to make sure his emotions were not distorting his rationale.

"Well, that really sucks!" Wayne agreed.

As the despondent trio drove back to Dr. Walsh's office, Hartley asked Walsh if he could think of any other angle to approach this from. "Doc, we're too close to give up. There has got to be another angle we can use."

Walsh needed the encouragement. He scratched his head as he was thinking. "Cody is supposed to be the father of this kid of Christine Browning's, right? This kid should have Cody's DNA, *if* Cody is the father. We checked for DNA a couple of years ago from the long bones, but couldn't get a good read because of the degradation from the fire. This body cooked in an auto inferno for an hour or so. Sitting underground in a casket for two years didn't help things. Or in a lab for twelve more years?"

Walsh paused to reflect. "But there is one other thing we could try. Half the teeth were burned off and the half that have been roasted. If—and it's a *big* if—the kid was really fathered by Cody, and *if* we can extract some DNA out of one of the molars, *and* if that DNA is stable, we could theoretically match those together. The enamel cover on each tooth is far more durable than bone. Those are some mighty big 'ifs,' but we struck out on dental X-rays, we really have no other choices."

Hartley and Akers were excited and optimistic; Walsh was cautious.

"Now Doc, listen to me. When you've worked as many cold cases as Hartley and I have, you learn to get fired up every time you get another clue. Let's see what happens. You've heard it before, when one door closes, another one opens up. Maybe your idea will work."

"Just don't want to get my hopes up. And you know what can happen if you get too close to a case."

Akers was on a roll today. "Now Doc, don't be too hard on yourself. First of all, we're all humans first, and a forensic team second. If you could be totally objective on all this, you might as well be a robot. We've come too far not to keep our chins up. I've worked cold cases all my adult life, and we have to keep on."

Walsh knew he was right.

81

Hₐᵣₜₗₑᵧ ₐₙd Aₖₑᵣₛ ᵣₐₙ ₑᵣᵣₐₙdₛ while Walsh finished treating his dental patients. By four o'clock, the trio was back at the morgue for a second look at Cody.

At the administrative desk, Dr. Walsh completed the paperwork to remove evidence for further investigation. A fundamental principle of forensics is to maintain a proper "chain of custody" of all evidence, so he documented the procedure the Cody skull was about to undergo. He wrote on the custody slip that he would be removing tissue from MEC-10-0123, limited to the upper left second permanent molar. Reason for operation: "to attempt a DNA read by extirpating any remaining pulp tissue from a cross sectional dissection of the clinical crown just coronal to the cemento-enamel junction."

"Lab should take note," Dr. Walsh read to the agents as he wrote, "this DNA has been subjected to intense heat from a motor vehicle accident, followed by burial for two years, and storage in an evidence room in a State Medical Examiner's Office for more than a decade." Walsh looked up, "You can't give the lab too much information," he said with a grin.

As they proceeded back to their decomp room, Walsh explained, "My hope is that since enamel is the hardest substance in our body, perhaps its encasement of its pulp, where the blood vessel is contained, would have protected it enough to salvage some important DNA."

Without his even noticing, Akers's pep talk had given Walsh an infusion of enthusiasm. "Tell you what we ought to do first," Walsh continued. "We need to talk to Christine on the phone and give her some instructions on how we might get her to help with this DNA procurement."

Akers was one step ahead. "Here's her phone number, let's call her."

Akers dialed the number, and Christine answered on the second ring. "Christine, this is Special Agent Akers with the Tennessee Bureau of Investigation. I've got Dr. Chris Walsh, our state forensic odontologist, who's working on Cody's ID case. He has a few questions for you."

"I've been hoping each day to hear from you. Thank you for following up on this." Akers handed the phone to Walsh.

"Ms. Browning, this is Dr. Chris Walsh. How are you today?"

"I'm fine, Dr. Walsh. I hope you are well."

"I'm fine, thank you. We are attempting to confirm identity of this body as that of Cody Britton."

"Cody and I were going to get married as soon as he got situated in Nashville."

"I understand that your son was fathered by Cody Britton. Have you ever had a paternity test to confirm this?"

"There's no reason. Cody is the only person I have ever had sex with."

"That's fine, ma'am." Dr. Walsh was already wishing he hadn't been that persistent with his questioning. "I'm sorry, but the dental X-rays and notes were not able to help us. There just isn't enough information to draw any conclusions. But we've got another avenue we want to consider.

"What we need to do is to get a DNA sample from your son, Britt. That could be done easily by stopping by the Albuquerque Police Department. The requirement is a Q-tip swabbed across the inside of his cheek. We may be able to compare his DNA with these remains.

"That's incredible. I knew you could do lots with DNA, but I never dreamed that might be possible. I'll have it completed by the end of today. Thank you for helping. I have a feeling that this is truly my Cody. I've waited for such a long time to put him to rest."

"Yes, I'm sure it's been difficult. It will take a few weeks to get this result, and we're not even sure we can get any material from the tooth to actually run the test, but we're going to give it a try. We'll call you when we have any lab results."

"Dr. Walsh, I can't tell you how much I appreciate what you're doing. This has been such an uphill struggle for a long time. I need some peace and closure and my son, Britt, needs to know what happened to his father."

"We're going to give it everything we've got to try to help. I have worked on this case for ten years and really feel like I know 'Cody.' I feel for your emptiness and loneliness. I don't want to give you false hopes because I don't know if this test will be successful, but I promise you. I will not give up until I help you find Cody." His voice was shaking.

Dr. Walsh said goodbye, and slowly hung up. He looked up at Akers and Hartley with tears welling in his eyes.

"Doc, let me tell you something," Akers said. "You are the real deal."

82

With that step complete, the three proceeded back to the evidence room. Dr. Walsh had brought some oral surgical forceps with him from his dental office.

Within a few minutes, Dr. Walsh had extracted tooth number 15. Agent Hartley made a few wise comments to keep from breaking a cold sweat. But Dr. Walsh had heard them all before: *"Do you think you've used enough Novocain?"* . . . *"Are you gonna charge extra for a more difficult extraction?"*

During the second return trip to Walsh's dental office, the three men were in a completely different mood. All three had a good feeling about this second chance they had been given to match the remains.

Back in the dental office, Dr. Walsh carefully sectioned the tooth vertically with a rotary disc. Agents Akers and Hartley watched with intense interest as Dr. Walsh narrated the procedure. As the two halves of the tooth fell apart like walnut halves, they revealed a somewhat hollow chamber, with tiny ribbon-shaped tubes extending from its chamber down toward the end of each root. Within this tiny chamber was a dark brown residue.

"This is called a pulp chamber, and these ribbon-like canals are called root canal spaces. It's where the blood vessel and nerve supply for each tooth is located. It is normally another place to search for DNA, if it hasn't degraded with fire and then decomposition. This part gets removed if you have an infected or abscessed tooth and you have to have a root canal procedure. Our hope is that this pulp tissue may have been insulated from the elements by its tough outer covering of enamel and dentin. Remember, it is harder than bone."

Dr. Walsh opened a package of tiny white paper points, used to dry the root canal spaces before its removal in a typical root canal treatment. He removed one point carefully from its package with a set of cotton pliers. Gently, he placed its tip down into the pulp space and rubbed against the dark brown residue. "If there is any remnant of blood still left in this pulp, it'll be a miracle. But we're due for a miracle. The tip of this point might pick it up, and we'll be able to do a DNA type from this. They'll try to match it against the cheek swab of the kid."

Agent Hartley's excitement was reignited. "Doc, this is so cool!"

"Let's wait and see if it works first." Dr. Walsh just wouldn't let himself get too optimistic, but he did have a pretty good feeling. "What is interesting about this, if this works, it will be the first time in Tennessee that we've done an ID on anyone using pulp tissue from a tooth and DNA. That would really be cool."

After collecting his sample, Dr. Walsh carefully placed it on a glass microscope slide with a single drop of sterile water. He gently stroked it back and forth, attempting to deposit some debris onto the glass slide. "Now we wait! Again! This time it's gonna be tougher 'cause all three of us know we're onto something."

The material was hand carried by the trio to the DNA processing lab at the TBI crime lab. Ted Knowles, chief DNA analyst for the TBI, told them they would have their results in three weeks. That was assuming that they got the cheek swab from Christine's son, Britt, within a few days.

Ted called Dr. Walsh three days later saying that Albuquerque police had sent the important data to be matched, and that all tests were underway on the two different specimens. The waiting game could officially start.

Dr. Walsh managed to be patient at first. Every morning over coffee he'd say to Brandie, "Maybe today will be the day."

She always smiled back. They had both been wondering who "Cody" was as long as they'd been married.

Brandie and Dr. Walsh weren't the only ones on edge as they waited. Walsh was getting phone calls daily from Christine. Ted assured him that another week would be needed to confirm all tests for reliability.

And, finally, the phone rang. Walsh was at his dental office when his receptionist told him Ted was on line one. Walsh made a frantic leap to run to the telephone. He had been waiting forever, and now, he was about to hear the verdict.

"Doc, it's Ted." He paused momentarily. Walsh tried to act casual, but was failing miserably. And then, came his words: "Doc, you guys nailed this one! We now know two things. The body is that of Cody Britton, *and* the kid is his son. Odds are 1.6 billion to 1. And, yes sir, that is billion with a 'B'! Pretty cool, huh? Good detective work to you guys! I'll email you the results when we hang up, but knew you had been waiting for a long time."

Walsh knew that Ted was strictly a scientist, and rarely got excited or showed emotion. He and Chris had developed a friendship working on several human bite-mark cases.

"Ted, can you friggin' believe it! I swore it would never happen! You were right, I admit, and I was wrong. Your encouragement kept us plugging away for a decade. I'm totally numb. It's like a dream."

Dr. Walsh thanked Ted, hung up the phone, and shouted at the top of his voice, "We finally got him!" He turned around, grabbed the first person he could, Lana, his dental hygienist, and squeezed her with all his might.

Lana, having been with Walsh long before Cody's death, and remembering the Body Farm, and had also heard the story behind every John or Jane Doe for the last decade. She knew how emptiness had haunted Walsh, even at his dental practice.

"Doc, that's awesome! I told you Cody would show up. You know that song Cody wrote, '*I Will Return.*' He tried to tell you that he would return!"

Walsh paused a moment to reflect. He got goose bumps. "That's weird. I see what you mean; you just might be right." Suddenly, Walsh lifted his eyebrows, remembering. "Hey, I need to call Akers and Hartley. They're gonna lay a gold brick!"

"Don't forget, you have three more patients that need to be seen right away. You're already a little behind. I don't want to rain on your parade, though." Lana's smile was contagious. She knew she could say anything and get away with it, as long as she smiled.

Walsh smiled back. Lana was right. He could call Akers and Hartley after Mrs. Campbell got her exam completed.

83

D<small>R.</small> W<small>ALSH'S AFTERNOON</small> was a blur. He would look back on the telephone call as one of the most significant moments of his career. When his last patient left, Walsh made a beeline for his office. With the punch of three buttons, the phone was ringing. He had Hartley and Akers, who shared offices at TBI Headquarters, on speed dial.

The phone rang once. "Special Agent Akers."

"*Bruce!* It's Doc."

"Hey! You been OK?"

"Yeah, man, thanks. Is Wayne there? Can you put him on speakerphone with us? I want to read you something." Walsh wanted to announce the news to both men together.

"Yeah, hang on." Three short clicks and the conversation resumed. "Hey, Doc. It's Wayne. You got us both now."

"Guys, how does the name 'Cody Britton' sound?! Ted just called. 1 in 1.6 billion, with a 'B'! Can you believe it?"

Akers was the first to respond. "Hallelujah! There *is* a God!"

Hartley was right behind Akers, "*Suuun*biiitch! I can't believe it!" They were as excited as Walsh, and they had five or six murder cases going on all the time.

Walsh giggled like a fourth grader at Akers's response. All three had prayed this day would come, but feared it never would. "Guys, I don't know what to do. This moment was not part of my long-range planning."

"Doc, not to be a smartass, but do you think it might be a good idea to give Ms. Christine a call? She and her kid have got a little something invested in this project."

"I will. Not sure how to say it. Bittersweet news. You guys are pros; you deal with this all the time. But I'm gonna tell ya, putting a name on Cody's face after eleven years . . . I feel like we just swam across the English Channel with two boulders strapped to our backs!"

"I second that one!" Akers chimed in merrily.

"All right, guys." Walsh cleared his throat. "I love you, and thank you from the bottom of my heart. You two are truly top shelf! I'll call you in a day or so with news from Christine."

"We love you too, Doc. You're awesome to work with."

Akers couldn't resist a moment to stir a laughter. "I'll just say this and then I'm hangin' up. In all my years with TBI, I've never heard one cop tell a doc that he loved him. There's a first time for everything because I love both of you. And I don't give a damn who you tell."

As soon as he hung up, Walsh fumbled for Christine's telephone number. He had called her so many times that he should have had her on speed dial.

"Christine, hey, it's Dr. Walsh. How are you today?"

"Well, Dr. Walsh. I'd been hoping each day that you'd call. Just like all those days when I hoped and prayed every day that I'd get a letter from Cody. I did get one. But I checked that mailbox six days a week for ten years, hoping for another one. I never gave up."

Walsh paused, and spoke very softly. "Christine, we have finally found your Cody."

There was a long pause. Chris wondered if his voice was cracking more than he thought. When he was checking to see if they still had a phone connection, he heard a faint, barely audible whimpering sound. It quickly turned into heavy sobs. In between, Christine did manage to get a few words out.

"Oh, Dr. Walsh, thank you. I just knew it in my heart. You'll never know what it means to me and Britt. I can't thank you and the TBI enough."

"That's our job. I'm just sorry it took so long to bring you closure." Dr. Walsh's heart went out to Christine. He knew that giving her this news was the best present he could give her short of finding Cody alive and well.

It seemed like Christine had already known the outcome before she ever received the call. She had her plans made and was just waiting to get official word before putting everything in order. "Britt and I want to fly to Nashville and have a memorial service for Cody. He loved that town. Will you three men attend the service? I don't know anyone in Nashville."

"Of course we will. You can have a small, private service at my church. Then, you could ship his body back to Albuquerque or cremate here and carry his remains back on the plane with you and Britt. We'll get the details set on the phone this evening, but I wanted to call you the moment we heard."

"You just don't know what this means to me, Dr. Walsh."

"Oh, my dear. You just don't know what it means to me."

84

Dr. Walsh pulled his car into short-term parking lot of Nashville International Airport. Southwest Airlines Flight 1607 was due in from Albuquerque.

Holding a sign marked "Christine and Britt," Walsh waited patiently at the end of the escalator near baggage claim.

Walsh collected his thoughts briefly as he waited for their flight to arrive. It seemed like an eternity had passed since the time when he had no idea Cody existed. There had been two different U.S. presidents in office since he acquired Cody's case. The way things had been going, J.D. and Clint might well have served their sentences and been released from prison before their victim got a last name.

The long and winding road was finally ending. Walsh started humming the melody to the famous Paul McCartney tune. From the top of the escalator, he heard a young voice exclaim, "Mom, look! There's Dr. Walsh! See the sign?"

Dr. Walsh looked up in eager anticipation. He knew it was Christine the moment he saw her face. Her bleached blonde hair was put up on top of her head. She was dressed impressively, with black slacks and a pink lacey top. She had Britt right by her side. He was a handsome young man, already tall and lean for his age, with sandy blonde hair and dark brown eyes. He sported a shiny pair of lizard cowboy boots, nicely pressed blue jeans, and a white button-down, long-sleeved shirt. Both travelers had big smiles on their faces.

Dr. Walsh's reflected over the history of this bizarre case. Never before had he gotten so emotionally involved in a case. He had developed a bond to a man he never knew. And he felt proud to have helped link Cody to his long-lost soul mate. He had helped Britt find his daddy.

"Christine? Britt?" Dr. Walsh awkwardly stuck out his hand to shake theirs.

Christine, beaming with tears streaming down her face, went right through his outstretched hand into a big hug. "Dr. Walsh, I feel like we've known you for years! Britt, say hello to Dr. Walsh."

Britt smiled broadly, reached his arms out and grabbing Dr. Walsh just like his mother had. "Hi, Doc," Britt said with tears welling in his eyes. "Thanks for helping to find my dad."

Walsh smiled. "You're welcome son. Sorry it took so long!"

Dr. Walsh drove Britt and Christine to their hotel. The Hermitage Hotel, in Walsh's mind, was one of Nashville's special places, located just across the street from the state Capital. Britt watched in amazement as the concierge and valet team pampered them like never before.

As Walsh, Christine, and Britt walked up massive marble steps, Walsh teased Britt's imagination. "Britt, wait 'til you see the inside of your hotel. It's bigger than a gigantic museum!"

Christine and Walsh both laughed as Britt's eyes doubled when a doorman held open the door for him. "Welcome to the Hermitage Hotel, young man. It's an honor to have you as our guest."

"Thank you, sir. This is my first trip to Nashville. I came to get my dad." Britt sounded so much like a grown man.

"I know he'll be glad to see you." The doorman smiled.

"He's dead. But my mom and I are bringing him back home with us, sir."

The doorman froze.

Having heard just the last part of the conversation, Christine jumped in, "It's okay, sir. Thank you so much for your kindness. It's just that neither Britt nor I have ever been to a place like this. We've come here to bring his dad home. It's alright. Long story. Please don't feel bad; you had no way of knowing."

Christine whispered to Walsh as Britt walked ahead, "You never know what kids are gonna say!"

Dr. Walsh grinned, "But he's a fine young man. You've done a good job. I know his dad would be proud."

Since their registration had already been finalized, the the customer service representative presented two keys to the guests. "Now Britt, you keep one and give the other to your mom. I told the lady you'd need your own key to get back in late tonight after you close down Printer's Alley!"

"What's Printer's Alley?" Britt asked.

"You'll find out tomorrow, and all the other sights and sounds of Nashville. This was your daddy's dream, Britt. I kinda think he'd be happy knowing you're getting to see it."

The next morning at 9:00 a.m. sharp, Brandie and Chris walked into the front lobby of the Hotel. The brisk winter chill made their topcoats feel warm and cozy. Christine and Britt were sitting on one of the massive sofas that adorned its marble foyer. Both seemed to be submerged by plush sofa cushions.

Christine grinned. "You must be Brandie. I'm Christine. You're probably sick of hearing my name around your house!"

"Not at all, Christine. Actually, I feel like I've known you for a long time. Mr. Britt, you certainly are a handsome young man!" Brandie winked at Britt.

"Thanks." Britt's bashfulness brightened his face to a deep red, and he shuffled his feet awkwardly from side to side.

As they walked out of their hotel, Britt stood tall and proud. This was his daddy's city and he couldn't wait to see it. The friendly doorman from the night before was back on duty. He opened the massive hotel door for Britt, greeting them with his signature broad smile.

"How's my favorite young man this morning?"

"I'm doing fine, sir." Britt returned the doorman's smile.

As they headed down the frosty sidewalk, they kept their pace to stay warm.

"Britt, we are going to be walking by the Ryman Auditorium, the original home of the Grand Ole Opry."

Britt and Christine seemed to be enjoying the personal tour. Britt got to spend two hours at the Country Music Hall of Fame looking at memorabilia from Hank Williams to Vince Gill and Amy Grant.

"Did you know I'm taking guitar lessons?" Britt said.

"I bet you're pretty good" Dr. Walsh said.

Christine was thrilled to see the void filled in her son's life as his love for country music was nurtured and reinforced.

After the museum, the foursome wandered aimlessly through the flashing lights, Elvis impersonators, and bluegrass fiddlers on every corner. People were wrapped cozily in warm blankets, taking romantic horse-drawn carriage rides through the streets of Music City.

Their last stop downtown was renowned Printer's Alley. Brandie narrated this portion. "Guys, this area is a famous alley between Third and Fourth Avenues, and runs from Union Street to Commerce Street. It's a district of nightclubs that dates back to the 1940s. The Alley was first home to a thriving publishing industry, including two newspapers and dozens of print shops and publishers.

"This is one of my favorite places. Probably the most famous club of all was the Carousel Club. It was famous for its jazz. Back in the day, you might have seen Chet Atkins, Floyd Cramer, or Boots Randolph performing there."

"Doc, would you take my picture with Britt in front of the Carousel Club?" Christine asked.

"Sure."

"Britt, this place looks like the Blueroom Cafe in Albuquerque. It's where your momma and daddy met about twenty years ago. Wow! This is really weird!"

Britt's interest definitely peaked upon learning this new information about his dad. One picture turned into six or seven. They even got strangers to take shots of all four of them. Then came the unexpected…

"Doc, can I ask you a question about my dad?"

Walsh held his breathe. He knew there might be questions this weekend and had reviewed the possibilities with Brandie. He just wanted to be certain that he answered everything in the most appropriate manner. "Sure, Britt. Go ahead."

"During the time that you were looking for my dad, did you have a picture of him to know what he looked like? How else would you have known it was him?"

Dr. Walsh paused. "That's a really good question, Britt. No, I never got the chance to meet your dad, nor have I ever even seen a picture of him. Sounds kinda weird, I know, but we've been basing his identification on other scientific things that we can measure. Does that make sense?"

"Not really, but Mom says it's complicated. Do you wanna see a picture of him?"

"Absolutely. Brandie and I would love to see his picture. There have been many times I've wondered exactly what he looked like."

Britt reached into his pocket and proudly pulled out a wallet-sized photo. "Here he is. Mom says I look just like him, but I can't tell for sure. What do you think?"

Brandie and Chris both couldn't wait to see the photo. It displayed a young man in his late twenties with dark brown hair and eyes and medium complexion. He was playing guitar on a stage. Brandie gasped, "Oh, my gosh, Christine! It looks like a spittin' image of Cody!"

"Can we take another picture, but this time get my dad in it, too?"

All three adults looked at each other in amazement. "We sure can, Mr. Britt. What a great idea! We should have thought of that."

They flagged down a passing tourist and asked her to take some shots in Printer's Alley. Just as the friendly young woman pressed the shutter, Britt proudly held out Cody's picture, so that his face was captured as a part of this heart-warming experience.

Their day ended with a limo ride and backstage passes to the Grand Ole Opry.

This is the perfect day, Christine thought to herself. *The only thing missing is Cody. And it almost felt like he was there.*

85

Dr. Walsh's pastor held a brief memorial service. In attendance were Agents Akers and Hartley, Chris and Brandie, Lana, a few staff members from Forensic Medical, Christine, and Britt. Unlike his previous funeral, those that truly loved him attended this special service.

The minister talked about kindness, love, perseverance, patience, family, and friends. He talked directly to Britt, as he highlighted the efforts that were involved in finally helping him find the father he never knew. He talked about Cody's song, "*I Will Return*," which had become a hallmark in this case. Walsh stood up and walked solemnly to the podium.

Pausing to look at Christine and Britt, he cleared his throat, looked at his notes, he surveyed the small group of friends and colleagues. He didn't know how far he would get before becoming emotional, but he was determined.

"Britt, when we started on this case to find your dad, we didn't know you existed. Christine, we didn't know you or anything about your life with Cody. Now, our lives have been blessed. You have become friends. If it took us this long to solve every mystery, we wouldn't get much accomplished. But this one has touched our hearts forever. We are sorry beyond words for the loss of this wonderful man, but feel fortunate to have gotten to know you and Britt. They say things happen for a reason. The problem is that none of us know exactly what that reason is right now. I feel confident that some day, maybe not in this lifetime, we will find out that reason." Walsh's voice was getting shaky. He reached behind the podium and pulled out a ragged, dirty notebook. "Britt, I have something to give you. As fate would have it, one of your father's killers ended up doing something very good. He saved something of your dad's that I think you're going to really like.

Even though this man was evil, he developed a love for your father and his music. I know this sounds crazy, but I truly believe that he is genuinely sorry for what he and his partner did to your dad. It was an evil act, done for no other reason than for greed and money.

"At his arraignment hearing, the killer told the story of how he had loved to hear your dad sing and how he sang his country songs for hundreds of miles as they traveled across the Southwest. For some reason this man couldn't toss away your father's notebook of songs. He presented it to the court at the hearing, and it was submitted into evidence.

"We have gotten special permission from the presiding judge to have this evidence released. It is with pleasure that I present, Christine and Britt, the entire collection of original songs that Cody Britton composed. I'm sure he would be proud for you to have it." Dr. Walsh opened the notebook, and turned it around. "The first song in the notebook is 'I Will Return.'" Dr. Walsh's voice cracked with emotion. He caught Christine's eyes in the front row. She placed her head in her hands and wept uncontrollably. Britt was right there to comfort her. He wrapped his arms around his mom and wept with her. "I'm told that this first song in the book is the last one he ever sung. And it was written for your mom, and for you, son." Walsh dabbed at his eyes as he left the podium.

Special Agent Bruce Akers came to the podium for his portion of the program. He laid his notes out, cleared his throat, and took a sip of water. "Thank you, Chris. I don't know whether I can do this or not. Christine and Britt, I have a letter from Jimmy Dale Scott to read. He is still in prison, but he wanted to say this to you." Agent Akers carefully opened the letter, crudely scribbled on a torn sheet of notebook paper.

Dear Folks

I am writing this to tell you how sorry I am for Cody's death. There's not a day goes by I don't regret what I did and my part in his death. I can only imagine the misery and tears I caused you. Cody didn't deserve this. We just did something crazy to get some money and Cody was in the wrong place at the wrong time. I hope that someday you could forgive me for the loss I caused you. I saved one of Cody's favorite things, his songbook. It's a great thing to keep, all his work. You need to have this. I am real, real sorry. Your dad was a good guy. I bet he could've been a big star had he never met us.

Jimmy Dale Scott

The room fell silent. There wasn't a dry eye among all in attendance. Brandie gently rested her head against Chris's shoulder. Reverend John openly wept at the sweet spirit and sense of true forgiveness that permeated the auditorium.

Britt leaned over to Chris and whispered something in his ear. Chris looked at him, thought a minute, and nodded his head in approval. Britt got up and went to the podium, carrying his backpack.

He opened the backpack and retrieved something. He placed it on the podium. He cleared his throat, just like the others before him had done. He looked deeply into the eyes of each person in the small audience.

"I'm just twelve—actually almost thirteen. I've never done anything like this. But my mom and I want to thank each person for what you did to help find my dad. You all have been so nice and made us feel like special people. The last song my dad wrote or sang was the song on the first page in the notebook you just gave me. It's in my dad's own handwriting. That is super cool. My mom told me this story. The last night he sang in Albuquerque she recorded him singing, 'I Will Return.' I'd like to play the song for you. It is dedicated to my dad, Cody Britton. He must have been an awesome guy. Awesome people keep their promises, and he did, as best he could. So, this is for you, Dad." Britt punched the button of the worn out cassette player, and held it carefully up in front of the microphone. The recording was worn and scratchy, but the words gave goose bumps to everyone.

> Your soft hands holding mine,
> Keeps me dreaming of what might someday come,
> To leave you now is so hard I can't hardly imagine,
> What life would be without you at my side.
> All I ever wanted to do was to sing my simple song, til I met you
> You've got my heart jumpin' and spinnin'
> I just don't know what I'd do if you weren't at my side.
> But I have a dream, it's been there since I was a boy,
> That dream will surely come true,
> With you right there with me.

So I must go, but it won't be long,
I will return to get you, you'll see, it won't be long.
So while I'm gone, I'll think about you daily,
And hope and pray our plan comes true,
This vow I make to you,
I will return, I will return.

I will return, it may be on a snowy day, it may be cloudy,
But when we are together, it will always be a sunny day.
It will always be a sunny day.
It will always be a sunny day.

The days seem long, and I miss you so much,
Please don't forget me
I love you so much. I love you so much.
So when the time is right, our home will be complete,
    together forever
For the rest of our lives. For the rest of our lives.
I will return. I will return. I will return. I will return.

Finally, this man who would be forever young had a past, a life story, a hometown, and a family who loved him and missed him. His remains would be taken to Albuquerque with Christine and Britt. His memory would be cherished forever.

After years of speculation, and many misses and false starts, Cody finally had his identity, Christine had found her soul mate, and Britt had found the father he never knew.

Cody Britton was a good man who wanted nothing more than to sing his songs, chase his dream, and share what he had with others.

It wasn't meant to be.

But Britt's father and the love of Christine's life had kept the promise he made in the very last song he ever sang on earth. He did come back again, for those who had the pleasure of knowing him before his death, and for those unfortunate ones who never got the chance, but who worked tirelessly to discover who he was even after death. He did come back. At long last, Cody Britton had returned.

Made in the USA
Columbia, SC
05 November 2017